Hearts, Hounds, and Haunts

By
Dakota Brown

Hearts, Hounds, and Haunts

Inkwolf Press
P.O. Box 473
Ault, Colorado 80610

ISBN: 979-8-9864144-8-5

www.inkwolfpress.com

PRODUCED IN THE UNITED STATES OF AMERICA

10 9 8 7 6 5 4 3 2 1

Dedication

To Isla

If not for your ways, we would not have our dogs, and this story would not contain Yakutian Laikas.

Acknowledgements

So many people have helped me with this project and I'm so grateful to all of you. Thank you to my proofers, Andrea, Kirsten, R. Knight, Angie, and Aeryn Havens. Thank you for all the encouragement Alpha Team: Angie, Becky, Chelsi, Janet, Kelly, Michael, Sarah, and Stacy.

And of course, thank you so much for your extra support on Patreon. You're all amazing: Lauryn, Tina, Museholly, Nina, Latisha, Kelly, Ruby, Julie, Arkay, Tabitha, Wendy, Michael, Teri, Shay, Jacqui, Melynda, and Yashi.

Thank you so much to my editor Lynn, my PA Becky Hodges.

On the subject of Yakutian Laikas. They're a fantastic breed. If you've read my "Only Human in Strangeville" book you've encountered a magical version of them already. These two dogs are directly based off the cover artist's dogs. She's read and approved of my rendition. They're an extremely versatile, do everything working breed and excel at any sport they've got a mind to do.

On the subject of the cover art… I could not be happier. Danni did such an amazing job. And the interior art just makes me grin.

Content Advisory

This book covers some heavy themes. It actually gets a little heavier than I intended. Here are a few key things a good friend of mine picked out for me. Thanks Mel! There are more that are much more minor so if you do have concerns please reach out to my PA Becky Hodges and she can get the full list to you or get you in touch with me. If we're FB friends you can also message me directly, but she responds more quickly than I tend to.

First, and foremost of importance to me… nothing bad happens to the dogs and none of this comes from the MC.

Okay, here's the list of the really heavy stuff.

"No Yakutian Laikas or ghostly reindeer were harmed in the making of this book."

- *Stalking*

- *Harassment*

- *Past mentions of suicide*

- *Implied domestic violence*

- *Emotional abuse*

- *Financial abuse*

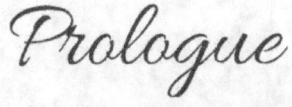

Grandmother

Grandmother sat in her rocker on the porch and watched as the realtor stood in the driveway and studied the house, her hands on her hips. She could tell the exact moment when the woman noted the chair rocking as if on its own. The woman visibly shuddered before turning away from the house, yanking the old, weather-worn For Sale sign out of the ground, throwing it into her car and slamming the trunk down. She got into her car and drove away without a backward glance.

Though Grandmother understood why the woman was glad to be rid of the house, it made her sad. She'd lived in this house for so many years and had such joy with her friends here. Still, the house was long overdue for a new owner.

Her needles clacked as she picked up her knitting project again, a blanket to keep her lap warm during the long, cold winters.

A new start

Chapter 1

Violet

The trip through the northeast had been like a visit to my childhood. The fall colors so vibrant; the air so crisp; farm stands selling apples, cider, pumpkins, and other produce; the environment so hauntingly familiar. Yet it was all as if it had happened in another lifetime.

I hadn't been back this way in years. The trip across Maine had felt like I was leaving one life and entering the next. The environment was so different from California, where I'd lived for the last fifteen years. I loved California, but I was glad to be home.

And now I stood at the gate across the driveway to my new house, one hand on the wrought iron, and stared. There was no way this was the right place. For one, it was huge. I couldn't imagine the amount of money I had paid would have even covered the land. Two, it was, well, a mansion.

I took my hand from the gate and dug my knuckles into my eyes. My realtor had taken care of everything for me since I'd been trying to survive—literally—a messy divorce. My ex had gotten away with nearly actual murder, but I'd come away with enough money to buy a house and live for a year, the dogs, their things, and the clothes on my back.

Pulling out my phone, I stared at the address and the picture of the house, then back at the address on the rusty old mailbox next to the gate. They matched.

"Well, this explains the giant key." I held up the actual old-fashioned key ring that had come with the paperwork and selected the biggest key. "Maybe this should have been my first clue that something weird was going on."

I'd selected Cliffside because it was not too far from my childhood home, it was near Arcadia, and I could afford a house there.

The gate opened with a metallic shriek of protest. I got back in the car and drove up to the house, leaving the gate open behind me. Creek and Shiner whined from their kennels in the back of the van.

"Almost time, buddies. Almost time." They'd always traveled well, and they'd seemed to enjoy this trip immensely, with all the stops on the way that we'd taken to explore and reconnect with a life that didn't involve watching everything I said or did for fear of reprisal, but we were ready for some rest from the time on the road.

I had thought Stacy, the realtor, would have met me here since we'd only ever spoken on the phone, but I hadn't heard from her since the sale was complete. Oh well, I had the keys and the paperwork. It was fine.

I parked in front of the porch and slid the door open on the Ford Transit. I'd only managed to snag the vehicle in the divorce because I'd insisted it was dog equipment, and the settlement had given me all of that. My husband would never have sullied himself with anything that was for the dogs.

Creek and Shiner darted out of their crates at my quiet release command and leapt out of the van, their fluffy coats waving in the slight breeze. I'd groomed them yesterday, so they'd be pretty for their new home. Since it was just me, I'd get some selfies or something on the porch to celebrate. I'd hoped for a family picture, but this would be good enough.

Pushing away the tinge of disappointment, the worry over the size of the house, and my general anxiety that hovered like a black cloud around me, I took a deep breath and put a foot on the front step.

This was it. This was my new life. My new home.

The rocking chair caught my eye first. It was beautiful. Old, stained wood clearly well cared for. The arm rests were worn smooth from use. No other chairs were on the porch, and it was otherwise empty.

Wood creaked slightly as I took a step, but it felt solid under my foot. I'd been worried that maybe it had been rotten or something. There had to be a reason the house was so inexpensive for its size.

The front door was unlocked when I tried it, which I thought was a little weird, but I took a moment to find the right key to fit into the smooth brass knob. The house was older, and hadn't been updated in quite some time, but according to Stacy everything was in good working order and so far, it seemed that was true.

I opened the door and before I could take a step inside, the dogs barreled past and clattered into the house. The house seemed to exhale as the dogs ran inside, its musty breath mingling with the fresh outside air until it came alive when I flipped on the light switch.

This was it. This was my home.

Creek barked at something and gave chase, scrabbling across the wooden floor and failing to slow down in time to avoid slamming through the swinging door and knocking a bit of dust into the air.

That had sounded like his "cat" bark. He liked cats, just not ones he didn't know. I wondered what he'd actually been after, since I doubted there was a cat lurking in the old house.

"Creek, come here, buddy."

He woofed from inside the door clearly not sure how to get back through. Shiner huffed as if sighing and trotted up to the door, batting it open with one big paw. The door smacked into Creek's freckled nose, and he backed up, warbling his displeasure.

The door swung shut again, but with Shiner to show Creek how to get through it, I figured he'd only get stuck for about a week. Shiner was the smart one. Creek… well…

"No thoughts, only spots" described him well.

They were a pair of Yakutian Laika dogs that I used to do shows and sports with back before the divorce. They were my best friends and the only thing that had kept me going through those last long years.

A door slammed, and I swear I heard footsteps upstairs. Maybe I wasn't alone? Maybe that's why the front door was unlocked?

Twisting my hands together, I debated for a moment, then shrugged. Whoever it was would know I was here already anyway.

"Hello?" I went up the staircase, hand caressing the smooth wooden railing. It was solid, beautiful wood. Probably hand carved. You couldn't get stuff like that anymore.

The stairs creaked as if talking with the voice of the old house, and I smiled despite the unease. Ignoring fear and putting on a mask had become a life-saving skill, unfortunately.

Their initial zoomies out of the way, Creek and Shiner trotted up the stairs behind me, sticking close while we explored the new place.

"Hello?" I called again.

No answer.

The house had two levels and lots of rooms. I'd never be able to use them all, but at least I could have an office, a library, a dog room, and, well, whatever I wanted. Someday, when I had the money to buy extras. For now, I had plenty of dog supplies, and I'd pick the best room for them.

Fortunately, the house had come furnished, or I'd be sleeping on the floor for a while. I had some money, but this place was going to cost a fortune to heat this winter. That thought had me reassessing what I could do with the little money I had left after its purchase.

"Well, I guess if there is someone else here, we'll find them. Maybe just old house noises," I said aloud to fill the silence.

Just to be sure, I quickly stuck my head in all the rooms before going back downstairs and checking everything on the main floor. No one. And no footprints in the faint layer of dust. Weird.

The basement door was locked and none of the keys worked, so I supposed I'd have to deal with that at some point. Not now, though. I had enough to worry about without exploring a creepy old basement.

The garage unfortunately didn't contain an old car. It would have been nice to have something to drive other than the dog van. Still, the van worked great, was safe, and while it wasn't fuel efficient, it would do the job. I had gone a little overboard with the crazy dog lady decals at one point and that was currently a little embarrassing, but oh well.

"Okay boys let's get a few things out of the van to make space for groceries and a few necessities, and we'll head to town. Plenty of time to explore more later."

Town wasn't large and was about a twenty-minute drive from the house. The coast was a safe distance away from the main part of town, most of which consisted of shops catering to tourists. Cliffside had the usual trinket shops, restaurants, local grocery, and things like that. Two shops caught my eye on the end of the strip, however. The pet store and the coffee shop.

I needed a good coffee so badly, and I needed a job. First thing's first, the pet shop."Paws on the Shore" had a grooming station attached, a pet bakery, and then the usual pet supplies. Mentally crossing my fingers, I parked the van. Hooking the dogs to their double leash, I put them in a side-by-side heel to my left, Creek next to my leg, Shiner on the outside. They both looked good and freshly groomed, though they didn't showcase my full abilities since the breed didn't require any fancy grooming techniques. Still, they looked fabulous when freshly floofed, and I doubted anyone here knew what they were, so they'd get attention. Especially if they were displaying their full manners.

They waited patiently until the door opened then trotted at my side at perfect heel. Not going to lie, that had taken some work, but we'd made it a fun game and now they thought it was the best trick ever.

For a time, I just wandered the aisles. I needed some supplies, and I thought maybe I should buy them first, so I got what I needed, plus a small bag of dog food to get me through until the auto ship reached my new house, paid, and put it all out in the van. Then I came back inside with the dogs and went to the grooming salon. We'd gotten some attention, but the shop wasn't very busy, so mostly it had just been the store clerk who'd asked about Creek and Shiner.

I'd given her the run down before taking my stuff to the van.

The grooming salon was currently unoccupied, and my heart sank. If they'd been busy, I would have suspected they needed another groomer, but with no Help Wanted sign, and no dogs on the tables, I could only guess that business wasn't brisk.

A middle-aged woman with wavy brown hair, lightly tanned skin, and a few laugh lines around her eyes smiled at me when I came in.

"How can I help you?"

"I was wondering if you were hiring?"

That got the woman's eyebrows to raise. She glanced from me to my dogs and back.

"I don't know you. Are you new to town?"

I nodded. "Yes. Just moved into the old manor house up on the hill."

If anything, the woman's eyes widened further. "You bought Hill House?"

"Uh, I guess."

She made the sign of the cross. "Bless you."

"Thanks?"

"Well, unfortunately, as you can see, we don't have much business, at least going into winter. We might have a summer position next year, but that's a ways off, yet. You have experience?"

"Yes, fifteen years." I'd known how this was going to go when I walked in, but I couldn't help but feel disappointed. "I groomed part time when I lived in California."

"Probably couldn't pay you what you're likely worth, anyway." The woman sighed. "We do well enough, but we don't have any extra work. I'll be sure to send a note around if we need you, though."

"Okay, thank you for your time. Is anyone else hiring?"

"Try the coffee shop. Lesbian couple opened it up and the locals take a while to warm up to new folks. Tourists love the place though. Pretty sure they're hiring."

I wasn't sure how to react to the woman's statement. She didn't seem bothered that they were lesbians, she'd stated that like she'd stated the sky would be blue. She did seem bothered that they were new. Like I was.

"Oh, okay."

"Well, Debbie's local, so it's okay but Katie just moved in." The woman behind the counter leaned forward conspiratorially. "She's from Boston. Got some big city ideas." And she shook her head as if that was ridiculous.

I had been very young when I'd left Maine, but I vaguely remembered the small-town ways and fought off a laugh.

"Well, I'll go see if they need some help. Thanks. I appreciate it."

"Sure. Say, what kind of dogs are those? Border collie, husky mixes?"

That was the most common guess I got from people. "No, actually they're Yakutian Laikas. They're purebreds and an ancient tribal breed from Siberia."

"Huh. Spell that."

I did and the woman pulled up an entry online.

"Well, would you look at that. Two very rare breed dogs in our little town. Are they friendly?"

"Very." I turned to the dogs, dropping the lead. "Go say hi. The one with the spots is Creek, and the whiter one with the black ring around his eye is Shiner."

"They're so soft." The woman cooed as she petted the two dogs. For their part, the dogs were thrilled with the love. "I'm Betty, by the way."

"Violet," I replied.

She nodded at me then went back to stroking the dogs.

"Well, thanks for the help," I said once she was done petting them.

"Come by anytime."

I promised to return, if nothing else to use the self-wash station, then left the grooming area and headed toward the exit from the store.

"Uh, ma'am," the clerk behind the shop desk called as I reached the door.

"Yes?"

"Uh, your dog?" She pointed.

I glanced, then sighed. I hadn't paid attention, but Creek had taken the opportunity to switch to the outside where he promptly attempted to shoplift. His fluffy tail was curled happily over his back, wagging as he trotted out with a bully stick. He behaved, but only when he was on the inside heel.

"I'm sorry. Thank you for catching the criminal. Let me pay for that."

I took Creek's prize and returned him to the inside heel position. The store clerk was laughing at Creek as he stared intently at my hand.

"I'm not giving this back to you, buddy. You're not supposed to steal."

He grumbled and pawed my leg.

"No."

The protest got louder. They weren't husky talkative, but they certainly knew how to use their words. He *rooed* loudly as I handed the clerk the bully stick and my card. She tucked it into a bag, which meant that as far as Creek was concerned the bully stick had vanished. Shiner knew it was in the bag.

Creek proceeded to have a mini meltdown as his brain tried to cope with the disappearing bully stick, while Shiner stared on, mildly disgusted.

It wasn't that I couldn't take things away from Creek. It was just that he got really confused when they vanished. Especially if it was something he really wanted.

11

"He's sweet and a fabulous show dog, but he's not the brightest. Shiner is the smart one."

The clerk giggled, gave them both pets, which distracted Creek enough that he forgot his treat had vanished, and we headed out to the car. I put the bully stick in with the other purchases, and we headed over to the coffee   shop.

Chapter 2

Violet

If I'd been home, I wouldn't have considered leaving Creek and Shiner out on the patio by themselves, but there weren't many people about at this hour of the afternoon and I'd taught Creek to do a Yakut scream if anyone but me touched his leash unless I handed the leash over. Even people he knew. That had backfired on me a few times, but overall, it was worth the security. It also scared people off. Sometimes good, sometimes bad. Well, looking back, completely good, but at the time…

Turning away from dark memories, I focused on my future.

"Stay," I told the dogs, and looped their leashes lightly over the railing on the coffee shop's patio.

Like the rest of the stores in town, the exterior was decorated with a nautical theme, fishing boats, lighthouses, and all that, though this one had a terrifying giant great white shark painted on the window, grinning at customers as they came in, a latte balanced on one fin and surrounded by coffee beans. I wasn't sure if they were quite on point with the imagery, but the painting was well done. The name of the coffee shop was Beans on the Bay.

Creek and Shiner both eyed the shark painting, but when it didn't move, they decided it was safe enough and settled onto their bellies to wait for me.

The patio was large enough for a handful of tables, none of which were currently occupied. The day was on the warmer side for September, though I was used to the California heat, so it felt cool to me.

The aroma of coffee and buttery pastries hit me when I opened the door. I paused, inhaling deeply. If they did actually hire me, I'd have to really start running again. I used to run with the dogs every day, but I hadn't in a while. I'd only just recovered from my ex's last attentions about a month ago, then we'd been dealing with the divorce and the move.

The inside of the shop was homey, with a gas fireplace, currently unlit, along one wall and couches and stuffed chairs on a portion of the floor that was done in old wooden planks. It felt like it could be someone's living room if they really liked stuffed chairs and small tables and had scattered them about. It also had a nautical theme to the décor. The rest of the coffee shop felt a little more "big city" to me. Linoleum floors, stainless steel tables and chairs, and the décor reflected the feel, with cityscapes as the artwork.

It felt like the two images should clash, but it really melded harmoniously.

In the center was where the bean-filled magic happened. Though I was surprised to see a wide collection of teas as well. I actually preferred tea most of the time, so that was nice. The pastry selection also looked delicious.

The woman behind the counter was a little darker skinned, with dark brown hair, dark eyes and a friendly smile which she aimed at me when I came in, then she glanced at the door. "Your dog?" Her Boston accent was thick, as if she'd just moved here from the city.

"Uh…" I turned. Creek had his nose and lips pressed to the glass in a ridiculous display. So much for his perfect stay. "Yeah, sorry. I'll wash the window."

"Naw, just let them in. They're welcome in the Maine part of the shop."

"Which part?" I didn't quite get what she meant.

She laughed and pointed to the fireplace. "Maine, like the state, not main as in the primary part."

"Oh! And the other part is the Boston part?"

The woman winked. "You got it, kid." She pronounced it *kehd*. "Let your dog in and then come get a coffee."

"Yes, ma'am."

That had her laughing again.

I wanted to scold Creek for breaking his stay, but we'd had so many changes, and he really did look completely ridiculous with his lips and nose pressed up against the glass. It was hard to be mad at these dogs. Even Shiner was basically absurd most of the time. The humor inherent in the breed had kept me going on more than one occasion. They were especially absurd now, as Shiner had tried to maintain his stay while attached to his rebellious brother. Creek had dragged Shiner a short distance to get to the glass door and Shiner lay on his back, feet outstretched toward his original position and a look on his face that said, "I tried."

"Okay, you win this time, Creek." I opened the door and called both of them to me, trying not to laugh. They politely came inside and laid down in the "Maine" part of the room.

"This time you have to stay, Creek."

He *awooed* but settled. Shiner gave a long-suffering sigh.

"Gawd, they're beautiful dogs. What kind?"

I actually appreciated that she didn't try to guess. I gave her the rundown of the breed, their names, and offered to let her pet them.

"Yep. Soon as I get your coffee. They want pup cups?"

Both dogs perked up at that.

"Yes, please. I'm Violet by the way." Belatedly, I remembered to introduce myself. "I just bought the manor up the hill."

Her eyes widened. "You're the one they convinced to buy Hill House? Good luck."

I wasn't brave enough to ask, so I simply nodded.

"Well, I'm Katie. Nice to meet you. Just moved here a few months ago myself. Debbie's my wife."

"Nice to meet you, too. I grew up in a different part of the state and came back just recently."

"Welcome home." Katie finished my latte, handed it to me and made a couple of pup cups, which she carried around the counter. "Okay, let's meet your dogs."

Especially with the pup cups, Katie was an instant friend for Creek and Shiner. She gave them their treat and pets and made a big deal of them until another customer came in.

"Ian, get your ass over here and meet the new owner of Hill House." Katie waved the guy over.

He was medium height for a guy, white, and had wavy dark hair that curled around his ears a little. His intense blue eyes fixed on me for a moment with a slightly surprised but friendly expression on his face. Then he glanced at the dogs and pursed his lips a little before coming over and offering his hand.

"Ian," he offered. "I'm the local weatherman."

I shook his hand, refraining from making any bad weatherman jokes. "I'm Violet. These criminals are Creek and Shiner."

"Hello." Ian gave them quick pats before glancing at Katie.

"Ian is Debbie's cousin. You want your usual?"

"Yes, please."

If nothing else, he was polite. Also cute. But he didn't seem very interested in dogs so we probably wouldn't end up being friends. Too bad, I could use a few friends. I'd lost most of the few I had in the divorce. My real friends had been other dog sport companions, but I couldn't get too close to them or my ex would have gotten upset and taken that away from me, too. I'd likely be able to regain contact with them once I settled. Especially if I ever found my way back into that world again.

Family, well, I'd sort of lost them in the divorce too. My parents were old school enough that they felt that's just how men were, and I should deal with it. So I'd walked away. The rest of my family I hadn't gotten along with well anyway.

I hadn't even bothered to go to my parents when he'd started hitting me. They wouldn't have believed me, anyway. Or if they had believed me, they wouldn't have cared. My ex made good money, and that was what was important to them.

So, it was just me. I'd partially chosen Maine because I'd grown up here, but I'd also chosen it because all my immediate relatives had moved elsewhere.

I settled with the dogs and sipped my latte, letting myself relax after the hectic morning.

Shiner put his head on my knee, and I rubbed his soft ears. I also unclipped him from Creek. He wouldn't go anywhere. Creek, on the other hand, might. Probably wouldn't, but I didn't want Shiner to get dragged around, either.

Once I'd finished my latte and centered myself, I went back to the counter and put my cup in the dirty bin.

Katie was cleaning up one of the machines, and I waved my hand to get her attention.

"Yeah?" She came over with a smile.

"You, uh, don't happen to be hiring, do you?"

That got another lift of the eyebrows and a considering look. "Figured you had some sort of fancy remote job."

"No. It's a long story, but I'm coming out here to start over. I have no experience in a coffee shop." I gave her a faint smile. "I'm a dog groomer, but they don't have enough business for another one. The groomer suggested I come over here."

"Huh. Betty's a doll, but I don't think she likes me." Katie shrugged. "Sure, come by in a day or two once you've had a chance to settle in and we'll talk about it. We do need the help. Long as you're reliable you don't really need much experience to work here. We can teach you all about coffee and tea. The rest is just running a register."

"I did some of that at the grooming shop I worked for in California. I can provide a reference."

Katie waved that away. "Like I said, take a couple of days to settle in, then swing on down. Debbie will be back from visiting her folks Friday, and we can all chat then. If we had another person, then she and I could travel together now and again." The woman laughed.

"Should I call first?"

"Nope, just sometime during business hours. Maybe toward the middle of the day when we're a bit quieter. Though Fridays do get hectic." She frowned as if thinking then shrugged again. "Any time, just be prepared for us to be interrupted."

"Okay, sounds good. Thank you, Katie."

We were interrupted by a human yelp of surprise. I turned in time to see Ian make a grab for Creek's leash as the dog dashed off, something in his mouth.

"Oh my god, Creek!" I shouted and dashed after the dog. He wouldn't have taken food, but other things like phones were fair game. "I'm so sorry," I said to Katie as I dashed after him. "We've been traveling and he's usually so well behaved."

"No worries, kid. No worries." She was laughing.

I reached my dog, who was coming generally in my direction with his prize anyway, when Ian finally grabbed the end of his leash.

"Give it," I said.

Creek obediently dropped the object into my hand and waved his plumed tail over his back, the biggest doggy grin on his face.

Ian came over to me, and Creek, getting a mildly concerned look on his face, bolted away.

"Creek!"

He twisted around behind Ian, who still held his leash, then dashed around behind me, before trying to bolt again, wrapping Ian and me up tightly in his leash in the process.

I was now nearly nose to nose with the poor guy, and we were absolutely chest to chest.

"Your dog—"

"He's a criminal, I know. I'm sorry. We've had a very rough couple of months. He's usually so well behaved."

Said criminal had wrapped us again and was now trapped against our sides. I wobbled, trying to catch my balance. Ian grabbed my arm, and we managed to keep on our feet while Katie came and untangled the leash from around us, laughing uncontrollably all the while.

"Gawd," she said, wiping tears from her eyes as we managed to right ourselves. "I'm so glad I had my phone. Please tell me you'll come by on Friday. I need these dogs in my life."

I would have also burst out laughing but Ian looked less amused, so I managed to keep it under control. Also, there was a fair chance I'd lose it if I did. I hadn't had a real reason to laugh in so long and I didn't want my emotions to get away from me and start crying. Then there might be questions, and I wanted to avoid questions. I just wanted to move on.

"Please tell me you didn't take a picture?" Ian groaned.

"I won't tell you then, but I'm going to send this to Debbie as soon as I have a minute." Katie handed me Creek's leash, and I handed Ian back what turned out to be his wallet.

"I really truly am sorry, Ian. He's just glad to be out of the car. We all are."

Ian wiped the slobber off his wallet on his pant leg then put it in his pocket. "It's fine."

His expression was annoyed but not angry, so I just went with it. I was very good at reading body language from years with my ex, so I didn't think he was truly mad. Certainly not interested in being friends, but not mad.

"I'll keep him under control," I said. "Looks like we need to brush up on some of our manners," I scolded Creek.

He waved his tail, looking pleased.

"We should probably get home. I need to get some food and things and get back. We need to unpack, and I've been traveling for a month, so I'd like to get settled in."

"Sure." Katie sobered. "If, uh, you need a place to stay we have a guest room."

"I have a house."

She twisted her lips as if thinking. "Yeah, you do, but... you might not want to stay there. Just, uh, let us know. I'll see you Friday?"

"You will." Completely confused by Katie's statement, I gathered my dogs and left the shop. I was ready to get some groceries and get home. Regardless of how everyone I'd met so far seemed to feel about my house, I was excited to get back to it. I didn't have many things, but I wanted to do something to make it feel like mine, so I'd set up the dog room.

Dakota Brown

Chapter 3

Violet

The rest of the trip in town was uneventful, except that I got more raised eyebrows when I mentioned which house I'd bought. One woman went so far as to make the sign of the cross before hurrying away. So apparently my house—everyone called it Hill House—had a reputation. Oh, well. Whatever it was couldn't be worse than what I'd come from.

When I got home, I put away the groceries, pulled the dust cover off the couch and after a quick glance to make sure it actually looked clean under the cover, collapsed onto it. I'd probably be sleeping here tonight. There was a lot to do to get a bedroom ready for me, and I wanted the dog room set up. Though I'd been on the go since early this morning, and the idea of organizing things was getting a little less attractive.

Shiner and Creek hopped up on either side of me, and Shiner climbed onto the back of the couch and sat his butt down on my shoulder. He'd only been able to do that when my ex wasn't around at home. No dogs on the furniture. So I'd taught them to stay off the couch when the ex was around. I just kept everything clean enough that he never really noticed the hair. I leaned against his back. Shiner wasn't lapdog sized, by any means, but a fifty-pound shoulder dog was comforting right now. Creek laid his head on my lap, and I ran my fingers over his silky ears.

"We're going to be all right."

Creek huffed and Shiner wagged his plumed tail, the soft feathers brushing against my cheek.

As I closed my eyes, something upstairs crashed and we all bolted to our feet.

After a brief pause, the dogs *awooed* and raced up the stairs. I hurried after.

I'd only just glanced in the rooms up here, but one of them looked like maybe once it had belonged to a teen decades ago. I wondered what the story was and why this room seemed to be a shrine to the late seventies or eighties and why it had never been updated. According to the realtor, the house had belonged to an elderly woman who had died, and the family hadn't wanted the house, or something. She'd been a little vague on the last bit.

This is where the crash had come from. A stack of brick-sized wooden blocks had crashed to the floor.

Interesting.

The part of me that was still controlled by my past went over and picked them up and restacked them in a tower. They were surprisingly heavy blocks of wood, and they'd fallen onto a rug.

The dogs sniffed around the room, plumed tails curled over their backs and wagging gently. Creek put his front paws up on a chair and sniffed at the air, tail wagging fiercely. Shiner came back over to my side, and I buried my fingers in his ruff for a moment before I led them back out of the room.

Weird.

Well, old houses had lots of noises. Maybe it hadn't been the stack of blocks falling over. Maybe it had been something else. I couldn't remember if I'd even noticed the blocks when I'd looked in the room earlier.

My energy was flagging, and I still wanted to set up the dog room, so I left the exploring for later. The dog room was going on the main floor. No way did I want to drag all the equipment upstairs.

I did, however, have to figure out which room to use. The house had plenty. I couldn't remember exactly which was which from my initial exploration, but the first room I glanced in was the library. An honest to god library with a fireplace, a reading nook, and a window that overlooked the cliff sides and ocean. I could even see the lighthouse in the distance. Fighting back tears, I backed out of the room. It would be a while before I was ready to face that. It had been so long since I'd read a book. The ex thought they were a waste of time. So had my parents, and most everyone else in my life. I'd given up that love quietly a long time ago, and now I had an entire library.

Shiner bumped into my leg, and I petted him again before looking in the next room down the hallway. It looked like it had been the previous owner's bedroom, and I wondered if she would mind if I made it mine. The bed itself was gone, but there was an old wardrobe and vanity with a lovely, older-style gilded mirror. In any other setting I would have thought it too much, but it seemed to fit with the rest of the room. It also had a window nook with a similar view to the library. Yes, I would take this one as my own. It felt welcoming.

The dogs and I went back down the hallway to the room nearest the living room where I'd stashed everything. Compared to a lot of show people I didn't have that much in the way of equipment. I'd had to keep it out of sight, so that had limited what I could own. I *did* have a solid grooming setup, though I'd look into installing a dog bathing area if I was able to keep the house. I had boxes of our show stuff, my show clothing, ribbons, their records, and other things I needed.

The tears started again. I'd be able to display all their ribbons. That little thing almost undid me completely, but instead, I pushed through the emotions and channeled it into a burst of energy. Yes, and they'd be up by the end of the day. Along with the rest of my things.

The last room was perfect. It looked like at one time it had been a gentlemen's sitting room, though it was sparsely decorated. The dust wasn't bad, and it didn't take me long to run a rag I found in the kitchen over the surfaces and get it reasonably clean.

I'd hire a cleaning service to come in next week. Once they got it up to standard, I'd keep up with it, but that was another small rebellion against my past. The ex had insisted I do all the cleaning even though we could have afforded to have someone come in daily.

In a flurry of activity, I uncovered and moved the armchairs and coffee table and shifted them out of the way for now. In a flurry of activity, I uncovered and moved the armchairs and coffee table and shifted them out of the way for now. Then I moved all the clutter on the shelves that lined the walls and put it all on one shelf for now.

That gave me space to get out my things and I attacked that project with enthusiasm. Now that I'd given myself permission to display our awards, set up a grooming space, and make a space completely mine, something in me healed a little. Never again would I hide this passion.

The dogs had curled up in the armchairs and watched while I got their space arranged. I even took out some of the dog exercise equipment I'd bought, hoping to be able to use it at home. Pulling the items out of the packaging and getting them ready to use felt like a special kind of freedom.

When I was done, I wiped away a few more tears.

"Look at this, buddies. Our very own space."

Creek hopped off the chair, trotted over to the grooming table, and jumped up on it, striking a pose.

I laughed and went over and gave him a quick brushing.

"You know what we haven't done yet? Pictures."

With all those ribbons now displayed, reminding me of the countless hours training and competing, and the fun we'd had together, I smiled and put the dogs in front of them. Then I set the timer, propped up my phone and took a few shots with our awards.

After that, we went out onto the porch, and I did the same thing with us sitting on the front steps. The car was in the right spot to serve as a phone mount, and I got a few cute ones. I'd print them in town tomorrow and get some cheap frames.

Tired after that flurry of activity, I sank down into the rocking chair and watched the sky change color as the sun sank below the horizon. If nothing else, this mansion I'd bought had an amazing view.

Chapter 4

Violet

After a surprisingly solid night's sleep on the couch and a good breakfast for everyone, I'd spent a little more time in the dog room, fiddling. We had even started training on some of the fitness equipment I'd unpacked for them. Then it was time to head into town to get my pictures printed and hit the coffee shop. I'd ask around for cleaners, too. Maybe I'd even take a hike on the shoreline.

Once I visited the general store that also served as the local print shop, the dogs and I headed over to "The Bean" as I thought of the coffee shop in my head. I guessed the name was a joke about what tourists often called Boston, where Katie was from.

She was behind the counter when we went in. I told the dogs very firmly that they were to stay put, and this time they behaved appropriately.

"What'll you have, Violet?"

"What's your specialty?"

"London Fog."

"Oh, that sounds wonderful." I grinned.

"Though because the tourists like it, we call it a Maine Fog here."

I laughed. "Great. I'll have that and one of those." I pointed to a delicious looking pastry. Yes, I was going to indulge. My ex could suck it.

"How'd your first night in Hill House go?" Katie's voice was almost too casual when she asked while steaming the milk for my drink.

"Fine. Why?"

She nodded. "Good, good." But didn't otherwise answer my question.

"I got my dog room set up, and I think I figured out what bedroom I'll use once I have stuff for it. I have no idea what to do with the other rooms yet."

"Big place for just you and the dogs."

I sighed. "Yeah. I wasn't expecting something like that. Honestly, I let the realtor handle everything. I was dealing with, uh, some other stuff, and I just needed to get a place I could live in once I got out here. Maybe I should have paid more attention, but if nothing else the view is stunning."

"Hill House does have one of the best views in the area." Katie handed me my drink.

"Why does everyone know about Hill House?" There I went, adopting the locals' name for it. "And why was it empty? It was such a reasonable price."

"Now, now, just enjoy your house, and your tea." Katie smiled. "Don't let local superstition influence you." She patted my hand and seemed about to say something else when the bells on the door chimed.

I glanced behind me. "Great," I muttered. It was Ian, the disliker of dogs and Creek's target for theft. I saw the criminal in question perk up when Ian came in.

"He's a good guy," Katie said quietly. "Just a little reclusive. He's here every day, though. Does a lot of his work from here so he can get decent coffee. Hi, Ian," she said more loudly.

"Hi, Katie."

Ian eyed me, then the dogs, before coming over to the counter. "Violet, right?"

"Yeah. Hey, I'm sorry again about Creek. We've had a rough few months and a long trip across the country. He was just feeling rambunctious. Can I buy your coffee to apologize?"

"It's fine. No harm done and all that." Ian gave me a cautious smile. "You don't need to buy my drink or anything."

"I want to."

Before he could object, I handed my card back to Katie, though they had a card reader like every other store these days.

She took it and smiled at Ian. "Your normal?"

"Yes, please."

"I'll bring it over in a few, hun."

"Thanks." Ian glanced at me, shoved his hands in his pockets, and clearly had no idea what to do next. Probably no one had ever bought him a drink before.

I got my card back, then took my own drink and pastry over to the table where I'd left my dogs in the "Maine" section of the coffee shop. Ian wandered over to the table where he'd set his bag and pulled out a laptop. I sat, watching out the window and tried to figure out what was next.

Should I pick up another hobby besides dog showing? Could I afford another hobby? Probably not. I doubted the coffee shop would pay a ton. Maybe I could find a cheap hobby, since I wasn't likely to be able to do much with dog showing out here either. Maybe there were some local clubs? I'd find out.

The streets were getting a bit more crowded as the day lengthened. Tourists wandered around and gawked, getting ready for lunch after their morning tours or staring at maps. Most seemed to be in a good mood. The coffee shop got busier, and Creek and Shiner got a lot of attention. I was considering printing up an informational sign about the breed by the time I decided to move on.

I took my dishes to the counter, and Katie waved me over to the register. "Hey, I wrote down a list of phone numbers for you. Put them in your phone, just in case you need someone. Sounds like you're otherwise all alone out here."

Grimacing, I nodded. I had a handful of dog show contacts saved in my new phone, but there wasn't anything else other than the pictures I'd taken with it yesterday. I didn't even have any apps or social media. The ex had never allowed it, and I had no reason to start now. I did notice Ian's number was on the list, but since he was a relative, that didn't surprise me too much.

I grabbed one of the business cards, jotted down my new number, and handed it to Katie. "You can give it to anyone on this list."

"We're glad you're here," she said.

"Thanks." That almost brought tears to my eyes. It had been a long time since anyone had been glad I was around, other than the dogs.

I gathered Creek and Shiner and headed out onto the sidewalk. The air was crisp, the sun warm, and I needed some exercise. Some of the hiking trails weren't far and that sounded like a fun way to spend the afternoon.

***

"I really don't know what's going on," Lee, the print shop owner said when I stopped back in the print shop later. He was an older Chinese man with a passion for photography. "I've never seen anything like it, but I can't get the orbs out of the picture without ruining it."

I studied the print he'd made for me. Six weird orbs floated around the dogs and me on the picture we'd taken on the front porch. When I'd stopped by to pick it up, Lee had looked embarrassed and now I understood why.

"I'm sure it's not something you did. It's probably my phone or something. Don't worry about it. The picture is perfect otherwise."

"It is lovely. Well, Hill House is an odd place. Maybe that has something to do with it." He glanced away uncomfortably.

"Well, I'll take it and the frame." I offered my card.

"I'll charge for the frame, but the picture is on the house. Call it a poor welcome gift, since I can't clean it up."

I laughed. "Okay, thank you, Lee."

"Welcome to Cliffside, Violet."

He shook his head and muttered about orbs messing up his prints as he checked me out.

Though the orbs were weird, I shrugged it off. I had a picture of me, the dogs, and my new house. That was all that mattered. I'd put it in the frame, and it could go on the mantel or some other special place when I got home. Eventually, I'd cover the place with pictures of the dogs, as I'd never been allowed to before.

***

Feeling lucky, though a touch confused, I watched Maria, and her daughters pack up their cleaning supplies and head for the van. I'd paid them a fair amount to clean the entire house except for the basement, which we still couldn't get in, and given them a fair tip as well. They were grateful, but they'd only taken the job once I'd agreed to stay in the house with them and I'd noticed that none of them went anywhere alone. I'd also noticed the wary looks they'd cast over their shoulders the entire time.

It had felt a little weird to have someone cleaning my house and me not helping, but the one time I'd impulsively tried, Maria had shooed me away with a friendly smile.

After the house was clean, I shut up the rooms that I wasn't going to be using right away and sank down onto the couch, and immediately bolted upright when something crashed upstairs.

The house had been quiet the last couple of days, but apparently it was going to be noisy again.

Barking, the dogs raced up the stairs and I followed. They stopped outside the room I had dubbed the shrine to teenhood. I pushed it open. We must have bumped that stack of blocks because they were scattered all over the ground.

Sighing, I restacked them. Creek and Shiner got in on it, bringing me blocks when I pointed. They were such good dogs. When we were done, Creek went over to the chair by the desk and sat with his back to it like he did when requesting pets. There wasn't anyone in the chair, obviously, but he had a pleased expression on his face, regardless.

I glanced around the room again, noting the one thing that didn't quite match. The room had an antique mirror much like the one in the room I claimed. Once I had a bed. The mirror didn't seem to fit with the otherwise teen feel of the room, but maybe it was a relic from the kid's childhood or a family heirloom or something.

When we left, I decided to try, again, to get into the basement. I didn't have the key, and my casual explorations hadn't produced any results, so I went outside and pulled my tool kit out of my van. The basement door was near the kitchen, and I headed for it, tools in hand.

Creek and Shiner both started barking in alarm, and I spun around. No one was there. They stared intently behind me, hackles raised, and Creek had his teeth bared. I twisted back around.

The toolkit slipped from my suddenly unresponsive hands scattering tools everywhere, and I whimpered. Written in bright red dripping liquid that looked like blood was the word "BEWARE" across the basement door.

That had *not* been there before.

I left the tools, collected the dogs, and headed at not quite a run onto the front porch.

Hands shaking, I settled into the rocking chair and stared out into the distance, letting the soft breeze and the gentle motion from the rocker take me away from my fear. It was an unfortunate coping device I'd developed from years of dealing with my ex.

The dogs sat with me, unwilling to leave even though they'd been alarmed as well.

Sometime later, when the sun had sunk to the horizon, I checked back into my brain. I hadn't expected the sun to be down. I covered a yawn and got to my feet. For a minute I couldn't remember why I was on the front porch. It came back to me when I put my hand on the knob to go inside. After a couple of deep breaths, I opened the door and went inside. My tool kit was on the table, closed, and I didn't see any scattered tools. There was no dripping blood on the door to the basement.

Though I was trembling, I grabbed the tool kit, went back outside, and put it in the van. Had I imagined everything?

What I did know was that I was tired, and the dogs would be hungry, and tomorrow I had my sort of interview with Debbie and Katie. I wanted to be at least somewhat rested for that. So, I went back inside, ignored the basement door, and got dinner ready. I wasn't hungry, but I needed something, so I had a sandwich. The dogs got their normal meals. I refilled their water bowl, tidied up, and headed back out into the living room. A quick glance around showed everything normal so I went into what would become my room for a shower. The dogs shadowed my every move and when I finally sank down onto the couch, they curled up with me.

I lay there for a while, heart pounding, ready for something to happen, but the house settled into sleep, and all was quiet. Maybe I had imagined it? If so, what did that mean? Could I be losing my mind, like everyone had accused me of when I'd demanded a divorce. I didn't think so. Besides. Creek and Shiner had reacted too. We couldn't all be losing our minds. Could we?

Chapter 5

Violet

The next morning the dogs ran to the door, yodeling their heads off. I hadn't heard anything, but I'd also been in the kitchen finishing tea. I left my cup on the counter and went to the door. A quick glance through the peephole revealed a young man standing back from the door, hands shoved in his jeans pockets. He had shaggy dark hair and wore a Ghostbusters T-shirt.

I opened the door enough to look out and blocked the dogs with my leg. "Yes?"

"Hi. I'm Josh. How are you today?"

"I'm fine. Thank you for asking. You?" I couldn't keep the confusion out of my voice, though I tried to keep it pleasant and mild.

"I'm fine. I'm a paranormal investigator and we've been researching this house. We were wondering if we could set up a time to come and get some readings?" His liquid brown eyes lit up hopefully.

"Oh, uh. I'm sorry, it's not haunted," I said automatically. Ghosts weren't real, after all.

"The rumors are pretty specific about the hauntings. The previous owner never let any investigators in, either, but we had hoped you might."

"Sorry to waste your time," I said kindly. "It's not haunted, and I just want some peace and quiet. Please."

He nodded and held out a card. "If you change your mind, you're welcome to call us. We won't bother you, but I do urge you to please reconsider. The advancement in paranormal science could be pivotal."

"If I change my mind, I'll call." I accepted the card, and he made a friendly goodbye before leaving the front porch and jogging over to an old, beat up half ton truck.

"Well, that was weird as hell," I muttered, taking the card back inside and putting it on the table. I reached for my cup to wash it and put it away, but it was already hanging on the mug rack. Maybe I'd already taken care of it? I really was losing my mind.

Though it was weird to take dogs to an interview, I wasn't comfortable leaving them behind, so I loaded Creek and Shiner into the van and headed into town.

***

"I'm so glad you brought them!" a woman who must have been Debbie exclaimed when we entered the coffee shop. She was as light-skinned as Ian, but her hair was honey brown and her eyes a softer blue, though I could see the resemblance. She had a heavier build than Katie but wasn't what I would consider overweight. My ex would have thought that, though.

Creek and Shiner took that as an invitation and went right up to her, not quite wrapping her up in their leashes, but it was a narrow thing avoiding a repeat of the tangle with Ian.

"They're delightful." She gave them both a thorough petting. "Katie told me about their breed, and I just had to look them up. What a unique dog. Let's grab a seat." She gestured toward the armchairs in the "Maine" section.

The dogs settled at her feet—traitors—and Katie brought over coffees.

"I hear you're going to help us out."

"Yeah, if you'll have me. My experience is in dog grooming, but I do know how to run a register, and I'll learn fast."

Debbie nodded. "I'm sure you'll do just fine. Do you know anything about event planning?"

The question threw me off. Event planning? Did I? I thought for a moment, scrunching up my brow. I doubted planning my ex's social calendar counted.

"Um, some, I think. I used to help the local kennel club plan events."

"Perfect. We need to bring in more local business. After you get the hang of things behind the counter, we'll get to work on events." Debbie handed me a piece of paper. "Okay, here is what we have right now. If it's not going to work out for you, I understand, but it's what we can offer at the moment." She named off a reasonable wage considering the work, plus tips, and part-time hours. That was fine, to start. "We have one other barista who works here very part time. You'll meet her during the busiest hours but otherwise she has her own business doing paintings for tourists."

"Okay, great. When do you want me to start?"

"How about Monday?"

"Sounds great."

"In the meantime, we have some hikes and other things you simply have to see while you're in the area." She handed me a list. "Not only will you enjoy them, but we get questions about them all the time, so consider it a request that you check them out sooner so you can answer those questions."

"Oh! Great idea. Thank you, Debbie. The dogs and I will love it."

She leaned over and ruffled Shiner's ears. Creek put his paw on her foot, so she pet him, too. Clearly, they already had her trained.

"As for the dogs…"

"Oh, yeah, I'll totally leave them at home. I brought them today because I wasn't comfortable leaving them yet."

"That's not at all what I meant. If they'll behave, we can set up a spot for them in the office. Hill House probably isn't the best place to leave them when you're not there."

I frowned. "Everyone, and I do mean everyone, has a thing against my house."

"Well, the old lady who lived there last liked it, but other than that, it has an unsettled reputation."

"A paranormal investigator showed up on my doorstep this morning." I took a drink of the last of my latte.

"Yeah." Debbie didn't elaborate, but also didn't sound surprised. "Katie is dying to know but she's too polite to ask. Men or women? She can usually tell at a glance, but you, she couldn't."

The change of topic threw me off. "What?"

"You date men or women?"

"Oh!" I laughed. "Men. Well, no one right now. Probably not for a long while." The idea of dating hadn't even occurred to me.

Debbie laughed. "There are a few eligible men around who might be worth checking out if you get it in your mind to date again."

"Thanks." I attempted to twist my lips into a smile, not at all sure how I felt about the idea.

"Well, enough of that. Go enjoy your day. Take your dogs hiking. We'll see you Monday."

"Thank you," I said again. The dogs got up when I did, and we headed for the door.

Ian was coming in as we were leaving, and Creek hooked his leg with a paw before I could stop him.

Ian yelped and Creek, gigantic Yakut grin on his criminal face, grabbed Ian's wallet and bolted for the door. He forgot he was still attached to Shiner and me, so he didn't make it very far. He still jerked me right into Ian in the process.

"Oh, my god," I gasped. "I'm so sorry."

Ian grabbed me to keep me from falling, a resigned grin on his face. "It seems like the spotted one has it out for me."

"He just really likes your wallet. I'm so sorry. I'll buy you another drink. Creek, give it back."

Completely unrepentant, Creek trotted over to us, his fluffy tail curled happily over his back. He dropped Ian's wallet into his hand and sat at my side like he was completely innocent.

Ian was still holding me, and we both suddenly realized we were standing very close. He blushed and I probably was too.

"Sorry," I stammered and stepped back. The spot on my waist where he'd caught me felt cold without the warmth from his touch.

"No trouble. Oh, uh, big storm coming in tomorrow. Keep an eye out."

"Thanks. I'll see you later, Ian." I rushed out of the coffee shop before Creek could do anything else embarrassing.

***

The area was absolutely stunning. I'd taken Debbie's request to check out the hikes on her list seriously. After our meeting yesterday I'd gone on one near the town that I'd been interested in anyway. Today I was taking a longer day hike out toward the lighthouse and back. I'd even put on running shoes in case the trail let us jog a little. I had a light pack with things for me, and the dogs wore packs with things for them. We were set for the day.

The sun shone brightly in the blue sky though clouds lingered on the horizon. It was early and the warmth from the rays felt good contrasting with the cool breeze. Tails up over their backs, the dogs led me down the trail.

It wasn't a difficult hike, for the most part. Some places had stairs down to the shoreline, with warnings to take an alternate route during high tide posted at the top. When I looked, the water was out, so we went down. The dogs romped on the rocky shore, but I wasn't sure what the local wildlife was like under the surface of the gentle surf, so I kept them out of the water. We eventually came to another set of stairs and the water seemed to be coming in, and we hurried up the steps. The wind kicked up a little once we were at the top, and the clouds thickened, but I had checked my weather app and it had said to expect good weather. I didn't think much of it.

This stretch of trail was rocky but flat. I picked up a quick jog and the dogs fell in ahead of me, attached at my waist and pulling slightly on their bungee lines. Their assistance gave me enough extra energy that soon we were running along the trail at a solid clip, the wind and my breath roaring in my ears and drowning out anything but the surf and some loud gulls circling nearby. It felt so good to simply run without having to worry about when I needed to be back to make dinner for someone who didn't even appreciate it or wonder about any of the other things that used to be my daily stress. There were certainly things I was concerned about, but right now they were a future problem.

The dogs slowed on their own, coming to a stop. Shiner turned back toward me and whined, bringing me back to the present. We weren't too far from the lighthouse. The overlook at the end of this trail was supposed to have an epic view.

It surprised me that the light was on. It wasn't even midday yet, but when Shiner pawed at me and I turned back, I saw what the problem was.

"Well, shit." A vague sense of panic tried to take me to the place where I simply existed and let the world go on by, but I couldn't do that out here. I shoved the fear away and stared at the dark clouds now dominating the sky.

The surf crashed against the rocks and the wind whipped at my hair and the dogs' tails. How had I not noticed the change in weather? I knew better, especially from growing up here, but I'd grown used to California I supposed.

I looked around to see if there was a parking lot or shelter. We'd need it before long. The trip back to town would take too long, even if I went out to the road and followed it down the coast. The only thing nearby was the lighthouse. This trail didn't go all the way, but I spotted the overlook and the parking lot nearby. If I could get to the road, I could go that way and hopefully someone would be there to help.

While I recalled pictures of lighthouses buried in crashing waves, I did know this one was far enough inland that while it might feel the waves in the worst weather, it hadn't been intended to bear that kind of punishment. I'd taken a minute to read about the historic building and the caretaker's cottage at the base.

Maybe someone would be home. Or if nothing else, the door might be unlocked, and I could leave a note for the caretaker.

Decision made, I picked up a fast jog and we ran for the parking lot just as the first drops of rain splattered on my arms.

By the time we reached the parking lot, my hair was plastered to my head and the dogs looked to be half their normal size. Their tails were down and their ears laid flat against their skulls.

I didn't let myself feel the cold, just ran as fast as I could down the gravel drive toward the cottage at the base of the lighthouse.

Chapter 6

Violet

Rain drove at my face, and though it was dark and water streaked my sunglasses, I kept them on to protect my eyes.

The dogs seemed to know we were heading for shelter and pulled me along, though we were now running straight into the storm. The wind resistance made it feel like one of those dreams where you tried to go forward, but your body was like molasses, and you could barely move.

The cold settled into my bones and made my movements clumsy. I was in real danger of hypothermia. The dogs were protected by their thick coat, for now, but if they continued to get soaked like this it would make it to their skin. They were bred for snow, not rain.

I didn't see the steps and tripped, going to my hands and knees and scraping my skin on the stone. I barely felt it through the cold and scrambled to my feet. The entryway was sheltered from the worst of the storm, though the wind drove the rain into the meager shelter.

We made it to the door and both Yakuts started barking. I fell against the door, grabbing for the handle just as the door opened, and we tumbled inside instead.

"Violet?" a familiar voice said.

I looked up from the ground where I'd tumbled. "Ian?" Did I know he lived at the lighthouse? Something tickled my memory, but I wasn't sure if I'd known that. Or maybe he was just out here visiting?

45

He helped me up and pushed the door shut. He had to put his shoulder into it to fight the storm.

"What are you doing out on the point? I told you a storm was coming in."

"You did?" I replied stupidly, shivers wracking my body.

"Yeah, at the coffee shop yesterday when we ran into each other."

"Oh."

"Shit, you're freezing. Come on, let's get you warmed up. Are the dogs okay?"

They took that moment to shake, sending water flying everywhere.

Ian winced.

"S-s-sorry," I stammered through chattering teeth.

"It's the entryway, it's gotten wet before. Come on." He helped me get my shoes and socks off, and I dumped my pack on the ground and insisted on taking off the dogs' packs before I let him get me inside.

The house was warmer than outside, but it was clear Ian hadn't had the heat on or anything. He led me and the dogs through the cottage to a bathroom.

"Just a minute." He disappeared, and when he came back, he handed me a stack of towels and a thick flannel robe with some slippers and thick socks on top. Clearly his, but it would be good enough. "I know the slippers will be too big, but just wear them all for now. I'll get a fire started." Then he left, shutting the door behind him.

For a minute I just stood there, stupidly. Then another shiver wracked my body and Shiner pawed me, jerking me out of my stupor.

I put the pile of towels on the toilet and stripped, throwing my soaking clothes into the shower for now. Then I dried off and wrapped myself in the flannel robe. It was a pretty charcoal color and very warm. The socks and slippers were a little big, but better than the bare tile floor. After I had myself taken care of, I rubbed other towels over the dogs to dry them as much as I could. They hadn't gotten wet to the skin, and both seemed fine, so I did my best to dry the floor before stumbling out of the small room into Ian's bedroom. I got an impression of scenes from forests and cloudy skies both from the color scheme and the décor. There was even a picture of a violent storm wracking the coast. I wondered if Ian had taken it, since it looked like a high-quality photograph. The one thing that stuck out in his bedroom was an old-fashioned vanity, much like the one I had in the "teen shrine" room. Surprised Ian would have something so feminine, I went over to take a closer look. I walked carefully, though truthfully, his slippers were only a couple of sizes too big. The vanity looked like it was almost a match for mine. Interesting. Maybe there had been a local craftsman at some point that a lot of people had bought these from. It was clearly an antique, as mine had been. Very strange. I'd take a closer look at mine when I made it home.

After another curious, quick glance around, I found my way out of his room, down the hall, and to the beckoning warmth of the fireplace, the dogs on my heels.

Ian had pulled an overstuffed chair close, and I curled up in it, the dogs at my feet. He came in carrying a steaming mug and handed it to me.

"Broth. It's warm, sip it slowly."

"Thank you so much." I accepted the tasty broth and sipped while we sat in silence and my shivering lessened.

The silence was comfortable, and I slowly warmed and relaxed. The rain beat against the cottage, and I could tell the storm raged outside, but the walls were thick, and the storm shutters were solid, so it felt distant.

"I'm really sorry to barge in," I said once I felt like I could talk without my teeth chattering.

"Not a problem." Ian looked up from the book he'd been reading.

From the cover it looked like some sort of weather disaster thriller. Surely he wasn't reading something like that? That he was reading at all made me oddly happy and sad at the same time.

"Next time, if I tell you a storm is coming, maybe don't go running out on the point." He grinned at me. "I really do actually know how to do my job."

I snorted. "I swear, I completely spaced it. I was so mortified by Creek that I just didn't process what you said."

"You're stuck here for a bit, unless you really need to get going but we'll get soaked getting to the car. I'll drive you back to your place once the rain lets up. How are things at Hill House?"

"Is that your subtle way of asking if it's haunted?"

He shrugged. "Is it?"

"Ghosts aren't real, Ian."

He winked. "Some would disagree. Still, I always figured the rumors were just rumors. The old lady lived there for years, and she was happy enough. Always had a kind word whenever she came into town."

"Not haunted. Thank you for the offer. Would you be able to take me to the trailhead where I left my van? You're welcome up at my place, but I still need to get the van."

"Oh, right. I should have thought of that. In the meantime, do you play board games? And I started some dinner."

I just about died. Board games? Dinner? What was up with this man?

"I would love that. Thanks."

He dragged over a table and pointed at some shelves I hadn't noticed yet. "What do you want to play?"

I'd had to admit that I hadn't played in years, so we started simple, but by the time the storm let up, we were both laughing at the game. Creek and Shiner had both taken to resting their muzzles on Ian's knees, where he was quickly trained to pet them constantly. He didn't even seem to mind. Dinner was simple. Soup and crusty bread, but perfect for the weather. I swore it tasted homemade, too, but I wasn't brave enough to ask. The time passed too quickly, for all that I was still mortified at getting caught out in the storm. When it abated, as promised, Ian gave me a lift.

I was almost sad when Ian dropped me off at my van. I hadn't had such a nice time in, well, I couldn't remember outside of show weekends, and I'd always paid for that once I got home with an angry husband.

"Thanks so much. I'll make sure I pay more attention next time you give me weather advice."

"See that you do," Ian said. He studied me for a few moments and seemed about to say something else, then he let out a soft breath and gave the dogs pets instead. "I had fun. See you around the coffee shop."

"Yeah, guess I'll be there a bunch for now."

"My cousin and her wife are good people. You'll enjoy it." Ian got back in his car.

The air was cool, and I was still a little off-kilter from getting so cold earlier, so I hurried to get mine started, get the dogs loaded, and the heat going.

"Have a nice night, Ian."

"You too." He drove away, and I stared after his car for a minute before pulling out of the parking lot and heading home.

I was having some feelings, but I didn't know what they were.

The car parked in front of my house distracted me from my nice afternoon, and a cold chill ran through me. The car was wet, so it had been here for a while.

I took out my phone and put my finger over the emergency button, just in case. I also left the dogs in the van and clutched the keys in my fist in case I needed a weapon. Who would come out here and sit through a rainstorm?

No one was in the car, but when I looked closer at the house, I saw someone sitting on the front porch. In my rocking chair, none the less.

Unreasonably incensed, I got out of the van and headed for the porch. By the time I got there, the man was standing. He was middle-aged, white, with sandy hair, sky-blue eyes, and a cocky smile.

"Hello, Mrs. Angleworth."

The sound of my married name nearly sent me through the roof. But instead of shutting down like I would have only a month ago, it pissed me off.

"You're at the wrong house," I said, voice firm.

"I'm quite certain I'm not."

"You are. And you're trespassing. There is no Mrs. Angleworth here, and you will leave now."

He smirked at me. "I'm here about your house. I'm a paranormal investigator and you have more than you can possibly handle in this house. We're prepared to offer you quite a bit of money to take it off your hands so we can study it."

"Fuck off." A month ago, I would have been horrified that I'd just been so rude to a complete stranger. Right now, I just desperately wanted him to leave.

"You're quite alone out here, aren't you?"

"No, you dumbass. Mr. Thompson will be along shortly. You've got the wrong house, and you're looking for the wrong person. Now leave before I call my husband, and the cops."

He smirked again. "Yes, well, you'll change your mind. We'll be in touch." The man sauntered off my porch and, after a long look at my van, got in his car.

I hastily snapped a picture of his license plate. It turned out a little blurry and I didn't have time to get another one before he was gone.

That I'd had to invoke an imaginary man to get the guy to leave just made me angrier. Unfortunately, I was well familiar with his type. The only thing that would have gotten him to leave was another man, so, I'd played the game.

He'd gotten one thing right, though. I was alone out here. That shouldn't be a problem, but now I was feeling uncomfortable about it. Maybe I should get a place in town? Hell, maybe I should start locking the gate behind me when I left. The fence around the property wasn't great, but it was better than nothing.

"Damn it," I muttered and looked at the poor rocking chair. I'd have to disinfect it, or something. Yuck.

I quickly went back to the van, let the dogs out, and then went to the front door. On impulse, I tried the handle. It was still locked by the deadbolt. I turned the key and went inside. The dogs ran into the back of my legs as I came to an abrupt halt.

The place was trashed.

Dakota Brown

Chapter 7

Ian

I hadn't expected to enjoy having company so much in my house, especially Violet and her, admittedly adorable, criminal dogs. Well, only the spotted one was a criminal, but still. I hadn't spent much time around dogs, and it wasn't that I didn't like them, I just didn't understand them well. Though, clearly Violet's were well trained. Hill House did have my interest. If nothing else, the rumors were persistent and compelling. I was willing to bet she'd let me come by and check it out at some point if I got brave enough to ask.

While I'd intended to spend the afternoon up in the lighthouse tower enjoying the storm, the afternoon spent with Violet had been fun and I wanted to do it again. Which surprised me. I didn't usually enjoy company that much, but her dogs had been charming house guests and Violet liked games. I was looking forward to seeing her at the coffee shop on a regular basis.

I turned my attention back to the latest weather reports, but my thoughts kept returning to Violet and the afternoon we'd spent together. Maybe there would be another storm, soon, and I could ask her to come out for another afternoon of stormy weather and board games. I already knew the key to her company was inviting her dogs, so maybe I could find some dog friendly recipes for treats or something.

53

Sighing, I wrenched my mind back onto work. The locals depended on my timely forecasts, and I had to get the evening weather report posted.

Chapter 8

Violet

"I didn't get his name. I took a picture of his car, but I was in a hurry." I showed the deputy who was standing in my living room the picture.

"Thank you, Ms. Thompson. Here's my card, if you could email that to me?"

"Of course." I accepted the card, hand trembling with emotion.

"And you have no idea how he might have gotten inside to do all this?"

"No, sir. Everything was fine when I left, but when I got home it was like this. The house was still locked. I don't understand." I waved my hand toward the mess. Furniture was overturned, the old pictures that had been on the wall were scattered around the room. One was broken, though amazingly the rest were intact. The kitchen had been upended, and broken dishes were everywhere. I hadn't even looked in the rest of the house. I was terrified to go into the dog room. I'd just gotten everything set up and hoped none of their awards had been damaged. I fought back tears at the thought.

The deputy glanced around again then tightened his lips for a moment. "I realize this sounds unprofessional of me, but have you considered that it was the ghosts, not your unwanted guest? Now"—he held up a hand before I could voice my protest—"I certainly am taking your unwanted guest seriously, and in my report, I will note that it is suspected he caused damage inside, but with no known entry method, unless he was able to go in through the front door and locked it behind him when he left to throw off an investigation, it's difficult to say exactly what happened. And this place is haunted. Old Lady Grace, who lived here for years admitted that it was, but that she'd come to terms with the ghosts. Perhaps they were upset?"

I stared at the deputy, mouth agape. "Ghosts? Really?"

He ran a hand through his hair and scuffed his foot on the ground. "I understand how that sounds. Lived here all my life, though, and Hill House has had a tumultuous history. Some deaths, some murders, in my lifetime Grace is the only one who's lived here for more than a few months before running in terror. Just, be careful, okay?"

"Sure, thanks." I couldn't think of what else to say. "Hey, I need to get started on this. Is there anything else you need?"

"No, ma'am. If anything turns up missing, or you find any other evidence, please email or call. Or both so we have a record. I'll be in the area for a bit, if the man comes back. Call me directly, right away."

"Thank you. I will." That, at least, was reassuring.

"People should be safe out here, and especially in their own homes. Makes me angry that someone is doing this. Don't hesitate to call if anything happens again." He took one last look around, then left.

I stared around the living room in despair. It was going to take forever to clean up. I wished I had a friend to call, but there was no one.

Well, I could probably call Ian. No, I'd imposed on him too much today.

Instead, I went and got my dogs out of their kennels in the van. I'd opened the door so they had plenty of air. I simply hadn't wanted them getting in the way of an investigation. Creek and Shiner stayed close, sensing that I was upset, and we went back inside together.

Both dogs *aroooed* quietly when they saw the house. Steeling myself, I went over to the dog room and pushed it open. *Please don't be damaged,* I said to myself before looking up from the ground.

Nothing had been touched.

The relief I felt was almost painful, and I sank to the floor, sobbing. Shiner and Creek pressed into me, and I put my arms around them and cried into their fur. They'd taken care of me like this for years and knew that their silent support was what I needed.

My dogs' awards and things were safe, and that was all that mattered. The rest of the house was mine, but the things had been here when I arrived, and while I was sure they were someone's important treasures, they weren't mine. So, it would just take time for me to clean up, nothing more.

Once I'd cried myself out, I got to work making the space at least livable again. I wouldn't be able to get it all clean until after work tomorrow, but I didn't want to be walking on glass.

After an hour of shuffling things around, sweeping up broken plates, and otherwise dealing with the mess, the exhaustion of the day hit me. It was time for a hot shower and bed. I went into the bathroom of the room I would eventually set up as my own once my bed and the other things I'd bought arrived. Things had been shifted around in here, too, but not quite as badly. I straightened up a bit, then leaned my hands on the counter and stared into the mirror.

Instead of my familiar reflection, an unfamiliar woman stared back. Wispy hair floated in an unfelt breeze, alabaster skin clung to a skeletal face, and sunken sockets outlined inhuman eyes.

I stared. Blinked. Stared some more.

The vision stared back. I knew I'd had a rough day, but it hadn't been that rough.

Haunted? Was the house haunted?

My hands trembled on the marble countertop, and I whimpered.

The dogs thundered into the small room, barking sharply.

I glanced at them, then back at the mirror, but all I saw was my own frazzled reflection.

Though I knew it was bad for me, I let my mind slip away into its safe space where the world couldn't touch me and all I had to do was exist. This was all just too much.

I went through the motions of my shower, getting ready for bed, and settling onto the couch, one dog on my legs and the other lying next to me on the floor. I trailed my fingers in his fur and let the exhaustion of the day claim me. It would all be better tomorrow.

***

The next morning, I'd managed to reclaim some of my calmness and put most of the events of the day before out of my mind enough to focus on my first day at a new job. Though I had no idea what to wear, I didn't have a lot of options yet, so it wasn't hard to throw on some capris and a light top, gather the dogs up—no way was I leaving them behind with weird people visiting and trashing my house—carefully locking the gate behind me, and heading into town.

When I arrived at the coffee shop, Katie was waiting for me. She showed me where to set up a place for the dogs in the office and how to go about getting the coffee shop open for the day. We spent about an hour going through various systems and procedures before she stopped and looked at me.

"You getting all that?"

"Yeah." I repeated a summary of what we'd done back to her.

She frowned. "It's just, well, you seem really distant, and that's unusual."

"Oh, uh." I scrubbed my face. "I'm sorry, Katie." *How much do I tell her?* "Someone was at the house yesterday waiting for me when I got home. They tried to get me to sell the place, and, well, somehow they trashed it inside. I'm just shook up. I disassociate sometimes, but I promise I am hearing everything you say and learning it all. Lots of practice doing both. Sorry," I said again.

"Oh, honey." Katie patted me on the shoulder. "I'm sorry. What did the police say?"

"They took me seriously about the so-called paranormal investigator who was harassing me but thought that the damage inside might have been ghosts." I sighed. "Ghosts? Really?"

"Dear, the place is haunted. Even Grandma Grace said it was haunted and she lived there for all her golden years."

I shook my head but didn't argue with her. "I'll work on not being distant."

Katie studied me. "I'm just gonna ask. What happened to give you so much practice disassociating?"

"Oh." I cast my gaze down, before hurriedly returning to my task, which was getting the espresso machine set up. "Just my ex. It's fine."

Katie looked away, and I settled into my work.

"Well, I'm sure it's not fine, honey, but I'm glad he's an ex. Good time to start over, right?"

"Well, I mean, I came out here to get away and to rebuild my life, so, I guess."

She grinned at me. "How's that latte coming?"

I went through the motions she'd shown me then handed her the latte.

Katie took a sip then set the cup aside with a laugh. "I'll make the drinks, you run the register."

"I…" Horrified, I looked back at the espresso machine. "What do I do?"

"Kid, don't worry about it. First one is always crappy. It's way better than chain lattes at least." She winked. "You'll be making perfect espresso by the end of the day."

"Are you sure?" I couldn't help the mild panic that built from not having done the latte perfect on the first try. A part of me recognized that it was a left-over reaction from my ex, but a larger part of me was fighting between shutting down again to take the abuse or trying to find a place to run to or a way to placate Katie.

"Oh, honey, you're way too good at that." Katie pulled me into a hug.

I stiffened for a moment then almost started crying on her shoulder. I couldn't remember the last time I'd been hugged, but I managed to keep it under control.

"Too good at what?" I finally managed around a knot in my throat.

"Presenting a distant but compliant image. In this shop, mistakes will happen, and it'll never be a problem as long as it's a mistake. And I can't imagine you being the type to do anything malicious, so don't worry about it, okay?"

"Um, of course. I'm sorry," I agreed automatically.

"I'm going to tell you to stop apologizing, too. But I'm sure both of those will be hard for you. Just know, this is a safe place, okay? Just work on it. I realize you have trauma." She shifted her focus back to the espresso machine. "Back to the lattes."

Grateful she turned the conversation back to work, I watched carefully while she showed me some tricks. I was already exhausted by the time the first customer walked in, but I felt pretty good about working the register.

Katie and I had worked into a nice rhythm by the time we had a steady line of customers. I almost didn't react when Ian came up to the counter, other than to ask for his order.

"Oh, hi!" I grinned when I recognized him. "Just in the zone, sorry, Ian. What will you have?"

"My normal is just straight coffee and I'll have that today." He handed me his card, and I rang him up after a quick glance at Katie, who nodded. She'd mentioned that there was a "regulars" discount, and I suspected Ian qualified.

After the morning rush settled down, I helped Katie spot clean, and then she started helping me make drinks when we had single customers and no line. I was shocked at how much time had passed when she shooed me back to the office for a lunch break. Creek and Shiner were thrilled to see me, but they'd been charming Debbie, so they weren't upset about being left.

I sank down into the spare chair and pulled out the sandwich I'd brought and gave both dogs a generous portion before feeding myself.

Debbie watched for a while before going back to her work. Once I'd finished eating, she looked up again.

"How's it going?"

"I think okay. My coffee skills are better, and the register isn't hard."

"That was a pretty busy breakfast rush. How'd it feel?"

"Oh, it was fine. Katie and I were in a good groove, and it seemed to go really smoothly."

Debbie raised her eyebrows. "Well, good. I'm glad it's going okay. Seem like something you want to keep doing?"

"Sure. It's actually kind of relaxing. I know it won't always be this smooth, but I can't imagine it gets horrible that often." I smiled at her to try and reinforce my sincerity.

"I'm glad to hear it, Violet. Well, I'll let you enjoy the rest of your lunch. I'm going to go help Katie, then she can have a break when you're done."

"Oh, should I go back now?" I shifted so I could stand.

"No, of course not. You take a solid half hour and relax, okay?"

"Right." I settled back into the chair and pet my dogs.

When my time was up, I took a deep breath and headed back out into the shop.

***

That evening when I got home from my first day at work, I really wished I had someone I could call and talk about how my day had gone. I considered trying to contact some of my dog show friends, but I didn't think I knew any of them well enough to call out of the blue just because I wanted to talk.

So, I did what I'd always done. I talked to the dogs. I told them about how calming working in the shop had felt, how safe and ordered it was, and how, once I got the hang of everything, I thought it would be a really good job to have. For now. In the longer term I still needed to address the need for actual money to keep up a house like this, but in the short term the coffee shop would do.

Chapter 9

Violet

"**O**kay, first event planning mission. Come up with a monthly event that will attract people who are local and tourists." Debbie leaned against the counter and watched while I made her a latte. My skills had improved drastically in the last couple of days.

"What about a monthly Paws on the Patio thing? The local pet treat bakery could have a table, and we could have dog-themed drinks, and maybe the grooming salon and the pet store could donate some stuff for a drawing. If anyone does animal photography, they could come show off some of their work, things like that. We could even do like a mini, for fun dog show. Costume contest? Something like that."

Debbie stared at me for a moment, and I wondered if I shouldn't have suggested something dog related. The coffee shop was dog friendly so I thought they might like it. Maybe I was wrong?

"We'd obviously have to have some sort of friendly dogs only thing and, uh, rules and stuff," I stammered.

"Relax, Violet, it's brilliant. Not only would it bring in some customers for us, but maybe it would get more business for others, too." Her expression softened.

"Oh, okay."

"Take the rest of the afternoon and hit up the other businesses on the street, see if they have any interest in contributing to the giveaway. We can go from there once we see who's onboard. Don't stick to just the dog-specific stuff though, ask everyone."

"Okay," I said hesitantly. "But we don't have any specific plans in place yet. Won't they want to know what the expectations are? Are we going to charge for advertising space, things like that?"

"No, free for everyone. Discount on coffee for pets in costumes, and, uh…" She hesitated while she thought. "Anyone who wants to put up a sign or donate to the drawing gets a discount for the day, as well for them and their employees."

"This won't cost us money, will it?"

Debbie shrugged. "We need to get the community to come to us. We'll plan one and see how it goes. If it goes well, we'll do more. If not, we'll try something else."

"Oh, okay." She seemed so unbothered by the logistics, but happy about the idea. I was surprised.

"Go on. You can leave the dogs here so you don't have to worry about them. Come back here once you've hit all the stores and let me know, then you can go home for the day."

"Okay." I hadn't expected to get paid for that part, but I guess if they were making it my job, they should pay me. I finished what I was doing and after an uncertain glance at Debbie, who shooed me toward the door, I headed out onto the street.

It was a lovely afternoon, warm in the sun, cool in the shade, breeze coming in off the ocean and chasing the humidity away. The air had crisp fall notes lingering from the cooler morning and had me dreaming of pumpkin pie and caramel apples.

Because this was a dog-related event, I headed over to the pet store first. The person behind the counter welcomed me in then went back to whatever task had their attention. I made my way back to the grooming area.

Betty was behind the counter looking a bit down. Her expression brightened when I walked in, then fell a bit when she didn't see any dogs.

"How can I help you?"

"Uh, so Debbie sent me over to see if you wanted to join in on our social event we're planning in a couple of weeks." I quickly gave her the details, and her expression brightened further.

"That's a great idea. I've been trying to figure out how to get more of the locals to come in for grooming. Maybe this would do it."

"Yes, that's exactly our hope."

"Well, count us in. We'll donate a gift certificate toward a groom and a gift basket from the shop." She gestured toward the store. "Treats and stuff. When you have all the arrangements set, let me know."

"I will. Thank you." Surprised at how easy that had been, I made my way down the main street. A few of the owners weren't present so I left information so they could get in touch with us and promised to check back later if the person working at the shop knew when they'd be around. Amazingly enough, everyone was excited about the idea, and most said they'd be happy to participate or help advertise. I'd brought a notebook to keep track in, and the first few pages were full of information by the time I made it to the last stop. This one was a bookshop. There was a small sign that promised an adult bookshop in the rear, and that surprised me a little for such a small town.

I went in not expecting much, but the selection of fiction and nonfiction was actually extensive, along with a section specific to Maine filled with guidebooks of various sorts. I wandered through for a few minutes, before heading to the desk.

"Hi, I'm Violet. I'm new to the area and work down at Beans on the Bay," I said.

"Oh, hi! I'm Janelle," the woman behind the counter said. She was a Black woman with short cropped black hair and a charming smile. "I own this place. What brings you in today?"

"We're trying to put together an event at the coffee shop. The idea is to get more people excited about the local businesses. Tourists too." I gave her a quick rundown.

"Oh, that sounds perfect. We'll donate a gift certificate."

"Thank you. Well, I'd better get back and let Debbie and Katie know that everyone seems interested. I'll swing by when I have some more information."

"Violet." Janelle frowned. "Oh! I have something for you."

"What? How could you possibly have something for me? I've never been in."

She laughed, and her laughter lit up my soul a little. I found myself grinning back.

"It's a gift from some mutual, undisclosed friends. Hang on." She went into a back room for a moment and returned with a gift-wrapped box. "Open it at home." She winked and handed the box over.

"Thank you," I said automatically, feeling flustered. Who could have sent me a gift? Especially something heavy like this. How many books were in here? I assumed it was books, anyway, since this was a bookstore. I guessed it had to be Katie and or Debbie because they were the only people around here I knew well at all. Or Ian, but I doubted he'd have thought to send me a gift. Unless it was a survival guide. Or several.

"Enjoy. Now, stop back in when you have the details, and we'll get something for you."

"Thank you, Janelle." I stacked my notebook on top of the mystery box and headed to the coffee shop. My shift was almost over, and I wanted to get back and report in, then head home. My bed was supposed to arrive today.

Neither Katie nor Debbie said anything about the box I set down in the office, which made me think they were probably involved. I gave Shiner and Creek scratches then went out to report.

"Most everyone is interested in advertising, contributing, or both. There are only a few owners I wasn't able to talk to." I handed over the list.

Debbie took it and scanned before nodding. "Excellent. Tomorrow when you get in, after the morning rush, start writing up the details and we'll start getting it organized."

"Okay. Great."

"Well, get out of here, then." Katie grinned at me. "Good job today."

"Thanks." I gathered up the dogs, my gift, and headed out back to the van.

The trip home was uneventful, though I couldn't help feeling a little anxious about what I would find when I got back to the house. Hopefully, everything would be normal.

I forced myself to take deep, even breaths as we went down the street to my house, but I was able to relax a little when I pulled into my long driveway. The gate was still locked, and I didn't see anyone around. I'd have to look at my finances and see if I could afford an auto opener for the gate, though. Getting in and out all the time wasn't my favorite.

At least today, I'd leave the gate open since my bed was supposed to arrive in a few hours.

The wind was brisk when I hopped out of the car to open the gate, fluttering my hair around my face and biting a little despite the otherwise warm day. Winter was on its way, and I needed to get some clothes that were appropriate for the extreme weather. At least the dogs would be plenty warm this winter. They'd probably love it, since their native land was Siberia, though these two were used to California.

The gate opened with a mild squeal that I mentally catalogued as a normal sound and one I should listen for, though I wasn't positive I'd be able to hear it from the house. Then I realized what I was doing. Finding signals that my ex was coming home so I could prepare. Grumbling, I stomped back to the van, got in, and headed for the house.

Creek and Shiner bounded around the yard, sniffing and peeing on things when I let them out. I grabbed my gift and went to the house. The door was still locked when I tried it, and I unlocked it and went inside, leaving the door standing open for the dogs when they were ready to come in. They wouldn't go far.

The rest of the tension left my shoulders when I came home and the house was clean and tidy, just as I'd left it.

No... I'd left it a mess, hadn't I? Well, not a huge mess, but I hadn't gotten everything cleaned up from when the paranormal investigator, or the ghosts, or whoever had trashed the place. It was clean now.

I put my gift down on the table and rubbed my eyes. Maybe I had cleaned? It wouldn't have been the first time I'd done chores in a foggy disassociated state to avoid dealing with my ex.

"Ugh."

The kitchen was also clean, but I knew I'd cleaned that up first. I hadn't wanted a stray piece of broken plate to cut a paw. The handful of dishes that had been left had been destroyed, so I'd thrown them out and gotten some paper plates to get me by until I figured out what I wanted to replace them with. Paper plates and plastic cups. At least the silverware hadn't been destroyed.

I fixed myself a meal, and like magic the dogs appeared at my side to receive their tribute. Laughing, I gave them both snacks, then went into the living room to eat and wait for the delivery people.

***

"I wonder what this is," I said aloud as I studied the box Janelle had given me. The wrapping paper didn't give me a lot of clues. It was black with pink hearts on it. There wasn't a card, and for a moment I wondered if maybe she'd gotten the wrong person. Still, I wanted to know what was in it. Carefully, so as not to make a mess, I slid my finger under the tape holding one flap down.

Then I paused.

Why couldn't I make a mess? As a kid I'd loved tearing paper off packages. It was only my husband who insisted on complete neatness all the time.

Screw it.

I grabbed at the paper and ripped it off, throwing it in the air and letting it lay where it fell. I twitched a little at that, then forced myself to leave it. The box itself was just cardboard. I pulled the tape off and opened the top.

As I did, the dogs barked loudly on the porch. Sighing at the interruption, I left the package and headed outside.

A van pulled through the open gates, and I tensed until I saw the delivery logo on the side. My bed was here. I waved them over to the house. The dogs stayed on the porch as the movers backed into the spot.

A Black woman hopped out of the driver's side and a white guy climbed out the passenger side. The woman approached with a big grin.

"Violet, right?"

"Yes, ma'am."

"None of that. I'm Rebecca. We spoke on the phone when you ordered. I own the company, and I hadn't been out this way in a while, and I love the ice cream shop, so I figured I'd come along. Danny, here, is my cousin. Family affair, this." She lovingly slapped her truck.

"I know it was a long drive. I really appreciate you doing this for me. There just wasn't anything local."

"Not at all!" Rebecca's grin widened. "We're happy to help and you were so understanding about the extra charge. We usually get a lot of push back."

I waved my hand. "You had to drive like three hours. Of course it costs more."

She turned her attention to the house while Danny opened the back of the truck. Then her eyes fell on the dogs and widened.

"They're beautiful. Are they…?" She trailed off and tilted her head as she tried to process what my dogs looked like. "I'm not even going to guess," she finally said.

"Yakutian Laikas," I filled in then gave her the "one of the oldest sledding breeds, herds reindeer, tribal primitive dog," spiel I'd perfected over the years.

"They're so beautiful."

"Do you want to say hi?"

"Hell, yes, I do."

I gestured to the dogs. "Go say hi."

They bounded down the steps and immediately showed Rebecca that most Yakuts have no sense of personal space. Fortunately, she loved it, getting on her knees and giving them all the attention they wanted.

Once they were all satisfied, Rebecca helped Danny unload the pieces of the bedframe and I showed her where to put them. She glanced around the house curiously and I wondered if she knew about this place's reputation.

Still, she didn't say anything other than to help guide the pieces into the bedroom and shoo me away when I tried to help.

"The décor is kinda eclectic," I finally felt compelled to say. "The place came somewhat furnished and, well, I haven't had time to redecorate."

"It's charming, honey. I love it." Rebecca took that as an invitation to look around a touch more. "And I'm serious. It's adorable. Now, I know you said you'd put this together yourself, but Danny and I are going to take care of it for you for the low cost of another chance to pet your dogs."

Her cousin, who was wrestling with Shiner, glanced up at that and nodded. "Yes, happy to."

Despite my protests, they quickly unpacked the pieces of the frame that needed it and swiftly assembled the bed. I'd have spent all day doing it, so I was grateful for their help. I'd indulged a little and gotten a canopy bed, though I didn't have drapes or a canopy for it, yet. My ex had always thought they were dumb, and I'd always wanted one, so now I had one and I couldn't wait to find the right pieces to go with it.

"Okay, time for the rest." Rebecca packed up her tools, and she and Danny bundled the packaging back out into their truck before getting the mattress. It was one of those that you could adjust the firmness of, and I felt very fancy having something that nice to sleep on.

They got everything set up, showed me how to use it, then spent the next half hour wrestling with Creek and Shiner. The dogs were thrilled, and I enjoyed watching the delight on Rebecca and Danny's faces at their antics.

They refused my offer of a meal once the dogs were done playing, congratulated me on the new bed, then left, saying they were heading into town for ice cream.

"They were so nice," I said to the dogs as they lay on the porch.

Creek was passed out, his tongue lolling out the side of his mouth. Shiner wagged his fluffy plumed tail and was soon snoring lightly. The porch had quickly become their favorite spot in the house.

I'd ordered sheets and they were washed and ready so I quickly made the bed, threw on the bright comforter I'd bought, then remembered the box I'd been opening.

My curiosity drew me back quickly, though I frowned when I looked inside. "What is all that?" I'd gotten it open enough that the contents were visible, but I hadn't paid any attention until now and my cheeks heated when I saw what I was looking at. Toys. Adult toys. Several of them.

There was a card tucked on top and I quickly read it.

"Just to get you through. <3 D&K."

While I knew what adult toys were, I'd never used them, or even really seen them before. Hands shaking with embarrassment, I pulled them out of the box.

"Well…" I finally laughed after several minutes of staring. "That puts my ex to shame." Nothing was overly large, but certainly enough to be satisfying. If I ever got brave enough to try.

There was a vibrator, a dildo, and a few other toys I wasn't quite sure what they were for, but I imagined I could figure it out, especially since there was also a book that I assumed had suggestions since it was certainly related to the toys. Oddly enough, she'd also included a couple of local guidebooks for hikes and things tourists should know.

"Wow, that's…" I didn't even know what to think. Still in a bit of a daze, I took everything to my bedroom and stashed the box in the bathroom before going back out onto the porch and sitting in the rocker. I stared off into the distance for a while, contemplating the gift. At least I wasn't supposed to be into work for a couple of days so I might be able to look at my bosses without blushing by the time I made it back.

Maybe.

Then another thought occurred to me. "Oh my god," I gasped. The box had been open, on the coffee table, the entire time I'd had guests. I really hoped they hadn't seen what was in the box. Mortified, I curled up on myself.

The sun sank low on the horizon and my eyelids drooped. I jerked awake with a shiver. Night had fallen and both dogs were dozing at my feet. They were likely enjoying the chilly air, but I was pretty sure the cold had woken me.

I stretched when I got up. "Come on, Shiner, Creek, let's go to bed."

They groaned and followed me inside, though my feet picked up as I remembered I had a real bed to sleep in. It didn't take long to go through my nightly routine, and Shiner and Creek had already claimed space on the bed by the time I crawled in between the silky-smooth sheets.

Grinning, I let myself drift back to sleep, only to be woken what felt like moments later by an alarmed bark from one of the dogs.

I bolted upright and screamed. Two little girls stood at the end of the bed staring at me. The light wasn't on, but I could see them as if they glowed from an inner light. I flailed around for the light, almost knocking it off the nightstand, and managed to flip on the light.

The images remained, as if burned onto my retinas.

"Fuck!" I shouted. The dogs barked, and with a flash of greenish light, the girls vanished.

"Oh, my god." I put my hand on my chest and tried to slow my pounding heart. All the calming breaths in the world didn't erase the image of the girls in pigtails wearing sun dresses and the sad eyes sunken deep into their faces.

If the dogs hadn't also been barking, I would have thought I was dreaming, but they were clearly affected by whatever it was, too.

Shiner plopped his butt onto my chest, trembling. Creek was prowling around the end of the bed, hackles up and soft growls coming from his throat.

I dug my fingers into Shiner's fur and didn't scold him for making it hard to breathe.

Was my house haunted? It wasn't possible, but I'd just seen two ghosts. Maybe?

It took hours before the three of us calmed down enough to go back to sleep. I finally had to turn some music on because otherwise any time the house settled or creaked, my heart started racing again.

At least I finally managed a few hours of sleep, knowing the dogs were also watching over me. If nothing else, they'd alert me, and ghosts couldn't hurt me. Could they?

Chapter 10

Violet

I woke bleary eyed the next morning. Shiner was sprawled over my legs, and Creek was perched on the end of the bed with his head tilted to one side, for all the world looking like he was getting pet.

I groaned and the dog stood and did a full body shake.

For a few moments I couldn't remember why I'd slept so poorly, but then the memories came back, and I darted my gaze around the room. Nothing.

Had I dreamed it?

I rubbed at my eyes and nudged Shiner until he grumbled and got off me. When I stumbled into the bathroom, my gaze snagged on the box of toys. What to do with those? I let myself consider actually using them before shying away from the idea. Surely not.

I took a quick shower and managed to wake up enough to stumble into some clothing and let the dogs out the front door. Then I managed a cup of coffee and went back out on the porch. The morning was as lovely as the view. I could just see the lighthouse in the distance.

The lighthouse reminded me of Ian. Ian embarrassingly got me thinking about the box of toys again. I'd never tried anything like that before. Hell, I'd hardly ever even touched myself before. That wasn't something you did. Was it?

75

It had been so long since I'd had any real pleasure. Probably the first year or so of our marriage, though it had never really been about me. Almost on auto pilot, I got up and went back inside. The box was where I'd left it and, irrationally nervous, I put it up on the counter and took out the vibrator wand. That was nice and safe, and I at least knew what to do with it even if I'd never used one. They'd thoughtfully included cleaner, and after a quick check of the directions, I cleaned the thing off and took it into the bedroom with me. It probably needed to charge, but it also came with an extra-long cord and the instructions said you could use it that way. I left it on the bed while I went to call the dogs inside. The last thing I needed was them alerting to something outside when I was in the middle of... Was I really going to use the toys?

After a moment of thought, I hardened my resolve. My hesitation was entirely based on my experiences with my ex and nothing more. There was absolutely nothing wrong with toys. I'd just been so focused on taking care of my ex when he wanted something from me, I'd forgotten I had needs too. And now that I wasn't worried for my life, or my dogs' lives, I could relax a little. Experiment. Enjoy the gift my bosses had given me.

That was a little weird, wasn't it?

Well, if they'd been men probably, but they meant well.

"Shiner! Creek! Get in here."

After a moment, the dogs rounded the corner and bounded up the steps. I glanced at the gate. It was still shut, though I'd left it unlocked just in case. Just in case what? I didn't know. But I was home, so at least no one was coming inside without me knowing it.

I shut the door behind them and locked it. Then, not sure how I should feel, I went back into the bedroom.

If there were ghosts, I hoped they weren't watching.

That was the most ridiculous thing ever.

I shed my nightdress and climbed back into bed feeling quite scandalous at being in bed naked. Which was also ridiculous.

Hesitantly, I pushed the power button, and the vibrator wand came to life. That seemed simple enough. There were several settings, and I tested them all out on my hand before I felt like I understood what it would do.

Creek and Shiner had briefly come into the room, but they'd gone out again and I was alone.

I lay back on the bed, head cradled on a pillow and held up the vibrator. I stared at it. Could I? Should I?

Fuck it. I turned it on to its lowest setting and gently touched it to the front of my pussy where the soft curls of hair had grown in after I'd stopped waxing.

I jumped, then started laughing, I couldn't help it. This entire thing was ridiculous. It was my body, if I wanted to touch it, I could. And I had every right to my own pleasure.

Once I'd gotten over the giggles, I turned the vibrator wand back on and touched it to myself again. This time I didn't jump. The sensation was pleasant, and I settled back and let myself feel what my body was experiencing. For so long I'd had to ignore my body to get through my day that simply shutting my eyes and feeling was pretty intense all on its own.

After a little while, I moved the vibrator around, trying to figure out where things felt better than others. None of it was bad, but there were certainly places that lit up my nerves more than others.

Finally, I settled on a spot that seemed a bit extra intense and turned the vibrator up one setting. A soft moan escaped my lips, surprising me. I never made sound during sex. I'd never enjoyed it enough and I was good at pretending, but not that good. My ex hadn't ever seemed to notice. I didn't try to suppress my feelings and moved the vibrator around until the sensations that had been focused around my pussy radiated deep inside me.

I liked that a lot and concentrated on the sensation as it built inside of me. I vaguely remembered this feeling from when I was much younger, but it had been so long, and I chased it eagerly. When it settled into a steady warmth that spread through me, I kicked the vibrator up another notch and groaned as it really sent the warmth and pleasant tingles all the way to my toes. My muscles tightened involuntarily, and I eagerly let myself sink into all the sensations that the vibrator was giving me.

When my orgasm hit, it surprised me. Somehow, I hadn't exactly expected to get that far. It had been years since I'd even hoped for one. I gasped, muscles trembling, pleasure rocketing through me.

I flipped the vibrator off and lay there, a cool draft playing across my sweat-soaked skin and intensifying the pleasure that still trembled through me. I trailed my fingers over my stomach and up over my breast, tickling my skin and enjoying the afterglow.

Had I ever felt this good after sex before? I didn't think so. If it was better like this, I was going solo from now on.

I curled up on my side and cuddled with my pillow and let a few tears trickle down my cheeks while I let my body rest and simply feel the powerful sensations of getting pleasure. I wasn't sure Katie and Debbie actually realized what they'd done for me, but this freedom to experience this kind of pleasure felt like power. Power over my own body and my own needs. I contemplated the other toys that had come in the box and decided I might have to try one out tonight.

Chapter 11

Violet

I was still feeling pretty good about life a few hours later. I'd puttered around the house, tried to decide what to do with some of the stuff that had been left, stacked more blocks in the teen's room because they'd fallen again, then went back into the main area of the house to stare at the basement door once more.

The key ring I'd been given felt heavy in my hands as I approached the locked door. I tried key after key. One of them did go in the lock, but it wouldn't turn.

"So weird."

I jiggled the handle then eyed the hinges, but they were on the other side of the door. It must open in.

"Damn it." I gave another hard shove on the door, just in case, but it didn't budge.

Creek came bounding into the house through the open front door just then and I turned to look at him.

He skidded to a halt, eyes going wide and ears going back, as he looked over my shoulder.

I turned, dropped the key ring and ran toward the door.

Next to the basement door in dripping red blood, the word DANGER was written on the wall.

Before I could get to the door, the two little girls I'd seen the other night appeared, blocking my way.

Shiner crashed through the middle of them, running toward my side, emerging from the apparition covered in what could only be described as green slime.

He skidded to a stop, ears drooping in dismay, before he shook, spraying goo everywhere. It splattered on my face, and I shrieked.

The image of the girls wavered then reformed.

Creek barked at something behind me, and I spun around. A translucent image of a man wearing a bloodstained white apron appeared with a meat cleaver in his hand dripping blood.

I watched as a drop of blood fell to the floor, but it vanished before it hit the old wood.

My legs trembled and I whimpered. It was only through years of practice not losing my shit in scary situations that I managed to keep my feet at all.

Upstairs I heard the blocks crash to the ground, and something rattled in the kitchen.

A flicker of light flashed across the floor right in front of Creek. He made to chase it then stopped and came over to my side, though his "cat growl" rumbled from his throat.

Shiner *boofed* at the little girls but otherwise just looked upset at being gross.

After a moment the swinging door between the living room and the kitchen moved as if on its own. A woman that looked for all the world like a housekeeper came out and pointed at the wall, then the big bald guy with the dripping meat cleaver, before putting her hands on her hips.

He hung his head then pulled a rag from his belt, floated over to the words and wiped them away.

I stared, flabbergasted. I couldn't believe what I was seeing.

Upstairs something else crashed, and the housekeeper looked up toward the teen's room and heaved an exhausted sigh.

"Uh…" I finally said aloud.

The ghosts all focused on me, and I froze again.

Another ghost appeared at my side. This one actually looked familiar, like I'd seen her picture before. Oh, she looked like the old woman who had owned the house before me.

"Uh…" I got out again.

She smiled and patted my cheek, an ice-cold sensation that would have terrified me if I hadn't already been scared out of my mind.

Then she floated over to the bald man and pointed at the wall. When the housekeeper raised a hand in objection, the old woman shook her head and pointed at the man again.

He proceeded to write on the wall.

THE ONE IN THE BASEMENT IS DANGEROUS

I gulped. Sucked in some air, then let it out slowly and carefully unclenched my hands. I wasn't in danger, just scared. After repeating that to myself a few times, I replied.

"Uh. Thanks." It was all I could get out.

He bowed slightly before wiping the words away with his rag.

Before I could think of anything else to say, both dogs barked again, this time ears perked up and attention pointed out the door.

The ghosts vanished, and I quickly grabbed at one of the sheets I still had on the couch from when I'd been sleeping there and rubbed the slimy goo off my face before going to the door, Creek and Shiner at my heels.

A black van with a dish on top pulled into the drive. They'd disregarded the closed gate, and it now stood open behind them. Two men got out of the van right away and came toward me.

I was again reminded of how alone I was out here. Though it wasn't the best response, I let myself fall back into my distant state where I could deal with just about anything calmly except danger to my dogs and waited for the men to come to me. I did grab my phone out of my pocket and pulled up the first number that came to my fingertips. Ian's. I'd call him if I needed to.

"Hello," I said coolly.

Both men were decently well dressed in khakis and polo shirts. Both were older white men, and both had that cocky self-assured look on their face that my ex and most of his friends had worn all the time.

"Mrs. Angleworth?"

"No. You have the wrong house."

The man who was speaking let his gaze roam my body. I was going to have to take a shower after this.

A low growl started in both dogs' chests. They rarely reacted like this to others. Anyone these dogs didn't like was automatically suspect. Normally, they loved everyone. They'd even tried to love my ex, but he hadn't let them, and they'd quickly learned to avoid him.

"I think we're right where we wanted to be. Now, about the house. What's your asking price?"

Something inside the house crashed, but I was in my calm place, and I ignored it. The dogs stayed laser focused on the men in front of me.

The one talking kept his attention on me, but the other glanced toward the house, then moved as if he might go investigate. I stepped in front of the door to block him.

"It's not for sale. Please leave. You're trespassing."

"Everything is for sale if the money is right," the guy said, and his eyes flicked to my dogs before returning to me.

Hot rage burned through me. I opened the camera and snapped pictures of the men and their truck.

"Leave. Now."

Then I dialed 911 because it would take a minute for the cops to arrive.

The dispatcher answered, but I kept my attention on the men.

"Hill House," I answered her question about where the emergency was. "You need to leave now!" I put as much force behind the words as I possibly could.

The man just laughed. "Why? Who's going to make me?"

Had he not noticed me call the cops?

"Leave."

Faster than I'd expected, the sirens from a police SUV reached my ears.

Normally, the dogs would have howled. Right now, they just continued to glare at the intruders.

The two men seemed to get the idea that the police SUV was responding to this location, and they headed for their van, though they weren't in that much of a hurry about it.

"You'll name a price before we're done," the man threatened.

I managed to snap a couple of pictures of the license plate without hanging up on dispatch. Then I put the phone to my ear.

"They're leaving right now, in a black van. They'll probably pass the deputy in just a minute."

"We have two units on their way," the dispatcher replied calmly. "Are you safe now?"

"I think so."

She asked a bunch of questions that I answered until the SUV arrived on my property then she turned me over to the deputy. It was the same one from before.

"Hi, Deputy." I glanced at his nametag to make sure I got his name right, hands shaking from reaction now that I was hopefully actually safe.

"Hello, Ms. Thompson. What happened?"

"I was, uh, cleaning, and these men came and demanded I sell my house to them. They used my married name, which I don't use anymore, and they threatened me and my dogs. The dispatchers might have heard some of it." I held up the phone.

He glanced back toward the road, shoulders tight. "I'm sorry you're being harassed, Ms. Thompson. Billy, uh, Ranger Milton, went after them, but we're not authorized to chase if they run, in this case."

"Yeah, I don't know if it's worth the risk," I replied, clasping my hands together. "I got pictures. I'll send them."

"You should really consider getting a security system."

"Yeah. I will. Thanks."

"My cousin installs them locally. I'll talk to him. He'll probably give you a discount."

"Oh, thanks." At home that might have been suspicious, but out here everyone was cousins or friends or neighbors, so I figured Deputy Maxwell was being honest.

"What happened to your dog?"

I glanced down. Creek had gone back to his normal cheerful self and had already tried to steal Deputy Maxwell's baton. Fortunately, the deputy liked dogs. Shiner, on the other hand, was sulking. Back turned and curled into a ball by the door.

When I looked closer, I could see his hair plastered to his body or standing out in spikes.

"Buddy, come here."

Shiner huffed but after a moment where it was clear he was thinking about disobeying, he got up and came over to my side.

"Oh, Shiner…" I hesitantly touched his fur. It had hardened into slightly green tinted spikes. Speaking of… The spots on my shirt that had gotten splattered when Shiner got the goo all over me had hardened too. I was really glad I'd taken the time to wipe my face off.

"He, uh, got into some, uh, baking. I spilled on him when, uh, the assholes in the black van came."

Deputy Maxwell kneeled and hesitantly touched the spiked fur.

"Ectoplasm comes out with saltwater," he said, but didn't elaborate.

"Ecto-what?"

"Well, Ms. Thompson, I'm sorry to see you again under these circumstances. There's a self-defense class at the station this weekend if you have time to come. We teach hand to hand and firearm basics. No charge to community members. I'll send my cousin by about the security system. He drives a white company van with Stan's Odd Jobs on the side. He's a good guy. Used to be a cop in the city."

"Okay, thank you, Deputy."

He nodded respectfully and left.

I shivered, fighting back tears as I went into my house. The house that was supposed to be my haven, and now all of this.

***

Though I hadn't expected to be using the self-dog wash any time soon, I was glad it was available. Feeling like an idiot, I'd even packed some salt from the kitchen before I'd left. Just in case.

Turned out Deputy Maxwell knew what he was talking about. Nothing touched the stuff all over Shiner until I put salt in the water, then it came right off. An hour of blow-drying later, and Shiner was clean.

Betty, bless her, didn't ask what he'd gotten into, and I made sure I completely cleaned out the sprayer so the salt wouldn't cause any damage, not to mention I had to get it all off my dog, before I went next door to the coffee shop. I needed a drink, and while I was in the mood to drown myself in alcohol, a London Fog was probably the better option. Especially since I had to drive home.

The dogs settled into a stay by one of the tables in the Maine section. Idly, I noticed Ian sitting at his normal spot working on his computer. I didn't want to bother him, so I went over to the counter and ordered. I hadn't met the woman behind the counter yet. She must be the artist who worked here part time. In an uncharacteristic moment, I decided not to introduce myself. I just wanted my drink, and to curl up on the couch and just exist in the coffee shop. She gave me my drink, and I curled up in the armchair and cradled it.

The dogs lay at my feet, and I let my thoughts drift. So, ghosts were real. People were trying to get me to sell my house for some reason and they kept using my former married name which made me wonder if my ex was involved. What could he possibly want from me or my house? Was it just to make my life even more miserable? Or was it something else. I knew I'd gotten a pretty poor deal in the divorce, but I'd been so afraid for my dogs and honestly, I couldn't really afford to pay a lawyer for very long, so I'd just done the best I could to get out. I probably was lucky the guy had gotten everything he had from my ex.

And I clearly could not leave the dogs at home until this was all resolved. Ghosts were certainly one thing, but the people? Yeah... that could be even worse.

Dakota Brown

Chapter 12

Ian

A familiar-sounding click of nails on the floor caught my attention, and I glanced up from my work. Violet and her two dogs had come into the shop. My mood brightened considerably just seeing them. I'd been disappointed when she wasn't at the counter earlier today.

My computer beeped and I glanced down at the model data that had finished running. The weather pattern distracted me for a moment and when I looked back up, Violet was curled up in one of the comfortable chairs in the Maine section where the dogs were allowed.

I sat over here by habit, not because I preferred this side or anything. Maybe I should go join her?

The more I looked, though, the more it seemed something troubled her. Her brow was furrowed, and she stared off into the distance. Maybe she didn't want to be bothered? Or maybe now was a good time to interrupt whatever darker thoughts troubled her.

I'd just finish this section of the report since it was due shortly, then I'd take a break and go talk to her.

Unfortunately, by the time I'd finished, Violet and her dogs had already left. I really didn't have to do anything else for the day, so I packed up and headed outside to see if she was still around. I didn't see her, or her van. Disappointed, I turned in a circle. When I turned back toward the coffee shop, my cousin, Debbie, was standing between me and the doors.

"Looking for someone?" Debbie had what I could only describe as an amused expression on her face.

"Uh, no?"

Her slight smile broadened.

"Looking for a set of fluffy dogs perhaps?"

"Oh. Uh, yeah, I guess. She seemed upset about something. I was going to ask, but she was gone before I finished the report I was working on."

"You know, I doubt she'd mind company if you went up to Hill House."

I tilted my head, sensing something from Debbie's tone of voice, but I wasn't sure what it was. "I don't want her to think I'm dropping by just to see the house." I'd actually considered going up to see her and not just because I wanted to see the house. I'd enjoyed our time when she'd been stuck at my house because of the storm.

"I'm pretty sure she hasn't quite comprehended how curious all the locals are about Hill House yet." Debbie patted me on the shoulder. "Go. She'll enjoy your company. She's very alone right now."

I frowned. "I doubt she really wants to hang out with me."

"You might be surprised, Ian."

"I, uh, should probably finish my work for the day." I let my shoulders slump, not sure why I felt so uncomfortable going up to see Violet.

"You said you were done. Go visit her. She needs some friends. She probably hasn't mentioned it. She's barely said anything to Katie and me, but her ex was an abusive shit. She hasn't said as much, but the signs are there. Go up to Hill House and make her feel welcome."

I took a breath and nodded. "Okay. Yeah. You're right, she probably needs some friends besides her meddling bosses."

Debbie's smile broadened into a full out grin. "Oh, we meddled. We'll meddle some more, but yes, she needs some extra friends."

"What did you do? Besides coerce me to go up and visit."

Debbie chuckled. "Same thing we did for your sister when she moved off to college."

My cheeks heated a little and my eyebrows rose. "I'm not sure I needed to know that. Either time, to be honest."

"Women have needs, too, Ian. Men must be aware of that."

"Yes, ma'am." I nodded acquiescence to her wisdom. She was right in that regard.

"Go on, then."

Still not sure she needed to tell me about sending Violet a gift box of the adult variety, I accepted her order and headed to my car.

The drive up to Hill House wasn't long compared to the drive out to the point where I lived. Even that trip didn't take very long. When I arrived, I noticed that the wrought iron gate that had always stood open was closed. I stopped the car, got out and checked. Locked.

"Well, shoot." I pulled out my phone, but before I could call Violet to see if she wanted company, her dogs came running up to the gate.

Creek barked and Shiner wagged his tail.

"Hi, guys." I kneeled, hand holding my phone going to the bars of the gate while I put my other one close enough for them to sniff. While I didn't know a ton about dogs, I knew that sometimes even when they were friendly, they might be aggressive around fences.

Not these two. Both stuck their heads through the bars for pets. I automatically went to pet their fluffy heads, and I managed to drop my phone. Before I could even react, Creek snatched the thing and took off, tail curled over his back and wagging.

Shiner stayed, glancing after the other dog before putting his head back through the bars for more pets.

"That dog," I muttered, not entirely upset. Though I did hope he didn't damage the screen. Shiner got a few more scratches before I stood up and eyed the gate and the fence. Could I climb it? I didn't want to just sit out here and honk, and I figured if Violet's dog had stolen my phone, I could at least somewhat justify climbing the fence to get it back. I was nearly positive she wouldn't be mad.

I waited a few more minutes to see if Creek would return or if Violet would notice the stolen phone and wonder where it had come from. When neither the dog nor Violet appeared, I studied the gate and fence again.

The fence wasn't very sturdy after years of neglect, but it wasn't exactly easily climbable, either. At least in its somewhat dilapidated state. The gate was taller but looked like it would be less likely to be damaged if I went over it.

Going up wasn't too bad. It wasn't that tall, something like eight feet. I even got my leg over the spikes at the top with no issues. Going down should be fine.

Before I could get my other leg over, Shiner barked, and a man shouted at me. "Get down from there."

"Ahh!" I nearly shrieked and lost my grip. Fortunately? The top spike caught my shirt and kept me from hitting the ground. Unfortunately, I was stuck dangling by my shirt. I kicked my feet, hoping to get some purchase, but my shirt was bunched up under my armpits and had kind of trapped my arms in an awkward position.

"Ian?"

"Yep," I managed to get out, voice a little choked from my shirt around my neck. I couldn't see who was talking to me, but they were on the other side of the fence.

Shiner stared up at me, ears perked, as if waiting for me to come down and pet him some more.

"What you doing up there?"

"Billy?" The voice finally clicked.

"Yeah."

"I was trying to get over the fence. Obviously. Creek ran off with my phone and Violet doesn't seem to have noticed yet."

The ranger laughed. "She did say he was a criminal."

Shiner warbled in that strange way that her dogs had, then stood up on his back legs and pawed at my foot before sitting very nicely. I swear he was presenting himself for more pets.

"Just a minute, Shiner."

My shirt wasn't stretchy, which meant it wasn't ripping with my weight. That was kind of good, but also not fantastic. I tried to twist again, or get purchase with my foot, or something, but I was left dangling.

"What are you doing out here, Billy?" Suddenly weirdly jealous, and not sure why, I hoped he had a good reason to be out here.

"Ms. Thompson's been having some unwanted visitors. I offered to walk the fence line and check for anything out of the ordinary, since I'm probably the most familiar with the area up here."

"Oh, that's great. Explains why I didn't hear your truck."

"Yeah, parked on the far end of the point and hiked in. Good excuse for a few different things. Anyway, maybe we should get you down."

"Ya think?" I liked Billy, and he was damn good at his job, but sometimes he was a little slow to get to the point.

At the very least, maybe I could get down before Violet saw me dangling from the top of her gate like a fish caught on a line.

Shiner's ears perked and he glanced back toward the house. I followed his gaze and saw Violet come to the door.

No such luck. Damn it.

"Ian?" She jumped the steps to her porch and ran over to me. "Hi, Ranger Milton."

"Hi, Violet. I was going to call, but Creek stole my phone."

She glanced back toward the house before shaking her head. "I believe it. You tried to climb the fence?"

"I'd shrug, but I'm trapped," I said. "Seemed like a good idea at the time?"

"He was doing alright until I startled him," Billy added in my defense. "If you'll unlock the gate, I'll come to that side and let Ian stand on my shoulders so he can get free."

"Sure," Violet said. "Be right back."

A small eternity later, Violet returned and unlocked her gate. She swung it open, which was a weird sensation as I was dragged through the air. Once he could get through the gate, Billy came and situated himself under my feet so I could stand.

That relieved the pressure on my arms and neck somewhat and I took a deep breath. Though my shirt was still stuck on the spike.

After a few moments of struggling, I sighed and undid the buttons, surprised none of them had popped. Once the shirt was unbuttoned, I was able to slide out of it and, with Billy's help, carefully get to the ground.

"Well, that was ," I said into the awkward silence that followed my successful landing.

Violet laughed. "You said Creek has your phone?"

"Yes."

"That explains his behavior. Let's go get it. Thank you, Ranger Milton."

"Billy, please. And you're welcome. Fence looks as good as it can, by the way. I'll check the other side, but so far, I haven't seen anything nefarious."

"Thank you."

He left as I struggled back into my abused shirt and hastily buttoned it up. "I'm sorry. I was going to call."

She laughed again. "Don't worry about it. You are always welcome. It's nice to have some friendly company up here."

"Billy said you'd had some unwelcome visitors? That's crazy. Everyone out here is friendly."

"I don't think they're locals." Her expression fell.

I let it drop for the moment and followed her into the house.

"Creek!" she called, then sighed and went up the stairs. "He loves the teen's room."

"What? I didn't know you had kids."

"Oh! No. This place was furnished, and it looks like a room a teen would live in. Creek seems to like it. This way."

I followed and we went upstairs.

She pushed open a door that had been shut to just a crack. There was the criminal, his chin pressed to the floor, his plumed tail wagging over his back.

"Creek, give it back."

His tail wagged harder, and he refused to budge.

"He does this." Violet kneeled at the dog's side and scratched his ears, before extracting the phone from under his chin. "Thinks he can hide it, or something." Violet wiped the phone off on her pants before inspecting it and handing it back. "If he damaged it, I'll replace it. Just let me know."

"Oh, I'm sure it's fine." A quick glance showed that everything seemed in order, if a bit slobbered on.

"Let me make you some tea," she offered. "And give you a tour while it steeps."

"That'd be great, thanks Violet."

"Don't mention it. Why did you come up this way, anyway?"

"Uh." I stammered and ran my hand through my hair. "I was just coming up to see if you, uh, wanted company."

"You wanted to see the house, right?"

"No. Well, yes, but actually I'd have come up sooner. I just didn't want you to think I only wanted to see the house. Debbie suggested I should get over that fear and just come visit. She meddles sometimes."

Violet blushed and turned her head away, busying herself in petting her dog for a moment. I could guess what might be on her mind since I knew what else my cousin had been up to.

"I'm glad you came up. Let me get tea started and then I'll show you around."

Warming at her happy smile, I held out my hand to help her to her feet.

She stumbled and I caught her.

"Ooof, I'm sorry." Violet righted herself and looked back over her shoulder, an annoyed expression on her face. "Seriously," she muttered.

"What?"

"Nothing. Just, more meddling. Anyway, I must have tripped. I'm very sorry. Tea?"

She hurried out of the room and, after a curious look around, I followed.

Chapter 13

Violet

The cold feel on my back was the only reason I knew how I'd tripped and fallen into Ian's arms. I had no idea why a ghost might have shoved me into him, but that had to be what had happened. Not that I especially minded being there, but at least it was less embarrassing than getting hooked on the top of an eight-foot gate. Of course, if Creek hadn't stolen Ian's phone…

The ghosts and I were going to have to have a talk about things here soon. Ghosts… I shook my head and went into the kitchen.

And stopped.

The paper plates I'd bought to replace the shattered ones were spread over the entire kitchen. The cabinets were open. A bag of rice had fallen and scattered all over the counter.

A flash of something caught my attention. Creek gave his deep "chasing a cat" bark and bolted back out the doors after it.

"Creek! Be careful!"

The thump of him slamming into something wasn't reassuring.

I sighed and went over to the coffee mugs, which thankfully hadn't been destroyed as they were the only ones I owned. They had cute little Yakutian Laikas that looked like my dogs on them. The one I picked up felt heavier than normal and I looked inside.

"Seriously?" I dumped a blob of ectoplasm into the sink. "Seriously," I repeated, then shut my eyes. It was better than my ex. Anything was better than him. Hoping I didn't sound crazy, I glanced at Ian, who was gazing around the trashed kitchen with a mystified look on his face. "Could you hand me the salt canister, please?"

"So, uh, tornado or dogs?"

I almost flat out told him it was the ghosts because my dogs would never do anything like this. Creek might be a criminal, but he wasn't a vandal. I took a few deep breaths and calmed myself. Ian didn't mean anything by it.

"I must have left a window open or something. A breeze probably. My dogs wouldn't do this."

Ian glanced around again, but didn't contradict me, simply handed over the canister of salt. I dumped a little into the mug and washed it out, then gave it an extra rinse. The other one with Creek on it was still clean, so I gave that one to Ian just in case ectoplasm left an aftertaste in the cup or something.

Then, acting like nothing was amiss, which unfortunately I was good at, I set about boiling water and making tea.

Ian shocked me by going around and picking up the plates while I was doing that. He set them uncertainly on the table, then he scooped the rice back into the bag as best he could.

"Oh, thanks. You don't have to do that."

"I am perfectly capable of helping to clean up while I wait for you to make tea." He continued to tidy up. "So, these unwanted visitors?"

"I don't know who they are. I've had a couple of paranormal investigators show up and want to test the house. One of them was polite, the other very threatening.

Then some folks outright tried to buy the house and made veiled threats against me and the dogs. I guess I'm putting in a security system." I stopped what I was doing and leaned against the counter. "I'm in small town Maine in the middle of nowhere. I shouldn't have to be dealing with this."

Ian came over and put his hand on my shoulder. "No, you shouldn't. I'm sorry this is happening. Can I help?"

I didn't know what to do. I hadn't been touched kindly by a man in so long. Part of me wanted to crumple in his arms and break down sobbing. Another part of me knew this wasn't Ian's problem and I certainly wouldn't subject him to that sort of behavior.

"I'm sorry," I said, trying to head off a dive toward disassociation and not quite succeeding. "I shouldn't burden you with this. Anyway. I don't know why they'd want the place."

"It's supposed to be haunted, and the house has a big history. Maybe we could do some research in the local archives to find out why they want it?" Ian squeezed my shoulder then let his hand drop. He backed away to finish cleaning up the spilled rice.

I felt emptier without his touch. That was weird. I'd always thought I didn't like to be touched, but suddenly the urge to wrap myself around Ian and never let go as long as he would hold me was strong.

Shivering, I finished the tea preparations and handed his cup over, along with sugar, honey, cream, and a plate to put his tea ball on.

"Yeah, I hadn't thought of that. I'll see what I can come up with."

"Tell you what, how about we go over next time you have a free afternoon."

"Is it dog friendly? I can't leave them here without someone around. Not with people showing up and trying to break in."

"I'll find out. If it's not, we can take them to my place for the afternoon."

"Oh, I couldn't impose."

Ian shook his head. "No, it'll be fine. I'll send you a message when I know more, and you can let me know your schedule." He took a sip of his tea. "This is delicious. Thank you."

I opened my mouth to say something and couldn't get any words out. He liked my tea? No one had ever even *acted* like they liked my tea before. My ex had sipped it, but he'd always made it seem like it was a chore.

"I'm sure it's not what you're used to, but thank you," I replied.

"Violet, it's the perfect temperature and perfectly steeped. It's like you knew exactly how I liked it. I only ever get coffee at the coffee shop, so you didn't figure it out there. It's delicious. What kind is it?"

"Uh, Irish Breakfast," I replied. "I'm sorry, I should have asked what you like. I have a couple of varieties."

Ian studied me for a minute before he glanced at the table. "Violet, this is perfect."

I felt like I'd done something wrong, but I wasn't sure what, so I just nodded and let myself drift a little more toward that safe place where I could deal with anything.

"So, um, yeah, just let me know about the research. I can't imagine what anyone would want with this place though. It's nice. I like it. But why harass me for it?"

"Is it haunted?" Ian glanced at me again.

I'd reached far enough into my disassociation that I didn't react, but something crashed upstairs.

"You believe in ghosts?" I couldn't bring myself to outright lie to him, but I couldn't quite tell him it was, either.

He shrugged. "I live in a lighthouse. I'm pretty sure it's haunted. I've never encountered anything, but it wouldn't surprise me."

"Interesting. How'd you get into weather forecasting?" I hadn't spent enough time asking Ian about himself and that was awfully rude, and maybe I could get him to forget about the ghosts for a while.

"My father was a fisherman. I grew up on the water with him and the weather was vitally important. He taught me how to read the clouds and the temperature and all that so when I went to school, I studied weather. I didn't want to be a fisherman, but I did want to contribute something and being able to accurately forecast the weather was something I could do for my community."

His story brought me back to myself a little bit, and before long we'd fallen into a conversation about our childhoods in Maine.

We talked through several cups of tea until Shiner pointedly brought me his bowl.

"Oh. Uh." Interrupting conversation to take care of dogs was just not something I was supposed to do, but Ian was already picking up his bowl and giving Shiner a pat on the head.

"Looks like it is dinner time. I should get going anyway. Let's get these guys fed and I'll make sure I've got my wallet and phone before I leave." He laughed and patted his pocket.

Creek perked up from the floor where he'd been watching us, and I scrambled to get to my feet.

"I'm sorry about them."

"Violet." Ian turned and held out his hand.

Automatically I offered mine.

Ian tilted his head slightly before gently taking my hand in his. "They're fine. Don't apologize for them. They're delightful dogs and while I've never considered myself a dog person before, they might be converting me."

I couldn't help it. I burst into tears.

Ian wrapped me in his arms and held me while I cried.

Chapter 14

Ian

"You were right," I said to my cousin the next day at the coffee shop. Violet wasn't in. She'd had to take the day to deal with the security system installation. "She desperately needs to see Lydia."

Lydia was the therapist who had helped me after the sea had claimed my father when I was twelve. I hadn't told Violet about that. I probably would, someday. It was somewhat common knowledge, but she'd had a lot of other things to deal with and I hadn't wanted to hit her with that sob story.

"What happened?" Debbie came around the counter and stood near me so we could talk quietly.

"She disassociates like a pro. She's super apologetic for things that aren't even remotely a problem, and when I told her I liked her dogs, she broke down sobbing. That was literally the only thing that cracked her mask."

"You didn't leave her up there like that, did you?"

"I'm not a total ass, Debbie. I made her dinner, which seemed to confuse her even more. I did have to leave at some point, but I made sure she was at least okay on the surface before I left. Do you have any idea what her ex did to her?"

"No. Do you?"

Ian shook his head. "I've never really had much luck with dating, you know that. I just know whatever she went through, it was bad. And that's only because I went through so much therapy after dad died that I can see the things I was doing in her."

Debbie shook her head. "What are we going to do about it?"

"I don't know that we can do anything except be there for her. I told her I never considered myself a dog person before but hers were changing my mind. That's what broke her. The dogs are so important to her, and they should be. They're hilarious and clearly completely devoted to her. She was really worried that the people harassing her would hurt her dogs. She wasn't worried about herself." I shook my head. "So, we make friends with her dogs and hopefully she'll feel safe enough with us to tell us one of these days. I might push a little and see if she wants to talk to Lydia. I didn't tell her about dad, but I might. We're supposed to research her house and try and figure out why people would be pressuring her to sell it. Maybe I can bring it up then."

Debbie nodded, her normally cheerful face somber. "I like her, Ian. We need to help her, if we can."

"How's that event you told me about coming along?"

"Good. Everyone is quite taken with the idea. It's scheduled around the harvest festival so we should have a lot of tourists to stop in, too. It's more for the locals, but it'll be good to have a big draw for the first gathering."

"Great. Let me know if I can help with anything. That's not really my forte, but if I can, I will."

"Just make sure the weather is good for us," Debbie joked.

"I'll do my best." Feeling troubled, I let my cousin get back to work. Not only was Violet on my mind because of how yesterday had gone, but I genuinely liked her. She needed a friend, so maybe I could be that for her.

I managed to get lost in my work after a while, though she was still on my mind when Katie came over.

"So, is it haunted?"

"She wouldn't say."

"Kid, it's totally haunted then." She took my dirty mug, and wandered away.

***

Hours later, I'd convinced the museum manager and the librarian into letting Creek and Shiner in. That way we could have the dogs with us, and Violet wouldn't have to worry. I told them what we were interested in researching and they promised to look into things if we gave them a couple of days.

After a quick text with Violet, I confirmed that we'd be able to go by in two days and headed back out to the lighthouse. I very much looked forward to spending an afternoon with her, and maybe we could figure out what it was about the house that the people wanted. If we knew that, at least we'd be able to come up with a better plan than just a security system. I'd have been nervous out there all alone if unwanted people kept showing up. I couldn't imagine how she felt.

Chapter 15

Violet

Shiner's deep alarm bark woke me out of a dead sleep. I bolted upright and screamed.

The twins stood at the end of my bed and stared at me.

I threw my pillow at them, then bolted from the room, my dogs on my heels.

Something crashed upstairs, and I heard my new plates shatter in the kitchen.

A terrifying ghostly visage stared at me from the mirror at the entryway when I ran out onto the porch and fell to my knees, sobbing.

I couldn't do this anymore. The ghosts, the paranormal investigators, the harassment from whoever was trying to buy the house. They'd been back, though this time the gate had stopped them. They'd left a large envelope at the gate. I'd not touched it, but I knew it was still there, waiting.

Creek shoved his way under my stomach and Shiner curled around me, letting me cry into his ruff. I wasn't sure how long I sobbed, but the dogs were the only thing keeping me warm by the time I cried myself out.

The rocking chair creaked as it rocked back and forth with no one in it.

I glared at it, but I imagined it was the grandmotherly ghost and I couldn't bring myself to be mad at her.

I was so tired. I hadn't slept well since Ian's visit. The ghosts kept waking me, or fear that someone was going to break in and hurt my dogs kept me up. I was going to have to call out from work, and I'd just started. I hadn't felt bad asking for a day to deal with the security system, but calling out because I couldn't sleep, that wasn't something I could do. But if I couldn't get any rest, I wouldn't be any use at the coffee shop. I needed the job, though. The security system had taken an alarming amount of my reserves, and I wasn't sure I'd be able to make it through the winter at this rate. Not that he'd overcharged me or anything. I'd found his rate quite reasonable. I just didn't have that much extra.

Wearily, I climbed to my feet, went inside, and collapsed on the couch. What else could I do but try to get enough sleep to show up to work the next day.

***

I guzzled tea at home, managed to get myself awake enough to drive, loaded the dogs, and headed into town. I just hoped no one wanted to chat while I was in the coffee shop today. I let myself retreat, and by the time I reached the coffee shop, I'd settled. I could get the work done and then go home and try to sleep.

"Hey, what's up?" Katie said as soon as I came in.

"Nothing. Just stayed up too late last night." I settled the dogs and got started on the morning routine. I had it down now and it didn't take long before we were ready to open.

Katie watched me while I worked. Usually she had some tasks, but I guessed she was checking to make sure I did everything correctly. That seemed reasonable to check in on new hires now and again. Though I'd been there a few weeks by now and the job wasn't difficult. It was demanding, and there were a lot of intricacies, but compared to dealing with my ex and his desires this wasn't hard.

Confident I was doing everything right, I kept on and eventually Katie went back to the office.

The morning went by in a blur as I selfishly let myself stay in my safe space while I worked. Ian came in like normal and acted happy to see me. I was glad to see him, too, but he came in during a quick rush so I didn't have much time to do more than say hi.

Once it was time for me to leave for the day, I got everything settled and said a quick goodbye. The dogs heeled quietly, and we headed out to the van. Tucked under my windshield wiper was another envelope. Even from here I could see the logo of the place trying to force me to sell my house.

I froze and stared, not willing to touch the thing, but not able to get home with it under my wiper.

They'd followed me home and now they were harassing me at work. I wasn't safe anywhere. A cold rage simmered just below the fear, exhaustion, and desperate need to protect my dogs from harm. Over that sat the calm that protected me. Despite all the layers of feelings, I had no idea what to do.

"Violet?" a familiar and welcome voice said. "What's wrong?"

I pointed at the envelope.

"Do you want me to get that for you?"

I couldn't reply, couldn't even process anything. It had taken a lot for me to even figure out how to get away from my ex, but this was so far outside my experience. Not to mention, no one had ever actually helped me even when I'd finally decided to get a divorce. Even the lawyer I'd managed to hire had done the bare minimum. Even I knew that. Still, I'd gotten away.

Ian gently lowered my arm and went and took the envelope from my van.

"Do you want it?"

I shook my head, and, on autopilot, loaded the dogs and left, leaving Ian standing there at the curb. It wasn't until I was home and soaking in a hot bath, legs curled to my chest, that I realized how rude that had been.

I'd apologize later.

The water cooled and both Shiner and Creek came over and rested their chins on the edge of the bathtub. I forced myself out of the tub and into bed.

No sooner had I felt like I'd gone to sleep than the dogs alarmed.

I bolted upright. It wasn't the house alarm; it was the dogs' ghost alarm. After the letter on my car, I was glad it was the ghosts. The twins stood at the edge of the bed and stared at me.

I stared back.

Exhaustion tugged at me, and I flopped back onto the bed and stared at the ceiling. The dogs whined but settled next to me. They were at least somewhat used to the ghosts by now.

Something crashed upstairs.

I hadn't bothered to replace the dishes in the kitchen this time, so I imagined my paper plates fluttering around.

I shut my eyes for a moment and when I opened them again, the twins hovered over me, staring at me from above.

I snapped.

Bolting upright, I stood on the bed and waved my pillow around until the twins dissipated. Right then, I didn't care that it would ruin my only other pillow. The first had been ruined when I'd thrown it through them the first time.

"No! No, no, no, no!" I shouted. "Leave me the fuck alone. If I have to sell this place, if the people trying to get it win, what do you think will happen to all of you! I have to sleep. I'm exhausted. If I can't sleep, I can't work and I can't pay the bills for this place! Clean up your own damn messes! Stop breaking my dishes! I don't have any extra money. I had to spend it all on the security system. Stop waking me up!"

I tossed the ectoplasm-soaked pillow to the floor and collapsed back into bed.

When the ghosts didn't return and the crashing upstairs stopped, I rolled over onto my stomach, pulled the blankets up over my head, and passed out.

Chapter 16

Housekeeper

I scolded the twins, shaking my finger at them. If they had scared the new owner of Hill House away, we'd be back to starving. Possibly for good.

Grandmother shook her head at me, but she was far too lenient with those two. She'd always indulged their ways. Even when she'd been alive.

If it cost us Violet, well, where would we be then?

We were going to have to clean this place up. Again. I loved cleaning, but the others? Well, they enjoyed making messes. Not this time. I wasn't cleaning it all up alone.

I pointed to the twins, then the mess, and put my hands on my hips.

They hung their heads, but after a moment sighed and bent to the task. Now I just needed to find that damn butcher. He was always making bloody messes for me to clean.

Chapter 17

Ian

The next day I got to the coffee shop early, before opening. I'd done something I shouldn't have, but I was so worried about Violet, that I'd opened the letter she'd had me remove from her van. Then I'd showed it to my cousin and her wife.

That had sent us to the internet to see if we could find out any more about Violet and her ex. There hadn't been much, but what we had found had turned all our rage meters up to full. I hadn't even known I could be this angry. And I had no idea how to approach any of this with Violet. I liked her. I wanted to be her friend. But what we'd done could be perceived as a huge overstepping of boundaries.

And yet, it was possible she was in real danger.

The company harassing her was a paranormal investigation company, but it had a very negative reputation and ties to California, where she was from, which was suspicious on another level. I'd also gone to the library and historical society directly and found as much as I could about Hill House, and I thought I knew what they were after. Part of me had been upset that I'd effectively canceled our day out doing research together, but another part of me thought this was more important.

When Violet and her dogs trudged in, they all looked tired. The normally bright and happy dogs were subdued.

Not in a way that made me worry about them, but I could tell they weren't happy about something. Violet looked, well, exhausted. As soon as she noticed Debbie, she plastered a smile on her face and slid back into that mask she wore sometimes. Usually, it was a pretty good cover for however she was feeling, but this morning it only sort of concealed the exhaustion.

When Violet first arrived, I was pretty sure she'd allowed us to see the real her with no mask involved. But the last couple of weeks, she'd slid more and more into that artificial place and every time I saw it, my heart broke a little more.

"Hey, Violet," Debbie said. "We're opening late today for a staff meeting. Grab a seat. Keep the dogs here."

I saw a flash of fear in Violet's eyes before she retreated further. She hadn't noticed me yet, and I knew where she was heading from my own experiences as a teen. She probably thought she was getting fired or something and I wasn't sure Debbie had caught on to that.

Katie put a sign in the window while Violet went over to the Maine section and sank down onto the couch. I got up from where I sat and joined her, sitting next to her though I hadn't planned to.

Creek and Shiner perked up and Creek, who was closest to me, sat up and put his chin on my knee.

"Ian?"

"Hey, Violet." I reached out a hand and she automatically put hers in mine. That hurt, but not on a personal level, just that she was so conditioned that she didn't even think, she just did what I wanted.

Still, I kept a hold of her hand and held it tightly.

"Why are you here?" She was focusing a little more but still seemed distant.

"Yeah, we're worried about you." I tightened my grip on her hand.

"I'm fine."

Katie pulled out the envelope from yesterday and Violet froze, retreating completely.

"Honey, we're here for you." Katie leaned forward.

Debbie came over and set a tray of drinks and snacks down on the table.

Debbie sank into one of the chairs. "Okay, first off, just to make this an official staff meeting. Your performance here is great, and you're getting a raise. We still don't have full-time hours, but we're very happy and hope you'll continue to stay as long as you're able to. If we do end up getting busy enough for full time, you'll get the hours. Second, plans for the gathering are going fantastically. Great job. If this event does well, that will be part of your duties moving forward."

"Thank you," Violet replied, voice soft, almost surprised sounding.

"Staff meeting is over. A-plus, great job. Okay, now we're on to personal matters and you can tell us to fuck right off if you want. We have a feeling you won't ask for help so we're getting involved, kid." Katie took one of the drinks off the table and took a sip before making a face and handing it to Debbie. Then she grabbed a different one and after a sip seemed content with her choice.

"What do you mean?' Violet replied with a frown, still not taking her own drink.

"You haven't said much, but we've pieced together a little bit. You're fresh out of a terrible marriage and you moved here to get away and start over."

Violet nodded. "It wasn't that bad. Just, not a good fit for me."

"Violet," I said. "You have so much trauma that no one knows you have trauma because you're so good at hiding it. I can tell because when my dad died, I pretty much did the same thing, and I can see the signs. It took a few years of therapy for me to come out of it."

"Oh." She frowned. "Yeah, I went to a therapist for a while. I couldn't afford that and the dog shows and, well, the dog shows were really important to me."

"Your husband is a CEO of a tech company. How could you not afford whatever you wanted?"

"Oh, I had to make my own money for dog shows, which is why I did grooming on the side." She said it so casually, as if of course her millionaire husband couldn't manage to pay for her hobbies. "As long as I kept the house up and all that and made sure I got home in time for his dinner, I could do whatever I wanted. I missed out on some big wins because of that." She shrugged. "That's life, I guess."

We all stared at her for a minute or two before I finally shook my head. "Violet. You're an incredibly strong woman, but you're not alone anymore. Let us help you."

"With what?"

I gestured toward the letter again. She didn't retreat quite as much. She did mostly avoid looking at it.

"You need to hire a lawyer, get some restraining orders, and to be completely honest, I want you to meet my therapist. I still go see her now and again." I squeezed her hand.

"Oh, I can't afford any of that." She shook her head. "It'll be fine. They'll go away eventually.'

That brought about another round of stares.

"Violet, your ex is a millionaire," Debbie finally said.

"Yeah. I know." Her brow furrowed, and if I hadn't had a hold of her hand, I might have reached out and smoothed them away with my thumb.

"You divorced him for very legitimate reasons," my cousin continued.

"I left him because he didn't like my dogs." Violet's free hand went to Shiner's head.

I swiftly moved my free hand, and Violet froze, her expression going placid. I felt like an ass, but all the signs were there. I had to know. I dropped my hand toward Creek, though I never would hurt an animal, and Violet came to life.

She jerked her hand free of mine and leaned forward, as if she were going for her drink. She interposed her body between me and Creek while she did it. She didn't even look at me, just took her drink and slowly straightened. I wasn't even sure she was completely aware of what she'd done. Creek had shifted away from me, but I didn't think it was because he was worried about getting hit. The dogs had never been touched, I guessed. But Violet…

Rage simmered deep in my chest.

"Violet," I said softly. "I will never, ever hurt you or one of your dogs. I want you to know that right now." I put my hand on her shoulder. She accepted the touch. She was trembling, though you wouldn't have known it just by looking at her.

"Of course not, Ian," she replied automatically. Her voice was even calm.

I met Debbie's then Katie's eyes.

"If I ever meet him, so help me, I'll kill him," Katie snarled in the thickest Bostonian accent I'd ever heard fall from her lips.

"Who?" Violet simply looked confused.

"Your ex."

"Oh." She shrugged. "He's unlikely to have any interest in me. I don't have anything he wants."

I scrubbed at my face. "Yeah, about that. We overstepped even more and did some digging."

"What do you mean?" She twisted to look at me.

"The paranormal investigators trying to get you to sell have a pretty bad reputation for harassment in several states. Not only that, but we think we figured out why they're after Hill House."

"I thought we were going to research this weekend?" She didn't sound upset, just accepting.

"Yeah, I know. When I called the historical society and the library to get permission to bring the dogs, I told them what they were after. They ended up getting curious, because, well, Hill House has such a reputation around here anyway, and we dug up some interesting stuff. As with most ancient, haunted mansions, there's a rumor of treasure. Thing is, it's entirely possible this rumor is real. Of course, it's also possible it's just a rumor. Regardless, I'll go into the details with you later. I think we need to do a few other things, first." I twisted my hands together nervously. This was so far outside my comfort zone, but I plunged ahead. Creek shoved his muzzle under my hand, and I buried my fingers in his soft ruff, much like Violet had done to Shiner once she'd calmed a little from my abrupt movements.

"Like what?"

"You and I are going to go visit a friend of mine." I glanced at Debbie and Katie who both nodded. They knew what I was up to. I'd also talked to Lydia already and she'd managed to free up her morning for an emergency session. "And then we're going to swing by the sheriff's office and fill out some restraining orders."

"Is someone bothering you?"

"Yes," I replied truthfully, hoping she wouldn't think too much about it until we were there.

"But I have to work."

"Paid day off," Katie declared. "In honor of your raise. Go with Ian."

"I couldn't…"

"Violet, paid day off," Debbie insisted. "The weather is lovely. Go with Ian for his errands, and then the two of you should take lunch on the point. Tomorrow is plenty of time to get back to work. We'll have extra for you to make up for it."

"Oh, okay." She nodded. "That's okay then."

I raised my eyebrows, and Katie looked like she wanted to get on a plane and go murder the ex right then. I wasn't far behind her. Debbie put a calming hand on Katie's arm and her wife got herself under control.

I was sure some part of Violet recognized Katie's mood because of her past experiences. However, she made no indication that she noticed.

"Not sure how you feel about this, but since we're taking your dogs, we should take your car. Do you want me to drive, or do you prefer to drive since it's your vehicle? I only offer since I know where we're going."

"You can drive if you want."

I clenched my fists and took a deep breath. She'd had way more life in her when we'd first met than she did now. She hadn't even objected to my opening the letter they'd put on her van. If Katie didn't get to her ex first, I was going to punch him in the face. I wasn't a violent man, nor was I very physically imposing, but a childhood spent on fishing boats had left me with some residual strength and a really esoteric knowledge of how to hurt people that you wouldn't expect from your local friendly weatherman.

Not to mention, I had access to boats and friends who wouldn't ask questions. Shaking my head, I took a calming breath. My emotions wouldn't help Violet right now. In fact, if I lost my temper, it could do completely the opposite, so I held on to my feelings.

By the look on Debbie's face, we were going to have a long, loud, yelling fest later. That was one way we'd both learned to cope years back. We'd find someplace relatively far away from others, like my lighthouse was now, and just vent as loudly as we possibly could about whatever was bothering us. We'd yell together and get the feelings out. Then we'd have hot chocolate and maybe cry a little, and then we usually felt a lot better. Maybe it was time to initiate Katie into the practice. It had been years since Debbie and I had needed that sort of emotional release, but I was so mad now, I could actually believe I might go through with my fantasy of dumping her ex in the deepest part of the ocean I could easily reach.

"I'll be out in a minute, Violet," I said, just as one more last sort of test. Not that I needed confirmation.

"Yeah, Okay. Thanks Ian. I'm glad I can help you with some errands. Come on, Shiner, Creek, let's go load up." She obediently got up and headed outside.

"Oh, my god," Debbie said as soon as Violet had left. "If you don't kill him first, Katie, I'm going to do it."

"I'll beat you to it," I said, voice quiet.

"If we hadn't seen her when she first arrived, we'd almost not even be able to tell. How long was she married to that asshat?" Debbie stormed over to the counter. "Don't leave until I get you both to go coffees. She won't leave without you, will she?"

"I doubt it," I replied. "But be quick. And I think ten years, right? Isn't that what we decided based on the internet search?"

"Thank goodness she never had kids with that monster," Debbie said while she worked.

"Yeah." I shuddered, thinking of what it would be like for a kid in that environment. "I wonder how she avoided that."

"Well, maybe someday we'll be able to ask. But until then, let's just be grateful. Clearly, she protected her dogs. If she left because of them, they saved her life, and I'm guessing that's why she finally got out." Katie twisted her hands together.

Debbie handed me large drinks and a bag of pastries then shooed me away before I could dig out my wallet. I took the offer and hurried out to Violet's car before she could leave without me. I really had to get her in to see Lydia because the next step really needed her to be present. Those restraining orders had to happen. No, a piece of paper wouldn't stop anyone, but they'd help if things got worse from a legal perspective.

Violet was waiting. The van was running, and she was sitting in the passenger seat.

I took a breath, balanced the drinks and opened the door.

"Oh, I'm sorry. I wasn't paying attention. I should have gotten the door for you." She put her hand over her mouth, eyes wide.

"I got it. It's no problem, Violet. Debbie sent us with coffee. I hope I got yours the way you like it."

"Thanks, Ian. That was awfully nice of all of you. I'm sorry to be any trouble." Her expression fell and she stared at her lap.

It was all very convincing. She truly felt that, I was sure, but the motions were perfect, as if she'd perfected exactly how she was supposed to look to appease her ex.

She hadn't been like this at all when she arrived. She'd been alive, vibrant, on the mend. Though clearly, she hadn't been far from the edge if she'd fallen back into her old habits so completely.

I got in the car, sent off a text to Lydia to let her know we were coming, and got the seat adjusted for my height. I didn't even know what to say, so I just concentrated on driving the larger vehicle safely. The last thing I wanted to do was mess up her car. Violet rode silently, occasionally taking a drink and otherwise staring out the window, except once when Shiner warbled in his crate. Then she turned and checked to make sure he was okay.

The trip to my childhood hometown took about forty-five minutes and we arrived at the small fishing town right when I'd promised Lydia. I parked next to her car in the small parking lot behind her office and went around to help Violet out.

She looked startled. "Oh, am I coming?"

"Violet, yes, I need to introduce you to Lydia. She can help better than anyone else I know."

Violet took my hand when I held it out for her to help her out of the vehicle. I wanted to give her a hug, but I didn't know how she'd take it. She'd let me, but that didn't mean she wanted me to hug her, so I refrained.

She eyed the weather then glanced at the car. "It's probably cool enough for a short visit."

It took me a minute to catch on, then I shook my head. "Dogs are coming."

"Really?" Violet perked up a little at that.

"Yeah." I offered a smile, and a hint of her old self shone through her mask.

Before long we were heading inside to Lydia's office. It was painted soothing greens and blues, and many ocean scenes were pictured on the walls. I stopped for a brief moment at the picture of the fishing vessel I'd gifted Lydia when I had returned from college. It wasn't my dad's exact fishing boat, but it was close enough. I wasn't sure I'd have made it through college without her help as a teen and I'd wanted her to have it.

"It's very pretty," Violet offered, seeing where my gaze had landed.

"It is." Someday I'd tell her about it, but right now this was about her.

"Ian!" Lydia's dark hair had a lot more gray in it than when I'd been a teen, and her dark face had a few more lines, but she still had that same cheerful, comforting smile.

"Hi, Lydia. This is my friend Violet."

"Hello, Violet. And these must be Shiner and the infamous Creek." She kneeled and when the dogs came up to her, offered them enthusiastic pets.

"Yes, hi, Lydia. It's nice to meet you." Violet had reverted to somewhat more automatic responses again and Lydia glanced at me and raised her eyebrows before nodding. Not that I'd needed any confirmation, but she already saw what I had.

"Why don't you four come on back and we'll have a chat. Then I'll kick Ian out, and we can talk."

"Okay." Violet tilted her head and glanced at me. At least she was thinking again.

"Lydia was my therapist. I think I mentioned her."

"Oh, yes!" Then she frowned. "But why are we here?"

"Because, dear, you are having a crisis and we need to help you," Lydia said kindly.

"I can't afford…"

Lydia waved her hand and Violet fell silent. "This one's on the house. We'll figure something out for the future, but right now you need some help."

Violet looked around the office again, eyes wide, and for a moment I thought she was going to bolt. Then her shoulders slumped, and she shuddered, as if she were coming back to herself. "I did it again, didn't I?"

"Yes, dear, you did. Let's go see if we can come up with a plan to help you from falling back into old habits." Lydia led us to the back. She'd already set up some blankets on the floor next to her couch for the dogs. I'd given her a heads up that I suspected Violet was literally living for them at this point, and she'd taken it to heart as I knew she would.

"Now, we have a lot to talk about. Let's get started with the most recent events," Lydia said as she got everyone settled.

I stayed until we'd given Lydia a clear picture of what had happened, and then she kicked me out despite Violet protesting that I could stay. I wasn't sure if I was glad to leave or not, but I was happy to occupy myself out in the lobby with the day's weather report while I waited for the two women to talk.

A couple of hours had passed before Lydia opened the door and called me back in.

Chapter 18

Violet

"I'm so sorry, Ian. I hadn't even realized…" I trailed off and wrung my hands. I couldn't even imagine why he'd taken the time out of his life to help me, but I was grateful. "I thought I'd gotten past a lot of this. I guess not."

"I'm not mad, Violet. Just worried. Everything you're currently going through would be a lot for anyone to deal with. I'd be terrified to be up in your house alone with the threats. At least at the lighthouse I have some seriously solid doors and storm windows. Please don't apologize for things that aren't your fault."

I sighed. "It's been a lot. Thank you for getting involved."

"Ian. Violet has given me permission to share this with you, and Debbie and Katie, too. But she would very much like it if you'd tell her she's disassociating when you notice her doing it. And if it ever gets really bad, my door is open. We have an appointment next week and we'd both be grateful if you'd be available to bring her by."

"Yeah, of course. Benefit to working from home." Ian grinned. "I'm happy to help."

"You're a good friend." I wanted to add that I didn't deserve his friendship, but I knew that was destructive.

"Okay, you two get out of here and get those restraining orders figured out. Ian, call my sister. She's a crack lawyer. I have a document I will be sending to her, again with Violet's permission. Her ex probably paid off Violet's original lawyer. That's the only way she wasn't able to take her ex for everything he had. He owes her, and big time. We need to fix some of this."

"It's not going to do any good. I told you, I signed everything away to get out like I did." I still didn't regret it.

"Under duress," Lydia replied. "I'm pretty sure she'll be able to get that overturned." She turned her attention from me back to Ian. "And I'm sure Violet has enough going on right now that I'm relying on you to talk to my sister for Violet, at least until Violet needs to get involved again. The information I sent her will be enough for now."

"Sure, no problem," he agreed.

"Well, you two get on out of here. It was very nice to meet you, Violet. I'll see you next week."

"Thank you." Impulsively, I gave Lydia a hug. She held me until I loosened my grip and then we went back out to the van.

Ian held out my keys, but I shook my head. "Do you mind? I'm still kind of raw."

"Sure."

He got the sliding door for the back of the van and helped me load the dogs, then shut my door for me when I got in. The actions almost brought tears to my eyes. I blinked a few times, and the feeling passed. He didn't have to help me like this, but I was glad he was here.

We drove for a while in silence. Finally, I felt I had to break it. "I'm sorry," I said. "I didn't mean to be so much trouble."

"No trouble, Violet. I'm just glad Lydia was able to help some."

"Yeah. Once she helped me see what I was doing, I was kind of able to sort of snap out of it. She gave me some strategies to try, too. I have gone to therapy before, and it was helpful. I had hoped I had moved beyond that, but this brought everything back." I gestured at the pile of papers he had put on the floor between us. "Do you really think there is treasure?"

"Honestly, probably not. But the story is solid enough that desperate people might believe." He slowed to take a turn. "But regardless, it's probably why this group is so interested. The other investigators you told me about are likely just wanting to visit a place that is almost assuredly haunted."

"Yeah." I shivered, remembering the woman in the mirror with the haunted eyes. I wondered what her story was. "I'm sure if there were ghosts they wouldn't want to be investigated."

"Probably not." Ian chuckled, then went silent.

Maybe he was waiting for me to tell him what I thought about the rumors of ghosts. Treasure would be nice, but even if there was treasure, it wasn't mine. It belonged to the ghosts.

I stayed silent on the matter. I didn't think they'd want me telling everyone about them, either. Though, if they didn't let me get some sleep, I was letting the next semi well behaved investigator in.

"Okay, let's get the rest of this done and then we'll go have lunch. I know a great little restaurant with a wonderful view." Ian turned into the sheriff's office lot and parked the van. He put the windows down. "Once I get you situated with Brody, I'll come back out and sit with the dogs."

"Sure. You all really do know everyone else around here, don't you?"

"Yeah, Brody and I grew up together over in Shoretown. He'll take care of everything for you."

"Thanks."

I followed my friend inside and he introduced me to Deputy Brody who sat behind the desk. He was a big white

129

guy with broad shoulders, blue eyes, and a kind smile. His expression darkened when Ian told him why we were there.

"Shouldn't be bothering folks like that." He shook his head. "I know we have increased patrols out there now. I'll make some notes for the other deputies and let's get that paperwork done."

"Do you need me, Brody? Her dogs are in the van, and I want to sit with them."

"Nope, but go ahead and bring them in. You can all hang out here," he said absently while he gathered paperwork for me.

Ian glanced at me.

"Sure. They'll come with you."

He went outside and returned a few minutes later with Creek and Shiner, which then necessitated an introduction to the immediately smitten Brody and the standard dissertation on their breed and repeating how to pronounce Yakutian Laika at least three times. Which I minded not at all. It was always a pleasure to show off my dogs to an appreciative audience. Though it did make me miss the show and competition rings.

After that was handled, Ian settled down in a chair with the dogs while I got the paperwork taken care of. Brody asked a lot of good questions, and I did my best to answer them. Once we were done, Brody loved on the dogs some more.

"How is it living up at Hill House?" His tone was too casual as he rubbed Creek's soft ears. I knew what he wanted.

"It's okay. It's a big house just for me. I had not intended to buy something like that, but I was dealing with a divorce and I let the realtor handle everything."

"Do you need a restraining order against your ex, too?"

"I doubt he'd bother with me."

"If anything changes, just drop by and let us know." Brody gave the dogs one last pat and didn't bring up the house again, though I hadn't answered his actual question.

After leaving the station, Ian cleared his throat. "Any type of food you don't like?"

"I'll eat anything," I replied automatically.

Ian stopped and turned to face me. "That's not what I asked," he said gently.

"Oh, uh." I fought with myself for a minute before I shrugged. "I do like most things. I'm not a fan of super greasy food."

"Great. Then the place I have in mind will be fine." Ian didn't elaborate, just drove toward the shoreline.

This was a part of the small town I lived in that I hadn't explored yet. The restaurant was nestled against the landward side of a rocky outcropping though the patio extended outward for an ocean view. Even mid-afternoon, there were plenty of cars in the parking lot and that boded well for a decent meal. Not that I didn't trust Ian's judgment.

Then I remembered I had the dogs. He didn't seem concerned though, so I watched while he parked. He didn't put the windows down, so I guessed we were bringing them.

He came around and opened the sliding door since I'd already hopped out and helped me get Creek and Shiner out of their travel crates. Then he led me straight to the patio. I followed a little uneasily, though there was nothing I should be worried about. I did relax when I saw another couple with a dog laying at their feet. So, it was dog friendly, and not just Ian assuming I could bring them. That was a relief.

"Is this table okay?" Ian pointed to a two-person table with a fantastic view.

"Yeah, it's great." I automatically moved to put my back to the view so Ian could have it.

"I'll take that chair, unless you don't want to look at the ocean."

"Oh, uh." I took a breath. "Yeah, thank you."

He winked. "My view will be just as good. Now wait here while I go let the hostess know we're out here."

He was gone before I could reply and I sat there, stunned for a moment. "Wait, is he flirting with me?" I glanced down at the dogs. Shiner had laid down at my feet, but Creek stared after Ian, his fluffy tail wagging. I had no idea what to do with that revelation and I sat in stunned silence until Ian returned.

The waiter was with him, and I totally missed what he said his name was, but I did manage to order water to drink.

"Do you want anything else?"

Automatically, I shook my head.

"Violet," Ian said gently. "If you want a drink, get a drink."

I gave myself a full body shake and dragged myself back to the present. "Mimosa. Please." I hastily added the last.

"Are you okay? If I've done something to push you back toward disassociating… or if I'm being too demanding, please tell me."

"No, sorry, Ian. I just… I'm sorry. I'm glad to be here. I'm okay."

He studied me for a moment longer before nodding. "Everything I've ever had here is fantastic. Get whatever you want. I'm serious. My treat. You've had a rough day, and I'd like to pay for your lunch. Please."

"Okay," I said. "I need to get a little for the dogs, too. I can pay for that."

"It would be my honor to buy lunch for the criminal and his accomplice." Ian grinned at me.

"If you're sure."

"Of course."

Then I caught on to what he'd called the dogs and laughed.

Ian kept me entertained with stories about the weather in the area, the natural features, and some local superstitions and lore while we waited for our food. Once it arrived, we ate quickly. We'd both been pretty hungry after the morning. The dogs enjoyed their chicken, and the view was amazing. This was easily the most enjoyable afternoon I'd had in ages. Especially contrasted with the previous day and the morning.

Ian had an easy laugh and an infectious grin, and I genuinely enjoyed hearing his stories about the weather. I'd mostly completely relaxed by the time we were done eating and had sat and talked just long enough. The view of the ocean was fantastic, though I found myself more focused on Ian than I was on the vista.

Had he been flirting with me?

I wasn't sure, and I didn't want to make things weird, so I tried to push the question out of my mind.

The trip back to the coffee shop so he could get his car went by too quickly, and I offered him a quick hug when I got out of the van to take back the driver's seat. He hugged me exactly as long as I hugged him and promised that he would see me soon. I'd almost expected him to go inside and let Debbie and Katie know how the day had gone, but instead he got in his car and was driving away by the time I got my seat adjusted and headed for my own house.

The happy glow remained until I reached my gates, then I remembered what I was coming home to. Ghosts. And chaos. And a mess, I was sure of it.

Desperately clinging to the good mood I would need to deal with the house, I locked the gate behind me. Maybe Ian would want a key if I got some made.

I banished that thought, too. He was just being nice. Probably. Still, between having the dogs at my side and remembering the happy glint in his crystal blue eyes, I managed to get up the steps on the porch and to my door without much hesitation. I just hoped I'd be able to reclaim the small amount of peace I'd found today, after I dealt with whatever I found inside.

Chapter 19

Violet

The house was spotless.

Like cleaner-than-when-I'd-hired-cleaners spotless. I rubbed at my eyes, but nothing had changed. Everything that had been in disarray from one of the many times the ghosts had rampaged was either gone if it had been broken or put back where I remembered it being if it was still intact.

If the ghosts habitually rampaged, that did explain the somewhat haphazard décor. I wondered how the old lady who'd lived here before me had managed to afford to refurnish the place every time they freaked out.

Maybe she'd had an arrangement with them. They could only break certain things.

I snorted. That was ridiculous.

The kitchen was just as clean, though I had to snort again when I looked at the dishes stacked on the counter. They'd been repaired. Sort of. The ghosts had taken the pieces of the plates out of the box I'd tossed them in to go to the trash and stuck them together. As best they could. For glue, they'd apparently used ectoplasm. The green goo had hardened and held the pieces together, but there was no way I was using those plates, even though I appreciated the effort. The first semi salty meal and they'd disintegrate. Not to mention, they hadn't exactly managed to get them all back together. Most of the plates had holes in them.

But I took the apology in the spirit—haha—it was intended.

Fortunately, they hadn't touched my mugs that had my dogs on them. And now that I thought about it, they hadn't touched the dogs' room, either. I'd have to be thankful for that, I supposed.

When I came back out of the kitchen, Creek was flopped over on his back for all the world like someone was rubbing his belly. Shiner had his head tilted like someone was petting his ears.

"If you get ectoplasm on my dogs…"

Motion caught my eye, and I turned. In the same spot as before, red letters dripping blood painted the word "SORRY."

For a moment I just stared at the bloody word, then I went over and sank down into the armchair that seemed to face the favorite writing spot.

"It's okay," I finally replied. "Just don't break my things. Please."

The words erased and were replaced with an "OKAY."

"What do we do?" I wasn't even sure exactly what I meant by that question, but it seemed like the thing to ask.

The reply got me to stop and think.

MUST HAUNT

Okay. So they were ghosts. They had to haunt. Fine. It was just like having a dog bred for a specific purpose, I supposed. If the dog didn't get to fulfill its needs, it would become difficult or possibly even dangerous.

"You have got to stop waking me up in the middle of the night. I can't deal with all the crap from the assholes trying to force me out of this place, work, and everything else, on no sleep."

"THE TWINS ARE SORRY" was the reply.

"The twins have watched too many Stephen King movies."

THEY DON'T UNDERSTAND

I frowned. "They haven't seen *The Shining*?"

NO

I pinched the bridge of my nose because I was having a really bad idea, but I didn't voice it just then.

"Tell me about yourselves?"

GRANDMOTHER YOU KNOW

I nodded agreement and waited for the words to vanish and reappear.

I WAS A BUTCHER FELL FROM THE CLIFFS

The words vanished and the pause was longer before he continued.

GOT DRUNK ENDED UP HERE

"Why aren't you manifesting?"

TAKES ENERGY USED IT ALL CLEANING

"Oh." I stopped myself before I could apologize. I hadn't asked them to clean, and I wasn't sorry they had.

POLTERGHEIST WAS TEEN

JUMPED

ENDED UP HERE

I shuddered.

GRANDMOTHER DECORATED THE ROOM FOR HIM

"I'll leave it."

TWINS GOT ILL DIED IN THE HOUSE

The words vanished and new ones bled onto the wood.

HOUSEKEEPER REFUSED TO LEAVE EVEN IN DEATH

The words vanished again and nothing else appeared while I waited.

"I'm grateful to know all of you." Then I frowned, remembering one other face. "The woman in the mirror?"

MARY SHE KEEPS TO HERSELF
GRANDMOTHER BOUGHT HER MIRROR

The words vanished and I waited, wondering if there would be more.

Finally, a few more words splashed onto the wall, sending a chill straight through my entire body.

SHE WAS LIKE YOU BUT DIDN'T GET OUT

I wrapped my arms around myself, but before I could slip away, Creek hopped into my lap and stuck his nose in my face. Tears poured down my cheeks as I thought about what could have happened. What would have happened if I hadn't walked away to save my dogs. It had taken my ex turning his attention on them before I'd stood up and said no more.

Once I'd had a solid cry into Creek's thick mane, I pulled myself together.

"Okay, so, you need to haunt. Can we, like, I don't know, have a set time for hauntings? Like, maybe once I get home from work or something. And, like, maybe less destruction?"

The butcher didn't reply. Grandmother appeared in front of me, her apparition faint. She patted my cheek, a cool breeze against my hot, tear-stained skin.

I took that as a yes.

"Great, well, I'm exhausted. Like. Completely. Let's start that tomorrow. I don't think I can handle it today."

The energy of the house stilled, and I hoped that meant they were done with me for the day. It was late enough that with everything else, I could probably justify passing out on my face.

I let the dogs out to potty, fed them their dinner, and headed into the bathroom to take a hot bath before bed. As tired as I was, I needed something to relax my body.

When I looked in the mirror, I saw the sad visage of Mary wavering in an unseen wind. Instead of screaming, I put my hand against the glass of the mirror.

She pressed her boney hand against the other side of the glass, and we gazed at each other. After a few moments, her lips turned up into a smile, as if she were proud of me. She nodded and swirled away into the depths of the mirror.

Oddly feeling as if I'd made a friend—or perhaps a few more if I considered the other ghosts—my heart lightened some. I held to that feeling while I ran my bath then let the hot water work its magic on my muscles.

So, a few problems were addressed.

That just left a million others, but with the ghosts at least partially handled and steps taken to deal with the people harassing me, not to mention the therapy session with Lydia, I felt like I could actually handle the rest.

Once I lay in my bed, I realized I hadn't asked about the basement.

A different sort of chill worked through me, and I decided that was a problem for another day.

I grabbed my vibrator out of my nightstand, partially to further help myself get to sleep and to distract myself from the thoughts of the basement, but also to distract myself from another problem.

What to do about Ian?

Chapter 20

Violet

Though no one had asked him to, Ian had stepped up to help with the event we were planning. It was nice working with him so closely. He was efficient, capable, and despite initial impressions, genuinely seemed to enjoy Creek and Shiner. He'd even made a game of having something dog safe stuffed in his pocket so Creek could steal it.

Creek was currently running around inside the makeshift fenced off area proudly displaying the bandana he'd stolen from Ian. Shiner looked on judgmentally, while a handful of the helpers laughed. We were all getting the area set up for "The Bean Has Gone to The Dogs." We'd been advertising for a few weeks now; the local shops were all in, and in a few hours we'd see if the event was worth repeating.

Though Debbie and Katie kept reassuring me that it was fine if we didn't get a lot of business, I was nervous. Fortunately, everything had been pretty quiet on the supernatural front. No more investigators had shown up, though I had thrown a few letters away. The people harassing me seemed to have quit. At least for now. I wasn't sure if that was because the restraining order had worked or if they were just focusing elsewhere at the moment. And the ghosts and I had set up a haunting routine. I was even starting to look forward to it. The butcher ghost had promised a surprise for this afternoon. I wasn't sure how I felt about that, but Grandmother had approved, so apparently it was okay.

Even though I was nervous, I was excited about the event. I'd put a lot of work into this over the last couple of weeks, even spending time pretending to be good at arts and crafts to make up some cute signs with dogs on them.

We had several gift baskets to draw for during the event that contained donations from all the different businesses, and we'd gotten the appropriate permits to take up some of the sidewalk space so everyone could have a booth.

Ian had volunteered to be a dog holder so people could go inside to order drinks since the dogs weren't technically allowed near the counter. They'd have to line up in the "Maine" section and Ian would help whoever needed a dog held. It was pretty cute how he'd really started taking an interest in dogs recently.

"Great job, Violet." Debbie patted me on the shoulder. "This event will be so much fun for everyone."

"I hope so." I couldn't help the proud grin though.

"It'll be fine. Now that we're all set up here, go get a drink and relax while we get this started."

"Thanks." I whistled and the dogs came up to my side in a heel, showing off for the crowd. The bandana Creek was carrying around, now quite soggy, ruined the effect a tiny bit, but did display the comedy the breed was known for. Since I knew there would be lots of questions, I'd made up a display about the breed and even brought some of my show pictures, pictures of us skatejoring, and doing other activities, and a few articles about the breed so that would hopefully cover some of the questions. While I didn't mind giving the dissertation on the breed, I didn't want to have to repeat myself all day.

When I went inside with the dogs, Ian came over to me and offered me a quick hug. I gratefully moved into his embrace.

"Great job, Violet," he said, holding me tightly.

I could have stayed there in his arms for an hour, and he was increasingly featuring in my thoughts as I went about my day. The dogs loved him, and I really was considering asking him on a date. Maybe today.

I tilted my head up to look at him. He gazed back at me, leaning over.

Instinctively, I matched his movement, stretching up as if I might kiss him, heart racing. Did I dare? Remembering we were in public, I quickly looked away and stepped back, mentally completing the movement where my lips touched his and we kissed for the first time. It was a nice fantasy, and maybe soon, when we weren't around others, I'd be able to experience it for real.

"Thanks, Ian."

He grinned at me. I blushed. Then Ian jumped and Creek scampered away, bandana forgotten at Ian's feet and something suspiciously wallet-like clutched in his jaw.

"Creek!"

The dog skidded to a halt on the smooth floors that led to the office where he and Shiner spent their time while I worked. He had enough momentum that he hit the doorframe, but not hard. It didn't seem to faze him. Instead, he used it to turn and disappear into the back room.

Shiner heaved a sigh before trotting after Creek.

"Sorry!" I squeaked and went after the criminal before Ian could get mad about it. When I reached the office, Creek was on his bed, plumed tail wagging and his muzzle pressed onto the top of Ian's wallet, as if he were trying to hide it.

"Creek."

He wagged harder.

"You're a terrible thief. Here, I'll trade you." I offered him a treat in exchange for the wallet and he accepted after a moment's consideration.

I ruffled his ears, gave him and Shiner another treat each, then headed back out into the main part of the shop where Ian, bless him, handed me a tea in exchange for his wallet.

"Trade you," he said with a grin.

"Sorry about that." I shook my head.

"All good." He laughed. "I'll just have to get more creative about what I keep in my pockets for him to steal."

"I don't know if encouraging theft is a good thing." I laughed.

"Could be a fun trick for him," Ian replied. "Some sort of trick dog competition or something?" He gestured outside. "Might be fun to organize an event along those lines in the future."

I raised my eyebrows, surprised he'd thought of something like that. "Yeah, that could be fun. I'll work on it."

Before we could continue, Debbie got my attention through the glass front of the coffee shop and waved me out. I hastily excused myself and went to see what she wanted.

"Ahh! Our woman of the hour! Everyone, this is Violet, our new employee and the mastermind behind this event."

I hadn't even realized how many people had gathered since I'd gone inside. The crowd was more than just regulars at the coffee shop and a few people I recognized from around town. I could tell there were tourists, and many folks I'd never seen before who looked like locals. That was exciting. Not to mention many of the other shop owners and workers.

Scanning the crowd, I gave a quick wave. "Thank you all for coming."

Someone started clapping. Something about the sound was weirdly familiar and it made me flinch. Confused, I shook off the uneasy feeling as more people joined in. After a few moments Debbie waved her hand. "Okay, everyone! Make yourselves at home. Don't forget to drop your names into the drawing. No catch! You just need to be here to win. We'll start picking winners in an hour so hang around! As a special surprise we're having our very own dog costume show here in half an hour. Violet will judge the classes. There are some construction materials over there. Get to work!"

"What?" I turned to look at Debbie. Though I had wondered what the craft table was all about.

She grinned. "Ian's idea. I think he's going to steal Creek from you."

I laughed. "Okay."

Many people had brought dogs, and a bunch of them headed for the craft table. The dogs themselves were surprisingly well behaved considering the crowd.

Released from duty, I made my way over toward the display I'd put together for the dogs. I knew I'd get questions. I always did.

Sure enough, as soon as I patted the grooming table I'd set out and Creek and Shiner hopped up, they were politely swarmed by curious onlookers. I stood in a spot where I could protect the dogs' space if I needed to.

"I might have mentioned we had a rare breed in attendance," Debbie said when she came by a little while later. "People were curious."

I laughed. "Fortunately, the dogs don't mind."

Ian came over just then. "Hey, can I borrow Creek?"

"Sure. Take the criminal." I handed over Creek's leash—there were too many dogs around for either of them

145

to be wandering at this point—and he went off with Ian, plumed tail wagging all curled over his back.

"Not even a backward glance, huh, Shiner." I patted him on the head then went back to crowd control, though it had thinned a bit by then.

It wasn't long before Debbie was signaling the start of the costume contest I was supposed to judge.

"Okay, Violet, come on over here and we'll get started."

Laughing, I scanned the crowd again, looking at all the different dogs that had gotten dressed up for the occasion. Some had come with premade costumes, but many had taken advantage of the construction paper, tape, and other odds and ends that Debbie had put out. Quite a few people had done very well in the half hour or so allotted.

Something else caught my eye as I looked around. Something that sent a chill down my back, so I looked again. Was that?

No… there was no way my ex would be anywhere near here. It had to be someone that looked similar enough to notice. I shuddered and turned my attention to the small area that Debbie had set up for the costume contest, forcing those thoughts from my mind.

"Okay, first up, exhibition only because this is our judge's dog, Creek the criminal and Ian the sheriff!" Debbie announced.

Unease shoved forcibly away, I laughed in delight as Ian led Creek out on a leash that had been embellished to look like it was made of chain links. Ian had taken black and white strips of paper and made stripes as if Creek were wearing a prison outfit. Ian himself had found a cowboy hat somewhere and wore a plastic sheriff's star on his chest.

Creek, at some signal from Ian, jumped up and stole the bandana from Ian's pocket and ran off. Ian dramatically dropped the leash and waved his hands around as if Creek had escaped. He didn't go far, though. He spotted me and came running, a big old grin on his face and his tail wagging like crazy.

He sniffed noses with Shiner, who inspected the stripes Ian had put on my dog, before putting his paw on Creek's forehead and *arooooing* at him.

Ian came over and gave me a hug. "Thanks for letting me borrow your dog."

"Sure. Nice trick."

Ian grinned, cheeks pinking slightly, but looking pleased. "He trained me."

"Okay, now for the rest of the show," Debbie interrupted the laughter from the audience.

I spent the next hour judging fairy dogs, dragon dogs, a few clouds, some s'mores, and many other fun costumes. We ended up dividing the dogs up into a couple of size groups just so there could be a few winners.

I finally selected the winners, and they got their prizes. Amazingly enough, I was exhausted after that and took a few minutes to take me and the dogs back into the office to relax.

Ian found me there.

"Hey," I said when he let himself into the office.

"Hi. Great job out there." He sat down in a chair near the couch where I had collapsed. Creek and Shiner immediately swarmed him for pets.

"Thanks. That costume you did with Creek was adorable."

He blushed, ducking his head. "Thanks."

We sat there in comfortable silence for a few minutes while Ian pet the dogs.

"Well, I should probably get back out there," I said.

"You doing okay?"

I nodded. "I just needed a few minutes after the show. That was fun, but oddly tiring. You two stay," I said the last to the dogs. They'd had plenty of interaction for now, too.

Both settled on their beds then Ian held the door for me, and we went back out into the crowd.

"The turnout is amazing." Ian again held the door for me, and we went out to what was becoming a kind of block party.

Debbie and Katie had switched places and now Katie was doing a drawing for one of the gift baskets.

I was looking for a place to help when familiar and very unwanted faces turned up. I stiffened, then hurriedly went over to the groomer's table. Hopefully they were just here for coffee and to see what all the fuss was about. Clearly the creeps trying to get me to sell my house didn't care about restraining orders. Though I wasn't sure how these things applied to public places.

The two men studied my display for the Yakutian Laika breed and my skin crawled.

I tried to find a way to avoid them, duck back inside, or something, but Katie saw me before I could vanish.

"Violet, come on over here." She waved.

Fortunately, it was the direction opposite the men, but they looked up at my name and we made brief eye contact before I managed to look away.

Good mood destroyed, I did my best to put on a mask without slipping away into complete disassociation and headed over to see what Katie wanted.

The next half an hour was progressively more stressful. The men didn't leave, nor did they get coffee. They simply made it clear they were watching, and to top it off, I swore I saw my ex again. I continued to try to

148

function, but it was getting difficult. I just wanted to vanish inside the store and hide.

"Violet, what's wrong?" Debbie came over and put her hand on my forearm. "The event is a smashing success. We'll certainly do more."

I sighed, almost said nothing, then remembered that I'd agreed to ask for help, or at least tell people I trusted when things were bothering me at my last therapy session.

"Those two men by the grooming display are some of the creeps trying to buy my house." I pointed. "And… this is ridiculous, but I swear I saw my ex in the crowd. I'm sure it's just someone who looks like him, and I'm feeling weird because of those two, but…"

Debbie's expression hardened. "Restraining order, right?"

I nodded.

Debbie immediately pulled out her phone. "You stay right with me. We'll handle this." She pushed a few buttons. "Hi, Deputy, yeah this is Debbie, we have some restraining order violators at our event. Great. Thanks." She hung up.

I wanted to protest that she didn't have to do that, but I managed to keep my mouth shut. The police would be here soon.

Ian, perhaps sensing something was up, came over just then.

"Ian, could you watch over our Violet for a moment, please? I need to talk to Katie."

"What's wrong?" He took a step closer to me.

"Some restraining order violation going on." She glared at the two men, who seemed to have realized they'd been noticed by someone other than me. They both smirked and went back to studying the grooming table display.

"Sure." Ian turned to me. "Mind if I put my arm around you?"

"Please." I stepped into his embrace, leaning against his solid warmth when he put his arm around my back. Something inside of me settled and I was able to take a deep breath and just relax. The feeling rolling through me was so comforting that it took me a long time to identify it. I wasn't alone. I glanced up at Ian and he met my gaze. The sounds of the crowd faded. For a minute the rest of the world fell away. My worries and fears vanished, and there was only me and him. We leaned toward each other.

"What are you doing here?" The shout, thick with Katie's Boston accent, interrupted my short moment of peace. Both Ian and I jumped back a little, though he kept his arm around me.

"Beg your pardon?" one of the men who'd been harassing me said to Katie. "I thought this was a public event."

"It is! But you're not part of our public. You have a restraining order against you for harassment and you know it."

The man waved his hand, unconcerned. "I have no idea what you're talking about."

Katie had timed her accusation well. I saw Deputy Maxwell and Ranger Milton approaching from the sidewalk.

"I'm sure you know exactly what I'm talking about." Then she went off on a tirade about their behavior.

By this time all the locals that were present were glaring at the two men and several more had gathered around Ian and me, as if to shield me from them.

Ian tightened his grip, and I leaned into him again, content to let others handle the situation for once.

Just as the two men protested their innocence once more, Deputy Maxwell came up behind them.

"Funny, because I hand delivered those restraining orders to you two myself. So now we're going to go down to the station and have a little discussion about what restraining orders mean."

At that point, the two men ceased arguing and went with the deputy and ranger quietly while everyone present glared at their retreating backs.

Silence reigned until the two officers drove away and then Debbie clapped her hands.

"I think this calls for another giveaway!"

Her declaration got the party started again. Betty and a few of the other shop owners reassured me that they would keep their eyes open, all the while grinning at Ian and me once they really paid attention to how he was holding me.

While the incident had scared me, the feeling of being supported and protected was something I wouldn't soon forget and when I finally stepped away from Ian to go help with the event, I felt a million times lighter than I had ever since I could remember.

Dakota Brown

Chapter 21

Ian

I was so proud of Violet. I couldn't even begin to express my feelings for her. I was definitely asking her out tonight. Not just on a date, but if she would consider being my girlfriend. I'd almost kissed her in the coffee shop, was still sort of kicking myself for hesitating. I'd wanted to be sure she was up for it, though. She'd stepped away at the last minute and we'd certainly have had an audience if we had kissed. I didn't mind, but it seemed like she did. I'd have to take that into consideration in the future. We could talk about boundaries. And hopefully I could make up for it tonight.

The local florist had made a beautiful bouquet just for Violet. It contained some of the standard flowers, but also some blues that reminded me of her dog's eyes, and many Maine wildflowers.

They sat on the passenger seat next to me and I glanced at them when I pulled up to her closed gate. She'd given me and a few others keys not long ago, and I clutched it like a talisman when I got out to unlock the gate. No more getting stuck crawling over her fence. I laughed at the memory while I opened the gate and went back to the car to drive through.

I didn't mind the whole procedure of getting out, opening the gate, driving through, then shutting it behind me, but it had me thinking of an automatic gate for the future.

Once I'd parked, I gathered up the flowers and the vase I'd bought because I wasn't sure if she had one and headed for her door.

When I got to the door, I set the vase down next to it, so I'd have a hand free and knocked.

No one answered, and the dogs didn't bark. Her van was parked here so she had to be home. Worried, I tried the handle. It wasn't locked, but I didn't want to go in without permission, so I knocked again.

I heard something crash, and a woman screamed inside. It didn't sound like a TV. Did Violet even have a TV?

Panicking, I threw open the door and ran inside to total chaos. Cushions and pillows floated in the air. A blanket swooped down from the top of the vaulted ceiling as if it were a ghost. More crashes sounded in the kitchen. Bloody messages splattered the walls, dripping down only to vanish before the ghostly blood hit the ground.

I froze. Not even rumors had prepared me for anything like this.

Violet screamed again, but before I could run to find her, she came running down the hallway, hands in the air, yelling as two apparitions chased after her.

She froze when she saw me.

So did everything else.

Complete silence descended on the house until the scrabbling of paws on wood broke it. I glanced up and stared as Creek and Shiner chased translucent—were those reindeer—through the upstairs hallway, down the stairs, and straight toward me.

I didn't even have a chance to dodge before the deer plowed through me, chilling the air and coating me with green slime.

The dogs skidded to a halt inches from my legs, saving me from crashing to the floor, but I was completely frozen in shock.

The bloody writing on the wall changed from whatever it had said to BOO.

"Boo?" I finally gasped out.

Violet twisted around to see what I was talking about.

The words changed again.

HI IAN.

"Butcher!" Violet shouted in dismay.

SHIT SORRY

The words vanished. The pillows crashed to the ground, and something clattered in the kitchen.

Violet and I stared at each other for a few more moments, before the dogs warbled at each other, darted around me to get out the open door, then raced away.

"Are those for me?" Violet finally said, pointing at the flowers.

"Uh. Yeah."

Hands shaking, I held out the bouquet of now slime coated flowers.

"Thank you." She didn't move and my feet were rooted to the spot.

More bloody words appeared on the wall.

IAN MOVE INCOMING.

I shifted to the side at the warning, and moments later the reindeer came bounding back into the house, Creek and Shiner racing along behind them, tails curled happily over their backs and big grins on their doggy faces.

The reindeer vanished into the door that I thought went to the dog room.

"That'll do, boys," Violet said, and the dogs trotted over to her side.

"Um, so. Uh. Yeah, the house is haunted. Do you want some tea? I… will… uh… have to find a vase." She said the last in a rush.

Just then the one I'd brought floated into the room.

"Oh, thanks, Petey."

"Petey?" I stammered while she took the floating vase as if stuff like that happened all the time.

"The teen. I don't know his name and they won't tell me, so I started calling him Petey. He's the poltergeist. Um, I think you met Grandmother in real life." Violet gestured to a rocking chair that was rocking on its own. A pair of knitting needles raised as if in salute.

Automatically, I waved back.

"Butcher is the one that likes to write on the walls. He's a cinnamon roll. These are the twins." She pointed to the pair of glowing orbs that had been chasing her. "The housekeeper is around somewhere. She rarely manifests, but she has started cleaning again."

"That's handy," I forced out.

Violet smiled sadly. "And that's Mary." She pointed to the mirror next to me.

I glanced. A woman floated in the mirror, white dress billowing in wind and her white hair floating as if in water. Her face was gaunt, her hand that she raised in greeting, boney, and I suspected she was putting on a friendly expression for me.

"Bloody Mary?" I managed.

"Yeah."

"Hi," I squeaked, trying, and failing, not to take a step back. "Tea sounds great."

A cold breeze rushed through the room, picking up pillows and cushions and folding blankets while I made my way to the kitchen.

"Uh, here." I held out the flowers and she hesitantly took them from me. "Great job today." Even to me my tone of voice was brittle.

"Thanks, Ian." Violet sighed, shoulders sagging. "I'm sorry about all this. Just, you know, ghost have to haunt people, so we came up with an arrangement. The reindeer are new though. Butcher found them for the dogs. They're actually herding dogs, along with sledding and all of that."

"Yeah," I replied. She'd told me before, but I didn't remind her.

"So, uh, saltwater gets the ectoplasm off." She put the slimed flowers in the vase and put a little water in it, clearly ignoring that they'd been encased in goo. "They're beautiful."

"Thanks." I rubbed at my face, finally noticing that I'd been completely slimed, too. I shuddered and tried to chip the hardening goo off.

"Let me help." She got a bowl, dumped salt in it, then water, and then scrubbed at my skin with a towel.

With her help, I got enough off that I wasn't in danger of not being able to move once it finished hardening.

"So, you play with the ghosts?" I said after an extended, extremely awkward silence in which I wasn't sure if I'd ever be able to break it, so I said the dumbest thing possible.

"Yeah, kind of. It's fun. I guess it's decent cardio. And then they don't wake me up in the middle of the night." She shrugged as if this was totally normal.

"Sleep is important," I agreed, lamely.

"Do you still want that tea?"

"Uh." I glanced down at myself. "I should probably clean up."

She nodded. "Yeah. I'm sorry." Her expression fell even more.

157

"It's okay, Violet. I just wasn't expecting to get slimed today or I would have brought some extra clothing." I forced a smile, and her lips twitched in response. I stood, not sure what I was feeling, other than a little gross because I was still covered in hard ectoplasm. "Salt, you said?"

"Yeah. Salt."

The house was quiet when I headed for the door.

"They know my name?"

"You've been over a few times, and I've talked about you."

A cold chill trailed down my spine, but I tried not to let the shiver I felt at that thought become visible. Hopefully, I'd been successful.

Violet was a master at hiding emotions, so I wasn't sure what she was feeling at the moment, and I wasn't brave enough to ask.

"Hey, I'll, uh, call you soon. I just, uh, really need to get cleaned up."

"Yeah, of course, Ian. I look forward to it." She smiled wanly.

I almost pulled her into a hug to reassure her, but I didn't think she wanted to hug someone covered in hard slime, so I waved instead and hurried to my car.

It was only hours later, after I'd taken a dip in the calm, frigid, salty, ocean, then hurried into the house to warm up, that I thought I might have screwed up. I should have said more to reassure her. I'd been so shocked, I hadn't really been able to cope with the situation properly. Hopefully, Violet would forgive me, and I could make it up to her. The ghosts were startling, and I'd never expected anything like that, but really, she was doing a great job of making the best of living in a very haunted house. Who was I to judge?

My phone was in my hand, and I was about to call Violet and see if I could come back over, when the phone rang. It was my aunt.

"Hi, Aunt Freida. What's up?"

"Ian, I'm so sorry to bother you this late. Your uncle broke his arm out on the boat." She sighed. "We could really use some extra help for a couple of weeks if you're willing. He'll be okay, but the only way he's going to sit, and rest is if things are still getting done. We know how you feel about fishing." She hesitated. "You were the only person we could think of who might be available. He said he promised you'd get enough time to work on your weather forecasts and get paid a fair wage."

I cursed the timing, but I couldn't say no to family. Not when I actually could help.

"Yeah, Aunt Freida. Sure. I'll come help. I'll leave first thing in the morning."

"Thanks, Ian. We really appreciate it."

"That's what family is for." I hung up and stared at my phone. I should call Violet and explain. I glanced at the clock. I had to pack, and it was getting late. It was a long drive to my aunt's place, and I probably should get rest.

Scrubbing at my eyes, I sent off a quick text to Debbie, letting her know what was up, then I thought about what to say to Violet. Finally, I settled on keeping it simple.

Hey, sorry I came by unannounced tonight. I was glad to meet everyone, despite my initial shock. I have to go away for a few weeks for a family emergency, but I'll call soon. Give the dogs pets for me.

I hoped that was okay. I hoped I wasn't making a mistake. I'd call her as soon as I could, and we could talk about everything.

Annoyed that my plans to ask her out had gotten completely derailed, I pulled out my suitcase and dug around in the back of my closet for my sturdy work clothes that I still had buried somewhere in the accumulated mess.

Violet and I would talk soon, and everything would work out fine. I was sure of it.

Chapter 22

Violet

I stared at the text from Ian, tears pricking my eyes.

I didn't blame the ghosts. They hadn't done anything wrong, and it certainly wasn't Ian's fault that he'd been scared away by them, but damn it! I'd never even gotten a chance to kiss him.

Well, I supposed if it was going to happen, it was better now than when I'd gotten really attached.

In a fit of emotion, I threw my phone onto the couch and stomped away.

"Damn it!" I swore aloud, headed out of the house, let the dogs out, and slammed the door behind me.

It was dark and the stars dotted the night sky. The vista would have been breathtaking if I hadn't been so upset. Instead, I glanced toward the lighthouse then back toward mine. I scrubbed a few more tears from my eyes then went to check and make sure Ian had locked the gate.

The dogs bounded around me, darting here and there, chasing rodents or scents, or coming over to me for pets. The crisp air felt good after the warm house. Unfortunately, I wasn't in the mood to really enjoy it.

When I reached the gate, I found it locked. A glint of metal caught my eye. The key I'd given Ian lay in the dirt under the lock, the small loop of leather I'd tied it with threaded through the hole but unknotted.

Wordlessly, I scooped up the key and put it in my pocket. I'd basically been rejected by my husband for years and nothing had hurt quite like this did.

When I got back to the house, Shiner cleaned the tears from my face. I fed both the dogs, ignored the question from Butcher on the wall, and fell into bed. I had to go to work tomorrow and pretend that everything was okay, because what else could I do?

Hopefully, at least, the assholes trying to scare me out of my house would be handled and I wouldn't have to deal with them again.

***

When I got into work the next morning, there was already a line outside the shop waiting for us to open. That had never happened before. A bunch of folks greeted me like I was a friend or acquaintance when I walked past, and that warmed some of the pain away from my heart. The excited murmur that followed Shiner and Creek further lifted my spirits. People always loved my dogs, and that thrilled me. The two made the rounds, getting pets as we walked past the line. I felt bad that I had to hurry them along, but I needed to get inside to help open.

Debbie was pushing open the front doors as I reached them.

"Come on in, everyone." She winked at me. "We'll open a little early today."

"Sorry!" I exclaimed though I was still a few minutes early.

"Not to worry," she said, with a satisfied smile on her lips. "You're early yet. Take your time. We've got it covered."

It occurred to me that this might be because of the event we'd held. That thought thawed more of the ice and

162

by the time I was behind the counter, I'd pushed thoughts of Ian and my aching heart into the back of my mind.

Everyone who'd been at the event had a kind word to say, either about the gathering, the dog costume contest, or my dogs, or even some of the other businesses around. That the community seemed to have grown closer over the gathering had me smiling through the morning rush, and by the time afternoon came around, I was feeling almost normal again.

"Hey, kid," Katie said. "Nice job yesterday. We might need more help if this keeps up. You available for more hours?"

"Absolutely." More hours would really help with winter heating bills looming on the horizon.

"Great. Debbie has a schedule in the back when you're done up here. She'll work things out with you."

Just then Betty from the dog grooming place came in. "Violet! Do you have a minute?"

I glanced at Katie, and she nodded.

"Sure, what's up?" I came around from behind the counter and we went over to a table. "Everyone is talking that they'd like to do organized community dog walks and one of them mentioned that there were other activities and stuff that there were actual awards for? We thought you might know something about that?"

"Oh! Yes, I do, actually." I spent a few minutes telling her about the programs for people with pet dogs and what kind of awards were available through the kennel club.

"Well, it sounds like you were just the person. We were hoping you could help us organize events. We want to do more with our dogs."

"I'd love that. Thank you for thinking of me, Betty."

"Of course, Violet. We'll see you Saturday morning?"

"Yes! Perfect. See you then."

Betty left and I went back over to the counter to fill Katie in.

"Let Debbie know, and we'll make sure to leave that blocked off as a day you're not available."

"Oh, is that okay?"

"Of course, kid. Now get out of here. You've done plenty today."

"Thanks, Katie."

I couldn't help the happy smile that stayed on my lips for the rest of the day. Even without Ian, I now had some hope that I really could call this place home.

Chapter 23

Petey the Poltergeist

Dogs were cool.

Everything else was lame, but the dogs were cool.

I tossed the ball down the hall and Shiner and Creek chased after it.

I'd always wanted a dog when I was a kid.

I liked that Violet had given me a new name. Something that was different from my old life. And I could pretend the dogs were mine.

Creek brought the ball back and I gave him a pet before taking the ball and tossing it again.

Dogs were definitely cool.

Dakota Brown

Chapter 24

Violet

"**H**ow long is Ian going to be gone?" Katie was saying to Debbie as I walked into the coffee shop, as a customer this time, a few weeks later. The weekly dog event went great. Today I'd taught them about the trick dog program, and we'd all started working on new tricks for our dogs after the walk.

I hesitated, then continued inside. I would have to deal with Ian, eventually. Unless he started getting coffee somewhere else while he worked.

"I don't know. I haven't heard from him, and you know Freida doesn't talk to me."

"That's not like Ian, is it?"

Debbie shook her head. "Freida isn't so bigoted that she wouldn't tell me if something happened to the kid, but otherwise I have no idea what's going on."

"Violet! Have you heard from Ian?"

"Uh, no. Why?"

"You two were getting on so well. I thought he'd have kept in touch while he was out of town."

"Oh." I sighed. "I don't think he's interested in me like that, if that's what you mean. He was just being nice. I haven't heard from him."

Debbie and Katie shared a look.

"Did something happen?" Debbie asked.

167

"No, nothing like that." I didn't think the ghost incident counted anyway. "It's just didn't work out I guess."

Both Debbie and Katie shared another look, this time a confused one.

"Are you sure, kid?" Katie handed me the drink she'd been making.

"Yeah." I shrugged and tried not to look too upset about it.

"Huh. Well, in that case, my second cousin from Boston is in town for a few weeks. He's cute, and single. Any interest in showing him around?"

I frowned at Katie. "Uh, sure?"

Debbie elbowed Katie, but her wife shook her head. "Why not? He's a nice guy. Anyway, I'll have him come by after your shift tomorrow. Take him hiking or something."

"Yeah, okay. Why not?" I wasn't sure I was really ready to date, but Ian had got me thinking in that direction, and really, what harm could a couple of dates do?

***

Jason hiked alongside me with occasional distasteful glances at the dogs. Ian hadn't been impressed with the dogs at first either, but he'd warmed up to them. Maybe Jason would, too. Still, I couldn't expect everyone to love my dogs, so I pushed the discomfort aside. It was surprising, really, how many people here did like them. I was sure it didn't help that neither of the dogs had shown any real interest in Jason when I'd introduced them. They'd allowed him to pet them, but otherwise they'd been more excited about sniffing the dirt. Though Shiner had tried to grab Jason's leg, perhaps to try and trip him or entice him to play. I wasn't completely sure. At least Creek hadn't tried to steal anything from him.

Thoughts of Ian taking me and the dogs out to lunch surfaced, and I pushed those away, too. Ian wasn't interested and Jason seemed to be.

So, we walked, and Jason talked about his favorite sports teams, his work—he was an engineer of some sort—and whatever else caught his fancy. I'd told him a little bit about the area, but he hadn't really been interested. This was familiar ground, though. I was just supposed to be present for him to talk to. He didn't really care what I thought about what he was saying. I nodded and occasionally made an acknowledging murmur.

When we reached the point, someone had parked an ice cream truck in the parking lot. Both dogs perked up at the sound and a few hikers were nearby. I glanced at Jason. "Interested in some ice cream?"

He let his gaze roam up and down my body before he raised his eyebrows. "I suppose we've hiked enough that ice cream won't hurt."

A thread of anger curled through me at that comment, but I let it go and followed him over to the ice cream truck.

In line I held back. The dogs would want ice cream, and I wasn't expecting Jason to pay for my treat or the dogs'. Though, as I scanned the menu, the truck carried frosty paws. Even better.

Jason ordered two lemon pops when the woman at the window asked what we wanted. It was the same thing my ex always ordered since it was low calorie and reasonably tasty, though I would have preferred actual ice cream. Unless Jason was ordering two for himself, though I doubted it.

He paid and handed me one without comment, then frowned when I didn't follow him away from the window.

"I'd like two frosty paws, please," I said to the woman. She glanced down at the dogs and her eyes lit up.

"Oh, I was at the event last month. I got to pet them. Hey, what are they going to be dressed up as for the Halloween costume contest?"

We'd decided to run a Halloween event with another show for the dogs, but this time we gave people advanced warning.

"I haven't decided yet." I did have an idea, I just wasn't sure yet.

She handed me the dog ice cream. I paid and joined Jason.

"Seems like kind of a waste of money," he commented.

"They like treats, too. And they're working hard and putting on winter coats. It's an unusually warm day and the ice cream will help them cool off a little."

The sun glinted off the ocean in millions of tiny diamonds and a soft breeze played with some loose strands of my hair, cooling the sweat on my skin.

The dogs, ignoring Jason completely, settled in to enjoy their treats while I tried to enjoy the lemon ice pop. Unfortunately, it brought back so many memories I had to force it down.

"Well, I was thinking that tomorrow I could take you to dinner."

"Okay. Where?"

"The Italian restaurant?"

"Sure, sounds good." I agreed automatically, but it made me uneasy. I hadn't tried them yet because they didn't have a dog friendly patio. I'd have to leave the dogs at the house for the first time since we'd gotten here. It wasn't like the dogs couldn't be left, I just worried about them with everything that had happened. Surely everything would be okay since I'd made peace with the ghosts. Besides, we had an alarm system and restraining orders.

Though I couldn't help but think he might have chosen that place since dogs couldn't come.

I pushed the thoughts away and forced down the rest of the lemon ice pop, collected the containers the dog ice cream had come in, and found the trash.

"Great. Ready to hike back?"

"Sure." He started up again about a project at work and I fell in behind him with the dogs at my side.

Creek hadn't even tried to steal Jason's wallet. That was good. Right?

***

Dinner the next night was more of the same. I kept wanting to pull out my phone and check on the dogs with the security cameras in the dog room. If Ian had been here, the dogs would be with us. But Ian wasn't interested in me, so now I was seeing Jason for the week. I didn't like him, and if Katie hadn't asked me to show him around, I probably wouldn't have agreed to dinner.

It was possible I was being overly judgmental, though. There was nothing wrong with Jason. He seemed nice enough, opened the door for me, paid for my meals even when I offered to pay for my own, and wasn't overly pushy or anything. He just wasn't very interesting. I'd even tried bringing up the weather to see how that would go. He'd pulled out his phone and checked an app. Ian would have cringed.

"How is your meal?"

This might have been the first time Jason asked my opinion.

"It's good," I replied. It was. The wine was a perfect match, and the shrimp alfredo was delicious.

171

And then he was off again on some other topic I half listened to while I worried about the dogs. Or rather, someone trying to break into the house while I was gone, and the dogs were alone with only the ghosts for company.

One other thing I did appreciate about Jason was that he didn't seem to be a complainer. While he wasn't overly positive, he didn't seek out negatives in stuff to comment on. My ex had done that all the time.

I got through dinner, and I didn't want to deal with any passive aggressive comments which meant I skipped dessert. I also used the old trick of taking half my meal in a to go box for lunch tomorrow. Or maybe I'd share some of the shrimp with the dogs when Jason wasn't around.

He took my hand while we walked back to the car. I let him have it. He also carried my to go box. That was nice of him. The night was crisp, with a slight breeze that carried the scent of brine from the nearby ocean.

"How do you like it here? Katie said you just moved in recently."

Startled to be asked something about myself, I hesitated, replayed the question in my mind, and then finally managed to answer.

"Oh, it's nice. I like it. Katie and Debbie are fantastic. The job is easy enough and enjoyable. The locals are starting to get to know me. You know, it's beginning to feel like home."

"Glad to hear it. You don't think you'll leave?"

I shrugged. "Why would I?"

Jason wandered on to another topic until we made it to the car. He opened the door for me, and I got into his rental.

The trip back to my place was punctuated by some music from the radio and the occasional comment from Jason.

I unhooked my seatbelt to get the gate and Jason held out his hand for my keys.

"Let me? It's chilly out and I have a heavier jacket on."

After a moment's hesitation, I singled out the gate key and handed the ring over to Jason. He got out and opened the gate. He didn't even hesitate to stop on the other side and close it behind us, though I told him to leave it unlocked for now. I was hoping he wouldn't stay long, and that would make it easier for him to go. I'd lock it again when I walked with the dogs before bed.

There was a sensor on the gate now that let me know every time it opened. That would ping my phone, and I didn't intend to leave that anywhere but my pocket or in my hand. Even though Katie and Jason were related, there was enough about him that set me on edge, that I wasn't completely comfortable with him here.

Jason, as I expected, got out and walked me to the door. He handed me my leftovers as if he wasn't expecting me to let him in.

"Thank you for a nice evening and a delicious dinner," I offered as I unlocked my door.

"You're very welcome, Violet. I know you're working tomorrow, but maybe I'll stop in and say hi."

"Yeah, if you want. I'm sure Katie would like that."

He didn't step into my space, or try to push his way inside, just waited until I was over the threshold and then turned to leave. I almost offered a hug, but I really didn't like him that much and didn't want to give him the wrong impression. At this point I really only was going out with him as a favor to Katie. It was a relief knowing he'd be leaving soon.

Then something crashed in the kitchen. I spun around and hurried to see what had happened and Jason came with me.

The dogs barked from their room where I'd left them shut in, just in case someone had broken in I'd hoped they'd leave the dogs alone.

The door to the kitchen swung open at my touch, and the box of plates that had already been broken a few times had fallen to the wooden floor and pieces of the dishes were everywhere.

I sighed. Petey was upset about something, clearly. Jason? Maybe.

"Damn it," I said aloud. "Must have been balanced funny or something. There's a cat that gets in here sometimes and I don't always notice because the house is so big. I'll find it and send it outside."

"Do you want help cleaning it up?"

"No, thanks, Jason. I'm good. But I'd better get to it. Have a good night."

"You too."

I walked him to the door and watched until he got into his car and drove through the gate, shutting it behind him. Then I let the dogs out of the room.

They *arooooed* and trilled and warbled their displeasure at being left behind while they danced around me, demanding pets and attention.

"I know, buddies. I know. I didn't like it, either. Well, let's go on a little walk and lock the gate."

I still had my keys in my pocket, but out of habit I reached for the loose key that Ian had left behind. It wasn't on the hook where I normally left it.

"Huh. Must have put that somewhere. Probably in a pocket. Or a ghost stole it!" I said the last a little louder. The stack of blocks upstairs crashed to the floor in protest.

I left the door open when we went outside. It was too cold for bugs, and the extra light was welcome while we went out into the dark night. After living in California for years, I'd forgotten how dark the night could get but seeing the Milky Way every night was certainly a highlight of living out here and I looked forward to our evening walks. At least until the snow got deep, anyway.

Creek and Shiner raced around, wrestling with each other and in general being goofballs. I locked the gate and headed back toward the house, hoping the housekeeper would have the plates cleaned up by the time I got back into the kitchen. In fact, I didn't want to deal with it tonight, so I just kept the dogs with me and headed for the bedroom. It wasn't so much that I was in the mood to try out one of my new toys, but that I'd promised myself earlier that I would, and I wanted to keep that promise.

Hopping a little in anticipation, I locked me and the dogs into the room for the night and looked through my handful of toys for one I hadn't tried yet, all thoughts of the somewhat boring dinner long gone from my mind.

Chapter 25

Violet

By this point I had tried most of the toys. There was one left that I hadn't been brave enough to attempt yet. Tonight felt like just the night to try it. I knew that all these things were tame by toy standards, but for me they were very daring.

I'd not yet tried the thrusting one yet. I had charged it, but it was intimidating. Still, I wanted to see how it would feel. I got it out and stared at it for a while. It was purple, decently sized, and had a little vibraty part. I'd looked at pictures, so I was pretty sure I understood how it was supposed to work. I just needed some lube and to give it a try.

Unfortunately, thoughts of Ian floated to the surface, and I lay back on the bed and stared at the ceiling while I tried to get my brain under control. Well, why not. Maybe not Ian because he wasn't interested, but someone like Ian. The same consideration for me and for my dogs, the same cute grin, but with a purple vibrating thrusty cock.

I giggled at my imagination, then did my best to put any thoughts of men out of my mind. Tonight was about me and this purple thing that would hopefully make me feel really good.

Reaching over, I dimmed the light and climbed into bed. It was cool enough that I pulled the covers up, then, feeling both excited and uncertain, I leaned over and dripped a small amount of lube on the end of the toy. While I rubbed it against myself with one hand, to get a feel for it, and help myself get in the mood, I traced my fingers lightly over my skin. The gentle touch combined with the feel of the toy against my folds was enough to get me completely in the mood. Apparently, my experimentation over the last few weeks had made a difference and my body was reacting eagerly to the attention I was giving it. I had gone so long without that this was becoming a highlight.

Once I felt I was ready, I slipped the toy inside me, groaning softly as it filled me up to a satisfying level. I'd already played with the controls, so I turned it on and hit level one.

Even at that level, it was instantly better than anything I'd ever had before from a human partner. I groaned a little louder as bliss spread through me, warming me at my core and spreading tingles of heat through me.

I turned it up a little and added the vibration on low. While I didn't quite crawl out of my skin, the extra sensation was almost too much and I almost turned it off, but, I wanted this, and wanted to enjoy it, so I left it and shortly I was back to relaxing into the feeling and enjoying what the toy was doing to me as it thrust along inside me. The heat built and sweat broke out on my skin, and I couldn't help the drift of my thoughts as they filtered back toward Ian.

Grumbling at my uncooperative mind, I attempted to focus on anything else, and eventually just turned the toy up another step. That got my attention focused back on the pleasure spreading through me and I let myself sink into the sensations. The toy kept up a nice, steady pressure. My inner walls trembled, and I arched my back up off the bed a little, pushing back into the little toy, though it didn't work quite like that.

The pressure built to a peak that was rapidly becoming familiar, and I embraced the fall as my body crashed over into its release. I had to turn the toy off then, leaving it inside me and enjoying the wave of pleasure that crashed over me and trembled out to the tips of my fingers and toes.

The aftermath left me feeling languid, satisfied, and more than ready for a solid night of sleep. I lay there for a few minutes, enjoying the sensation, before slowly removing the toy, shivering as my body continued to react to the stimulation, then reluctantly climbed out of my warm bed to head to the bathroom and clean up.

The dogs had gotten up on the bed while I cleaned up, and I snuggled in between them and fell into a deep, contented sleep.

***

"It's a beautiful morning, buddies," I said as stood on the porch and watched the sun peek above the horizon. Ian's lighthouse was east of me, and it was backlit by the dawn light. I turned away and watched as the dogs ran and sniffed the yard.

I had to leave in an hour for work, but I wanted to enjoy some tea on the porch for now. I left the door open and went into the kitchen.

"Oh, shit. Guess that's no good anymore." I went over to the counter where I'd set my leftovers and forgotten them. No big loss, really. It had been good, but I didn't really want to eat more. I had a brief thought that I could have fed the rest of the shrimp to the dogs. Maybe if I'd thought about it last night. Certainly not after sitting on the counter all night.

179

The broken dishes in the box rattled. The housekeeper had cleaned them up as I'd hoped. However, the ghosts still seemed agitated.

I grabbed the box to throw it away and jumped, barely suppressing a scream. A mouse lay next to it.

The ghost cat manifested briefly and pounced on the thing before vanishing through the table and leaving some green slime behind. The mouse twitched but otherwise didn't move. Was it asleep? Poisoned?

I inspected the box and noticed a small chew hole.

Fuck, was something wrong with it other than it being out on the counter?

Now I was really grateful I hadn't given any to the dogs. I felt okay, so clearly whatever had gone wrong, hadn't been an issue when I'd eaten at the restaurant. Spooked, I bagged the leftovers in a couple of plastic bags, kind of scooped the mouse into a box, and took the leftovers straight to the outside trash can. The mouse I left in the box on the patio in the shade to see if it recovered. I didn't know what to do, other than go on with my morning and head to work.

"What happened?" I asked when I went inside.

ATE FOOD WENT TO SLEEP

The words appeared on the walls.

"That's scary."

YES

"Okay, well, we're going to work. Um, keep an eye on things while I'm gone? I guess."

OKAY

I hurried through the rest of my morning, skipping food. I'd replace everything in the house, because I didn't know what else to do. The dogs could have some egg sandwiches at the coffee shop. I didn't necessarily think someone had gotten into the house and poisoned my food. This was leftovers that had never even had contact with my food, but I couldn't get that sleepy mouse out of my mind and I knew I wouldn't be comfortable eating anything in the house now. I certainly wasn't going to feed my dogs anything that could be contaminated. What did I do? Store their food in the van?

Good mood from last night shattered, I hurriedly got Creek and Shiner loaded and headed into town early. If I was going to get something to eat for all of us before my shift started, I needed to get going.

I tried not to think too hard about what was going on and just focused on driving. When I got into town, I relaxed a little. At least here I was surrounded by people instead of off by myself.

Hurriedly, I parked and got the dogs out, carefully locked my doors, and headed inside the back entrance. Once Shiner and Creek were settled in the office, I hurried up front to ask about paying for some food before I started. I stopped when I saw Ian leaning against the counter talking to Debbie. His back was to me, so he didn't see me, and Debbie only spared a quick glance before refocusing on her cousin.

Ian was talking loud enough that I could hear what he was saying.

"Yeah, asshole didn't like that I was working on other stuff while I was out on the boat, even though Uncle Owen specifically required them to give me a chance to get my other work done during the day. He claims he didn't get the message, nor did he know I wasn't just a newbie off the streets. I think he was just being a shit. Anyway, he grabbed my phone and tossed it overboard. I don't lose my temper very often, but that phone was really expensive and necessary for my actual job, so I punched him. Fortunately, I'm stronger than I look, or he might have handed my ass to me." Ian shrugged.

Debbie laughed. "I'm assuming you're okay since you're standing here?"

Ian snorted. "I got a black eye out of it. The other guy got a broken nose, and he had to replace my phone and apologize. I'm not sure which one he was more upset about. Owen set him straight and the rest of the time went fairly smoothly."

"Why didn't you call?" Debbie scolded him. "We've been worried."

"I don't have anyone here's number memorized because"—he shrugged again—"well, cell phones. Who memorizes numbers anymore? I gotta apologize to Violet for vanishing and not calling like I promised. Is she going to be in today?"

Debbie pointed over his shoulder and Ian spun around.

"Violet!" His expression lightened for a moment, then grew concerned. "Violet, what's wrong? What happened?" He had the faintest trace of a shadow of a bruise still around his eye.

"Uh." I tried to process what Ian had said, comparing it with what I had thought had happened. He'd left the key, after all.

Before I could answer, Jason walked into the coffee shop. He came up next to me, but I stepped away before he could put his arm around me or make any sort of weird possessive move. I needed to sort things out with Ian, and hanging out with Jason had been more of a favor to Katie anyway. Well, at least after I'd gotten bored, that's how I'd looked at it.

Ian tilted his head, obviously sensing something. Jason focused on me for a moment.

"Still up for tonight?"

"I didn't think we'd planned anything?" I tried to remember, but I was sure we hadn't made plans. Maybe the thing with the dishes distracted me and I'd forgotten? Or it was possible he'd meant to ask and thought he had.

"Yeah, I was going to come over for dinner."

"Uh, yeah, I don't think tonight is good." I really didn't want him coming back to the house. Something about him was just kind of off. Or at least wasn't on enough to risk having him over again.

"Okay, well, I'll be in touch." He hesitated as if he were going to take a step toward me and try to get a hug or something.

I didn't move and he managed to read my body language enough to back off.

"See you later, Debbie." He ignored Ian. Maybe he didn't know Ian.

"I take it Jason isn't your type," Debbie said.

"Uh, no." I shivered. "Weird vibes. Speaking of…" I plowed ahead when my stomach grumbled, and I heard a warble from the back room. "I need to buy some breakfast sandwiches before I start, please."

Ian stared at me while I came over to the counter and ordered.

"Your type?" Ian finally said.

"Katie set Violet up with Jason on a few dates. He was in town. Her second cousin or something," Debbie explained while she made my sandwiches. "You extra hungry? Not judging, but you usually only get one."

"Oh, the dogs need breakfast, too."

"What happened?" Debbie stopped what she was doing and both she and Ian faced me.

"I don't know. I'm probably being overly paranoid with everything going on, but I accidently left some leftovers on the counter last night and a mouse got into it. The mouse was not looking the best when I found it this morning. Spooked me. Now I don't think I can eat any of the food in the house in case something happened to it.

What if they broke in and poisoned the food while I was gone? I couldn't feed the dogs any of it, either."

Ian's look of concern darkened his brow. "Were the leftovers ever in the house without you there?"

"No. Look, I know I'm being dumb but…"

Ian held up his hand but otherwise didn't interrupt. I still stopped talking, casting my gaze downward.

"I don't think you should take the chance," Ian said. "It probably was only the leftovers, but you didn't get sick after eating at the restaurant, right?"

I shook my head.

"So something happened to them, or to them and the rest of the food in your house. I wouldn't eat it, either."

I looked up at his validation of my fears, surprised.

"Did, uh, any of your, uh, security cameras pick up anything?"

Hunching my shoulders, I crossed my arms. "I haven't had a chance to check any of them, and there were, uh, no messages, so, I don't know."

Ian took a step forward, glanced toward the door, then kept his distance.

Debbie had gone back to finishing my order for me.

I didn't speak for a few minutes and the others let me have my silence. Once Debbie handed me my plate of sandwiches and drink, she gestured toward the office. "Take your time. Get those pooches fed, and when you're ready, I'll turn the counter over to you."

"Thanks, Debbie."

I took my food and headed for the office.

"So I take it you are still interested?" Debbie said to Ian quietly enough that I didn't think she meant me to overhear.

"What? Yes, of course." Ian's tone was shocked.

I hurried into the back before they could catch me listening in, limbs shaking in reaction to the emotions roiling through me. I couldn't really process what I was feeling, so I just sank to the ground, pulled out the dogs' bowls that I kept here, and offered them the sandwiches while I ate mine. They were more than happy to snarf the unexpected treat then both laid next to me while I finished mine more slowly.

Exhausted and emotionally drained, and the day hadn't even started yet, I tried to get myself to move and head back into the coffee shop. I needed to get to work, but I was suddenly so tired. Not like in a something was physically wrong with me way, but in an emotional, soul deep way.

Ian finally joined me, sitting on the floor across from me.

Creek and Shiner perked up, both wagging their plumed tails, but they didn't leave my side. He leaned forward and pet them.

"I'm sorry, Violet. I didn't handle that well. I could have tried harder to get in touch, but working on the fishing boat is so time consuming. Uncle Owen was in a pinch."

"I just thought you'd gotten scared off. Especially since you left your key at the gate."

"I didn't leave my key," Ian said. "It's right here."

He pulled out his keys from his pocket and looked through them before sighing. "Well, I guess it's not. Damn it. The knot on the cord had come undone a couple of times. I was meaning to get a ring for it. I admit I was a little rattled, but I'm not scared off. Well, unless you want me to be."

Confused, I frowned. "But…" I shook my head and tried to think about what had happened. It took a few minutes but finally I worked around back to my trauma from my ex. "I'm sorry, Ian. That sort of thing was exactly what my ex would have done, and I shouldn't have thought you would do the same."

"Violet, you have had so many bad experiences, it's going to take a while to reframe your expectations."

"You sound like Lydia."

Ian laughed. "I've spent a lot of time in her company."

I tilted my head quizzically.

"I guess that sounds weird. When I was twelve my father's fishing boat went down. Bad storm that no one at the time had predicted. Even his trusty weather sense missed the signs. All hands lost. I checked out pretty hard for a while. Lydia helped me a lot, which is why I brought you to her. I was upset for a couple of reasons, one, obviously, I'd lost my dad, my hero. We were very close. And the other was that it was summer and when I wasn't in school, I was usually out on the boats." He held up his hands, palms toward me showing red marks and abused skin. "My hands weren't always this soft. Before I went off to school, a couple of weeks on the boats wouldn't have bothered me at all. Anyway, I'm digressing. I was supposed to be out on the boat, too. I'd caught a cold or something. I don't remember what, and I was feeling bad enough that Mom insisted I stay home. I'd tried to go anyway, but Dad had agreed with Mom. So, not only had I lost my dad, but I would have died, too. We knew it was bad when the storm hit land, but it wasn't for a few days that we were able to confirm the boat had been lost." Ian shook his head. "I'm not saying any of this to get sympathy or anything, just to say that I know how valuable therapy can be and Lydia is fantastic. I don't expect you to get over your past right away, or even for years, but just promise you'll talk to me if something is wrong? If you can. If not, maybe have your butcher friend pass messages for you, or something."

I raised my eyebrows at that. "I'd have to ask him. I don't know, Ian. I'm so broken, I don't know if I should even try to be in a relationship. Maybe it's better if I just didn't see anyone, ever."

Ian put his hand on my shin and squeezed gently. "It's not, but if that's what you want, that's okay. I'm happy just being your friend, if that's what you want or need. If you want more, well, I was going to ask you out. I got a little distracted by the ghosts. That, at least, I feel is a little understandable."

I managed to crack a smile at that. "Yeah, very. I won't hold that against you. Or anything, really."

"I'm sorry I didn't get in touch. I should have tried harder."

"Ian, I'm surprised you even went back out to help your uncle."

His expression turned inward for a moment. "Yeah, it was a couple of years before I was willing to go back out. Unfortunately, that was the main source of income for my mom and me, and I hated the dockside jobs, so after a couple of years ashore, I went back on the water. It was hard, but I managed to do it. It's still hard, to be honest. Probably why I lost my temper with Mack so badly that I started a fight."

"I think he started it. And Ian, it's okay. You don't owe me anything, you had no need to try and get in touch with me."

"No, Violet, it's not okay that I didn't. I think I probably disassociated a little bit, myself, but that's not enough of an excuse. I know I do it any time I have to go out on the water, and I should have gotten in touch with you before I did. I had time. I just wasn't sure what to say."

"Okay," I replied quietly.

"Think about us. Or, you know, Jason, or whatever. Even though you have such fine companions"—he pet the dogs again—"I'd like to be a part of your life. Just let me know what you want from me."

"Okay," I said again.

Ian climbed to his feet. "I have to go take care of some things, but I'm pretty available if you want to call me."

"Thanks, Ian."

"Thank you, Violet."

I managed to hold off tears, but I did take the time to hold Creek and Shiner close for a few more minutes before I finally got to my feet and headed out to start my day. If I was going to replace all the food in my house, and the dogs' expensive food, I needed to get paid.

Chapter 26

Violet

The day dragged on. Worry about what had happened to the leftovers and if I was being overly cautious thinking I needed to replace everything preoccupied me. Worry about when the assholes trying to buy my house would try again, worry about Ian, and just general worry about money and life, kept me from enjoying the normal rhythm of the job.

I hurried through my shopping trip because the dogs had to stay in the van. It was plenty cool enough out this time of year, but I was feeling anxious about so much, I didn't want to risk taking too long and someone stealing my van, too. That wasn't common around here, and I knew if it happened it would be a targeted thing from the people harassing me. I got more dog food, some food for me, and headed back to the house. I hoped that the delivery I was expecting would already be there and I wouldn't have to leave the gate open for the driver, but when I arrived, I didn't see any boxes and I didn't have a notification in my email, so, feeling uncomfortable, I left the gate open behind me and made sure the security system was responding to motion at the gate.

The dogs happily leaped out of the car when I released them and did a quick circuit of the property while I lugged the food inside. I put it all in the living room for now then went back outside.

Both dogs sat on the porch, tails wagging, and stared at something up in the rafters. I went over to look. A sleepy looking tabby cat lounged on one of the beams, tail flicking lightly as it soaked up the last of the afternoon warmth that had collected up under the roof over the porch.

I glanced down and the mouse was gone out of the cardboard box. Well, the cat had probably gotten the mouse, and the cat wasn't dead, yet, so hopefully whatever had affected the mouse hadn't been that bad.

"Nice to meet you," I said to the cat. "The dogs are friendly, if you don't run. If you run, they'll chase you. If you stick around, I'll get some food for you, too."

The cat yawned and stretched before settling back onto the wide rafter.

I shook my head and called the dogs off. "Let's go get food, guys."

While the dogs ate, I snacked on what I'd bought and cleaned all the old food out of the house. Fortunately, except for the dog food, it really wasn't that much, but I just couldn't risk any of it. I did keep everything that was still sealed, like the new tin of tea, but I thought that was safe enough. Something had happened to that mouse, and I had no idea what. I didn't think anyone could have gotten in and poisoned my food, but I just couldn't bring myself to eat it, or feed anything to the dogs. If anything happened to them…

I dragged all the trash out to the trashcans, grateful that the service was due soon, and went back inside.

The dogs were playing ball with one of the ghosts when I came back inside. Probably the teen.

Before I could question the ghosts or ask them how they wanted to do their haunting hour, someone knocked on the door.

I sprang to my feet, hoping it was the dog stuff I'd ordered. Since I couldn't easily get to any shows, I'd thought about setting up some stuff here to at least stay in practice. I really shouldn't have spent the money, but at some level, I just didn't care.

Instead, when I opened the door, Jason was there.

"Hi?"

"Hi, Violet." He pushed past me into the house.

"What are you doing here?" I felt my pocket, but I'd left my phone in the kitchen. Damn it.

"I'm heading back to Boston today, but I had to swing by first."

"Oh, well, okay. It was nice spending some time with you. I hope your trip home goes smoothly." I really wanted him to take the hint and leave. I really didn't like how he'd barged into the house.

Both Creek and Shiner lined up on either side of me, staring at Jason.

"How'd your food reheat?" he asked as he wandered around the living room, peering at the old pictures on the wall.

"Uh." How did I answer that? The question wasn't weird, but in context it was. "I accidentally left it out on the counter, so I had to throw it away. Why?"

Jason turned and looked at me, expression darkening for a moment.

I almost apologized, but then stopped myself. It wasn't any of his business, anyway.

"Jason, you should leave. If you're taking off today, you don't have a lot of daylight left and wildlife is a real danger driving in the evening and after dark."

He squared up on me, leaning forward.

I took a step back and the dogs rumbled a warning. They *never* growled, and that told me I was right, Jason wasn't acting right. They'd never even growled at my ex, though I'd been careful to keep them away from him as much as possible.

191

"Where is it?"

"What?"

"The treasure!"

I stared at him. "What!"

"We know this place is haunted. We know there is treasure. Where is it? Hand it over and we'll leave you all alone."

I continued to stare, fear momentarily forgotten. "There's no treasure. It's an old mansion with a lot of dust, but not much else."

"Yeah?" He proceeded to throw open the door to the dog room. "Well, just remember, we'll find it, and until we do, no one will be safe. Not you, not your dogs, not Ian," he sneered as he said Ian's name.

"Get out of my house!"

Jason stomped around the dog room for a moment before snorting in disgust and trying the door to the basement. It didn't budge and he yanked hard on the handle.

"Keys!" He held out his hand, demanding them.

"Get out!" I shouted.

Just then I heard footsteps on the front porch. I'd left the front door open and a woman wearing a brown uniform knocked on the open door.

"I have a delivery."

Jason glared at me, then turned to the woman. "Just leave it."

"No, you just leave, Jason. I didn't invite you over, or in, and you need to go." I returned his glare.

The woman came in and stood next to me, pulling out her cell phone. "Do I need to call the cops?"

"Yeah," I said.

She immediately dialed 911.

Jason stormed out of the house as the dispatcher answered. The delivery driver quickly told the dispatcher what was going on.

I hurried to the door and watched as Jason left. Had he been working with the people trying to buy my house all this time?

***

Tamara, my delivery driver, stayed until Ranger Milton showed up. She left my packages on my porch, gave her report, gave me a hug and her phone number since she was a local, and headed off to finish her route.

I invited Ranger Milton in for some tea, which he accepted, and I went through everything that had happened since the last time we spoke, including letting him know about the weird occurrence with the mouse and Jason's questions about how the leftovers had been.

"They're after some treasure?"

"Yeah, I guess there's some rumors of like, treasure from early in this house's history. It was connected with—" I frowned, trying to remember. "Some smugglers or something, Ian said. I'll have to look into it more, but really, there's nothing here. I thought they just wanted the place because of the ghosts."

"The ghosts?" Ranger Milton raised his eyebrows.

"I mean, everyone thinks it's haunted, right? I thought they were like the other paranormal investigators, just more aggressive about it. Turns out, they think there's treasure. Which, honestly, is ridiculous. I mean, I guess I haven't been in the attic. But, otherwise, it's a pretty normal, old mansion." I didn't mention the basement, because that was weird and I knew it was connected to the ghosts, so I left that alone.

Ranger Milton shook his head. "Some people will do anything for treasure or money. I'm sorry you're experiencing this. We'll dig into the folks behind this more, but it may be more than the local sheriff's office can handle. Deputy Maxwell is out on the water right now or he would have come. I was in the area, so they called me since it was urgent."

"Yeah, I appreciate it."

"We'll get Jason on our list of people to hopefully bring in and question, and I'll have a word with Katie and see what she knows."

"Oh, Katie would never…"

Ranger Milton interrupted. "Sorry, I didn't mean that she's a suspect or anything, but she is related to Jason, and she did suggest you go out with him. It will be helpful to see if she has any idea how he might have fallen in with the others."

"Oh! Okay. Sure."

"Well." He put his teacup in the sink. "Thank you for the tea, Ms. Thompson. We'll be in touch."

"Thank you." I followed Ranger Milton to the door and watched him leave. After he was gone, the dogs and I went out, locked the gate, and did a quick evening patrol. Then I moved the boxes that would go inside off the porch and left the other ones for later. After everything, I just didn't have the heart to deal with the things I'd ordered, and I collapsed on the couch instead.

"Can we have a pass on haunting tonight?"

The dog ball bounced down the hallway and Creek went after it.

"I'll take that as a yes." An idea occurred to me. "Oh, hey, what about a movie? You've all got to see *The Shining*. I'm sure I can find it on streaming somewhere. I think you'll like it."

While horror movies might not have been the best to watch after the day I'd had, since the ghosts were on my side, I didn't think the movie would leave me feeling unsettled. At least not any more than I already did, so I found it online, set up my laptop so we could all see the screen and grinned as the ghosts manifested around me. The twins sat one on each side of me and the others crowded in, with the dogs at our feet.

It was an excellent way to take my mind off the horrors of the real world for a while, and the twins, at least, loved it.

Dakota Brown

Chapter 27

Ian

Kicking myself again and again over how I'd handled things with Violet, I slammed the top down on my laptop and leaned back in my chair. Debbie was behind the counter, and she glanced at me, but I ignored her.

"I'm going to kill him!" Katie came storming into the coffee shop from the front entrance. A few of the other patrons looked up, curious. The locals, Judy and Trudy, *friends and roommates* who were old enough that they just couldn't admit that they were a couple even to Debbie and Katie, were playing checkers in the Maine section and immediately stopped and gave their full attention to Katie's impending tirade. The others were from out of town, but still leaned in for the details.

"What's going on, hun?" Debbie leaned against her side of the counter.

Katie shoved a chair back under a table and stormed through the coffee shop, fixing things up, before she turned around and leaned against the counter.

"And I'm the one who told her to go out with him. Damn it!"

Well, at least she wasn't mad at me. I'd been a little worried about that.

"Katie, what happened?" Debbie asked again.

"Jason, that sorry son of a bitch, if I ever get my hands on him…" She stormed through the shop one more

197

time, then sank down into one of the chairs as if exhausted. "Apparently he was working with those goons trying to scare Violet out of her house."

I clenched my hands as she continued. Why couldn't they just leave her alone?

"Treasure, seriously?" Debbie shook her head. "The only thing in that house is a whole lot of dust. Well, maybe not as much in the main area, but you know what I mean."

Now I felt even worse. She'd been willing to go out with Jason because she thought the ghosts had scared me off.

"Ian, honey, why don't you go out and see if she's doing okay?" Debbie glanced at me. "She's off for a couple of days."

"Yeah, I'll do that." I packed up my stuff and left to the litany of things Katie was going to do to Jason when she caught up to him. He was family, distant, but family, and family wasn't supposed to fuck up like that.

I ran my hand through my hair, before tossing my stuff into the backseat of my car and backing out of the parking spot. It was possible she wasn't home, but I'd check there first. If she wasn't home, I'd call her. Of course, I didn't have my key anymore, so I'd probably still have to call her when I got there. If a certain criminal dog didn't steal my phone again.

The trip out seemed to take forever, though it wasn't any longer than normal. I just kept playing the things Katie said over and over in my mind. She'd been alone with Jason enough that he could have really hurt her. I wasn't sure what her dogs would do if he tried, but they were not guard dogs. She shouldn't have to be worried about going out alone, though.

I was fuming by the time I pulled up to her gate.

The first thing I noticed when I pulled to the side of the driveway was her van. So it looked like she was home.

Then I saw that she had some sort of playset or jungle gym set up for her dogs. She was running Creek over a bridge at the moment.

Huh.

I watched for a while, fascinated. There were jumps and a tunnel, and all sorts of things. I had no idea what she was doing but I was sure she and the dogs were having fun.

"Violet!" I yelled once she'd finished with Creek.

The dogs barked and after a quick word from her, they bounded over to me, fluffy tails curled over their backs.

I reached through the bars and pet both of them, marveling as I did every time at how soft they were.

"Hi, Ian." Violet jogged up to the gate but didn't act like she was going to open it.

My heart sank a little.

"Hey, I was just coming out to check and see how you were. Katie told us what Jason did. That's… I don't even have words." I was trying to keep the anger I felt out of my voice, but something must have flashed across my face because I saw her lean back for a moment before she shook her head.

"Yeah, messed up. I just wish I knew what they were really after. I mean, treasure? Seriously?"

"Yeah, pretty messed up. Anyway, are you okay?"

She shook her head. "As much as I can be. I don't even know what to do at this point."

"So…" I trailed off, not sure what to say. Finally, I shrugged. "Yeah, I have no idea, either. We should talk to Lydia's lawyer friend."

Violet shook her head. "Ian, I can't afford a lawyer. I'm not even going to be able to afford to heat this house this winter."

I stood and leaned against the gate, staring at the ground. "We'll figure something out," was all I could offer.

"Ian, it's best if we don't get involved any more than we already are. It's not…"

Shocked, I looked back up at her, meeting her gaze.

Violet clenched her jaw, and it was her turn to stare at the ground. "It's just not a good idea."

I'd told her it was okay if she didn't want to be anything more than friends, but it sounded like she didn't even want that. Had I screwed up that badly?

I had to accept what she was telling me. Pushing wouldn't help anything, and it would make me just as awful as the people who were hurting her.

"Okay, Violet. If that's what you want."

I didn't miss that she scrubbed at her eyes, but I didn't say anything.

"Yeah, it's for the best."

"All right. Hey, I still want you to feel free to call me if you need anything?"

"Yeah, of course. Thanks, Ian."

She was clearly dismissing me, so I turned and headed back to the car. How had I screwed up this badly? I knew I hadn't had a lot of relationships. Most people thought my obsession with weather was nerdy and lame, but she'd seemed like she appreciated all of that about me. Maybe she just needed time to deal with everything she'd been through. I'd be careful not to burn any more bridges, and if she wanted to try again in the future, I'd be there for her.

That didn't really ease the pain in my chest now, but maybe in time I'd feel better about all this. I was also careful when I got in my car to drive away that I didn't slam my door or drive like an asshole. Nothing that might hurt her more than I already had. Violet had enough to deal with, without having to deal with my emotions too. I wasn't giving up on helping her with her situation, regardless of everything else, so there was that, at least. And Lydia had asked me to talk to her lawyer friend for Violet. Well, I'd touched base once, but it seemed like I needed to make another phone call.

Not sure what else to do, I headed back to the lighthouse to finish my work for the day.

Dakota Brown

Chapter 28

Violet

Finding the words to push Ian away had been surprisingly easy. Living with it was not. Unfortunately, until the situation with the people harassing me was resolved, I didn't want to risk Ian, or anyone else, more than I had to. Images of the possibly drugged mouse haunted me. What more could they have done?

The cat who had eaten the mouse had decided to stick around after an extremely long slumber, and I was wondering if Jason had put some sort of sleeping something or other in the leftovers. Maybe to knock me out so they could search the house? I probably would have been fine, but the dogs? What if I had shared my food with them?

I shivered and went back to cleaning up the counters during a break in customers. Ian hadn't been in as much as normal, and I knew that was my fault. I'd seen him a few times and he'd been friendly, but distant. That was completely understandable, and I didn't blame him at all. Every time I saw him, I wanted to apologize, wanted to ask him to forgive me and tell him about the threats, but it wasn't safe.

Debbie and Katie didn't say much, just let me go about my work in peace. I was still working on the next event for Halloween. It would be a good one and I was looking forward to the costume contest, though I still hadn't decided what to dress the dogs up as. This kept me reasonably occupied, as did the extra hours they had for me to work now that business was picking up. Tourist season was winding down, but the locals had started coming in more, so the first event had accomplished exactly what it was supposed to. I was proud of that. It didn't do much to improve my mood, though.

The Saturday morning dog club we were developing was also keeping me busy. I was going to have them out to try the agility equipment once this mess with the paranormal investigators was over. If it ever was.

I'd had one other session with Lydia, but then put that on hold, too. I didn't know what would happen if they really went after everyone, and I just couldn't put the people around me in danger.

I know they wanted me to isolate myself. Unfortunately, until the police were able to do something about the situation, I didn't actually know what else to do but push everyone away for their own safety. And even then, I knew it wouldn't be enough. I hadn't been safe with my ex, but at least I'd known what to do. Play along, keep my head down, don't make a fuss, everything would be all right. Now? I just had to keep my dogs and everyone around me safe. The ghosts had promised to watch the house and let me know if anything happened while I was away, and I had the security system. Unfortunately, I was back to having a hard time sleeping and this time it wasn't because of ghosts.

"Ian said there's another storm brewing for tonight," Katie said while I cleaned the espresso machine.

I winced at Ian's name. "Yeah, the sky was really dark, and the wind brisk when I came in." Those were things I just knew to look for. Ian had given me other tips, like types of clouds and wind direction and stuff, and I'd guessed we had a storm coming in from his lessons and my childhood growing up here. I glanced at Katie, and she studied me, brow furrowed. Quickly looking away, I went back to cleaning.

The bell on the door chimed just as I picked up the pot of fresh hot coffee to move it back to the warmer.

"Hi, what can I get for you?" Katie asked.

"Just coffee," a horribly familiar voice said.

I turned, dropping the pot of coffee and not even feeling it as the hot liquid splashed all over me. The crack and clatter of the glass shattering on the floor jerked me out of my shock. My hands shook as a hot rage burned through the initial fear that had trembled through me at the sound of my ex's voice.

He leered at me. "Looks like you're just as useless here as you were at home, Violet."

The sound of my name on his lips disgusted me.

"Leave," I said quietly.

"I'll have coffee, if there's any left." He ignored my quiet words.

"Leave," I managed more loudly.

"Coffee," he repeated, pointing at the brown liquid all over the floor. "I'm sure you can manage that."

"Get the fuck out of here. Leave!" I shouted.

Katie turned her attention from me back to my ex.

"You can't tell me what to do," he said with a smirk.

"Do what she says." Katie backed me up. "Get out."

"Oh? I'm sure the owner will have something to say about you turning away customers, not to mention all that." He gestured to the mess on the ground.

"I'm the fucking owner," Katie said, accent thickening with her rage. "Get the fuck out or I'll call the cops."

My ex gave an exaggerated sigh. "So much drama. I'm sure the coffee isn't worth the ridiculous price, anyway. Be seeing you around, Violet." He sauntered out of the coffee shop and went down the road.

Once he was gone, I gasped for breath and noticed how badly my heart was racing. I clutched my chest and leaned against the counter, trying to breathe.

"Violet, honey, who was that?"

"My ex," I managed to get out.

Katie straightened and looked back toward the door. "I'm going to fucking kill him."

The pain from the hot coffee all over my legs hit. I winced, then suppressed the pain. It was nothing compared to the rage I felt at my ex following me here.

"Kid, are you okay?" Katie gestured toward my legs.

"Yeah, I'm fine. I'm sorry about the mess, and the coffee pot. I'll replace it."

"Don't worry about it, Violet. I've broken a few myself. They're cheap. Come on, let's get you cleaned up, and then we'll take care of this."

Katie carefully avoided the spilled liquid and went around the counter to lock the door and flip the sign to closed. "We'll have the shop opened again in a few minutes everyone," she said to the handful of customers inside. "Come on in the back, Violet and let's get your legs taken care of."

A little numbly, I followed.

"Do you have any spare clothes in your van?"

"Yeah, I usually have some yoga pants, or something stashed in the back."

"Do you want to give me your keys and I'll go get them for you?"

I handed over the keys and went to the restroom. My legs really did hurt, and the thin fabric of my pants was not much protection against the coffee I'd spilled. The pants, a light blue, were probably ruined, but oh well. I could wear them around the house, I supposed.

I kicked off my shoes and socks, also wet with coffee then pulled off my pants. My legs were red in patches, probably burned, as were the tops of my feet where the coffee had pooled a little before cooling and being wicked away by my socks. It really didn't hurt that badly, but some of that might be shock. As long as I didn't blister, I figured it would be relatively easy to ignore. I had a lot of practice ignoring injuries, after all.

I cleaned off my legs and rinsed off my pants, but when Katie still hadn't returned, I grimaced and pulled my wet pants back on to see what was going on. I couldn't quite manage the socks, so I pulled my shoes on without them and went out of the office after giving the dogs a quick pat and telling them to stay.

I'd parked behind the store, like normal, and went out the back.

A tow truck idled blocking the exit to the employee parking area, and Katie and the driver were having a heated discussion while the wind whipped at Katie's hair.

"What now?" I groaned. I could easily believe my ex would try to get my van towed.

When I got closer, that seemed to be exactly what had happened. He hadn't taken into account the small-town nature of Cliffside though. Katie jabbed the truck driver, a Black man who's name I thought was Joel, as we'd met before, in the chest and he held up his hands.

"What's going on?" I asked tiredly, one hand tucking my hair behind my ears in a vain attempt to keep it out of my face.

"Got orders to repossess this van, but Katie says it's a mistake."

"The van is paid for. I don't know what's going on. Well, I'm sure my ex is behind it, but the van is mine." The hot anger burning through me was split by icy shards of fear. I had to leave, to go somewhere he couldn't find me.

"Hmm, well we can't be misusing the tow service, now can we." Joel scratched his head and grimaced. "I'll swing by the sheriff's office and file a report. If it turns out the order is legitimate, I'll come back and talk to you, and we can figure it out. That okay, Katie?" He glanced at my boss.

"Yeah, Joel." Katie shook her head. "This is ridiculous."

"Yeah, I'm sorry you're getting caught up in all this. It's more than anyone should have to deal with. I'll have to go somewhere he can't find me." I scrubbed at my face.

Katie didn't say anything as I took my keys back and got into the back of my van to find spare clothing. I even had some jogging shoes, so I shut the van and quickly changed before rejoining Katie and Joel.

She seemed to be explaining something to him and his expression darkened with every word she said. He glanced at me when I slammed the side door shut and by the sympathy, I had an idea that Katie had shared what she knew of my ex with the driver.

"Ms. Thompson," Joel said.

"Violet is fine, Joel."

"Violet, this harassment is ridiculous. I'm going to have one of the deputies swing by after I go file my report, okay? I'm the only tow truck in town so don't you worry none."

"Thanks, Joel." My shoulders slumped and I stared at the ground, defeated.

Katie put her hand on my arm and squeezed gently. "Let's go back inside and get everything cleaned up. You can add your ex to the restraining orders, and we'll see if there's anything else we can do."

I shook my head. "There's nothing else we can do."

Katie gently led me inside, and I lost myself to the task of cleaning up the spilled coffee and making sure the counters and floor were as spotless as I could make them. Selfishly, I allowed myself to disassociate. Even this coffee shop that I'd come to love was no longer a safe haven. Where could I go that he wouldn't follow me?

I had a few dark thoughts, but Katie reappeared from the back with Creek and Shiner in tow and tucked them in behind the counter with me. Their fluffy tails were curled over their backs and they both gave doggy grins when they saw me. They banished my dark thoughts, and I knew I'd have to figure out how to deal with this situation, if nothing else, for them.

"Today, they are service dogs. If you need any breaks at all, just take them, okay?" She gave me a quick hug before going back and flipping the sign back to *Open* on the front door.

I took a minute to pet the dogs before making sure my hands didn't have hair on them. They were on perfect behavior, and both laid down out of the way, their eyes focused on me.

Katie disappeared for a minute then returned with her laptop. She grabbed a table near the counter and got to work on something or another.

It wasn't long before one of the non-locals approached the counter. She'd been here for a while, sipping on coffee refills and working at her computer. She was not at all our normal customer, wearing a pantsuit and carrying an expensive briefcase.

"Another refill?" I held out my hand for her cup before I saw she held papers instead.

"Violet Thompson?"

"Yeah." An icy shard of fear cut through the numbness. What now?

Before she could continue, Deputy Brody came in, expression furious.

"Violet, we've got calls in to the city, see if we can figure out what to do about this BS situation of yours. In the meantime, let's get that other restraining order sorted. Katie, do you mind?"

"Not at all, Dennis." Katie shut her laptop and came behind the counter.

I couldn't understand how she was willing to deal with all the disruption I'd caused her, but the dogs followed me, flanking me on either side, as I came out from behind the counter and went with Deputy Brody.

The woman in the suit followed.

"Ma'am, can I help you?" Deputy Brody turned to face the woman.

"I'm Violet's lawyer, and I would like to be present for this. It might be better if we use a back room."

"Uh, what now?" I shot a look back toward Katie, but she was focused on a customer.

"Oh, right, Violet, is there some place we can go?"

On autopilot, I led them to the back office.

Deputy Brody sat behind the desk so he could write, and I sank down onto the couch. The dogs continued to flank me, and the mystery woman sat on one of the chairs.

"Who are you?" I asked while Brody got out his paperwork.

"I'm your lawyer. If you recall, you gave Lydia permission to share things with me?"

"Oh! Uh, yeah. But, uh, I don't have any money."

The woman waved her hand. "Handled. We'll discuss that later."

"But…"

"Ms. Thompson…"

"Violet."

"Violet, then." She smiled. "My name is Charlotte Mallory. There's a fund. You qualify. Don't worry about my fees. What you should be more interested in, is that your ex is going to go to jail, probably for a long time."

I raised my eyebrows. "What?"

"May I speak in front of Deputy Brody, or would you rather wait until he's done with the restraining order?"

"Uh, no, that's fine."

"Good, because it's relevant to his task. Though, Deputy Brody, I must ask that you keep this in confidence."

"Of course, ma'am," Brody replied, leaning forward, elbows on Katie's desktop.

"Do you remember those wavers you signed for Lydia, granting legal access to your medical records?"

"Yeah."

"Good. Well, they were very enlightening. What was even more interesting was that your ex didn't go to jail when you divorced him."

"Uh, well, I mean, it was just a divorce."

"Violet, the pictures alone from the last time he put you in the hospital should have had him behind bars. I went digging. I've got friends out in California, and they found some very interesting information. Not only is your ex going to jail, but your so-called lawyer is going to, at the very least, face charges as well. Your ex absolutely paid him off and we have the proof. I've already initiated things in California, and now we'll have legal proceedings here, as well. It seems he's involved with the harassment you're experiencing, and the incident this morning that I was fortunately able to witness, and record is more than enough to have some action in this state, as well."

"Um."

"Here's the unfortunate part. Outside of selling his home, he's in so much debt I doubt you'll get much other than him behind bars, but that's something at least."

"Debt?"

"It appears he's had some rather large bad habits for years, outside of how he treated you. They've caught up to him. I'm sure part of the reason he fought so hard to keep you from getting any more in the divorce was because he was in such a bad financial situation as it was."

"Huh." I wasn't even sure how to feel about that.

"He's after Violet's house because of the ghost treasure?" Deputy Brody asked.

Charlotte raised her eyebrows. "Ghost treasure?"

I groaned. "My house is supposed to be haunted. There are rumors of a treasure, but, like, I'm pretty sure every old, haunted house has rumors of treasure, doesn't it?"

"Probably common, especially on coastlines where piracy and smuggling were once an issue." Charlotte shrugged. "The men your ex hired are paranormal investigators as they said, but they're pretty shady and that community has blacklisted them, too. So, he's after your ghost treasure. That's, by itself, interesting information to add to the lawsuit, as it shows his mental state as becoming increasingly unstable." She made some notes.

"We should get this restraining order filled out," Deputy Brody said. "Is there any way we can arrest him, too?"

"If you can find him, I believe there are now warrants. If there aren't now, there should be soon. Violet, I'm so sorry for everything you've been through, but hopefully we can put this behind you before too long. The investigators will likely leave you alone once your ex is no longer paying them. Especially with the threat of real jail time on top of the lack of funding."

"I hope so."

"Ma'am, did Violet inform you about the ex's latest abuse?"

"Outside of his visit in the coffee shop?"

"Yes." The deputy filled Charlotte in on the incident with the tow truck.

The malicious glee on Charlotte's face as he added more fuel to her case against my ex was a bit validating and hints of hope started to shine through my dark despair.

"Okay, last thing for now," Charlotte said. "We'll set up a meeting for later this week when you're not working to discuss more details. Do you have someone who can stay with you out at Hill House? That is what your place is called?"

"The locals call it Hill House, but it doesn't officially have a name."

"Is there someone who can stay with you, so you aren't alone? Or maybe a place you can stay in town until we get your ex behind bars?" Charlotte held out her hand to Shiner, who was closest.

He pushed his muzzle under her hand and her eyes lit up as she pet his soft head.

My thoughts flashed to Ian, but I'd already pushed him away. I couldn't ask him to take me and the dogs in. Even if I hadn't, that was a lot to ask.

"No, not really."

"Aww, Katie and Debbie have a spare room," Deputy Brody said. "Or what about Ian. Aren't you two seeing each other?"

"Uh, no, I can't impose on anyone like that," I automatically replied before remembering that I'd promised Lydia I would try to ask for help when I needed it.

"Well, I'll ask for you." Charlotte stood. "You should not be alone until your ex is safely behind bars. He is dangerous."

I shuddered. As much as I tried to shy away from those memories, I knew he was. The lingering pain from the coffee burns served as a reminder. Thinking of that, I

213

realized I hadn't actually put any burn cream on them. I'd have to do that, soon.

"We will increase patrols, too," Deputy Brody said. "We're already out that way a lot, but when we're not doing anything else, we can park out there. Not too many of us in this county, but we'll do what we can."

"Okay, well, Violet, it was nice to finally meet you and your furry friends in person." She held out her hand. "I'll let you get back to work, but I'll be in touch later this week."

I stood and shook her hand. "Great. Thank you."

She and Deputy Brody left. The things Charlotte had told me weren't especially surprising, but at the same time, I was also shocked. Perhaps it was more that my lawyer had been purposefully incompetent. On some level, I'd known I should have gotten more out of the divorce, but I'd just been trying to get out with the dogs and their things and my life. Suddenly angry at the injustice of it all, I fantasized about taking all this to my family and forcing them to see what I'd been going through. I wondered if it would change their minds. Probably not. Well, his financial situation might, but the rest? Sadly, probably not. Still, I had my life out here, and that was certainly something.

I quickly found the first aid kit and put some cream on my legs, washed my hands, then headed back out to finish my shift, Creek and Shiner glued to my side. Hope pushed through the dark cloud hanging over me. Maybe, just maybe, I'd be able to rebuild my life for real.

Chapter 29

Butcher

The reindeer had been a hit. I wondered what else I could dig up for those mangey mutts to chase.

Oh, better not let Violet hear me call them that.

Well, she couldn't hear me. I'd have to be careful what I wrote on the walls.

All dogs were mangey mutts to me, though.

Did dogs like to chase pigs? They probably liked to chase everything.

Maybe some sheep to go with the reindeer.

I floated around the kitchen, dripping blood, until Housekeeper shooed me out with an annoyed swat of her broom.

Well, I knew they liked the reindeer. I'd better go make sure they were ready for the dogs to herd around later today when they got home.

I drifted upstairs to the room where their scrimshaw tether—an old decorative piece of bone with carvings on it—was stashed to check on them.

Yes, the reindeer had been hit. What else could I find for them? I faded out while I considered the problem, drifting into the ether to await the next haunting hour.

Chapter 30

Violet

The rest of the day went reasonably smoothly, and when I clocked out, Debbie took Katie's spot behind the counter.

"I'm going with you, kid. We'll get your stuff, and you can stay with Debbie and me."

"I can't impose, Katie. That's too much."

"Nope, that's what friends do, Violet. You're staying with us until it's safe."

Surrendering, I sighed in relief. "Okay, thanks."

Katie nodded. "Yep. No problem. Now, let's go get your things, and I'll finally get a chance to have you over for dinner." She gestured toward the back door. I glanced at Debbie who grinned at me.

I took that as her approving, too, so I followed Katie out back. After a quick glance at the van to make sure nothing seemed amiss—my ex knew jack shit about cars, so I wasn't too worried—I loaded the dogs, and Katie and we got in out of the cool, damp wind. The sky had darkened considerably, and thunder rumbled in the distance.

The trip out to the house was quiet, outside of the wind against the van and the occasional drop of rain on the windshield as the storm teased the fury to come. Katie didn't say anything, and I was almost never inclined toward small talk. Ian was about the only one who ever had gotten me to just sit and talk about nothing. Though, come

217

to think about it, talking about the weather with a weatherman probably didn't qualify as small talk.

"What's on your mind?" Katie asked as I turned onto my long driveway.

"Nothing, why?"

"Oh, you just got the first smile I've seen from you in a while."

I sighed. "I was just thinking about the weather. Sorry."

"For what?"

"Everything." I slumped my shoulders.

Katie gripped my arm. "Don't be."

Not totally reassured, I stopped at the gate, hopped out and opened the gate, pushing against the wind.

"I could have gotten that, kid," Katie said when I got back.

"Oh, it's fine. Habit." When we went through, I got out and locked it behind me, double checking to make sure it was actually locked. Normally, if I was leaving right away, I would have left it, but with everything that was happening I wanted to be as safe as possible.

I let the dogs out. They ran and pottied, then joined me on the porch. Usually they'd run around, but they clearly sensed the storm or that something was going on, so they stayed right with me.

Katie glanced around curiously when I let her inside. I couldn't blame her. Hill House had such a reputation, and the décor was extremely mismatched. The house creaked and groaned as the wind picked up outside.

"It came furnished," I felt I had to say.

"Oh, I wasn't judging," Katie assured me. "Just curious."

"Feel free to poke around." I went into my bedroom and grabbed a bag and my clothes. I still didn't have much, and, except that I would have to buy winter clothing soon, probably wouldn't have much for a while.

An alarmed bark had me rushing back out to the main room. The front door banged in the wind, and my ex and the two paranormal investigators he'd hired stood there. How had they gotten in? Had they cut the fence?

Creek and Shiner's hackles were up, and deep growls rumbled from their chests. My normally friendly dogs were in full defense mode, standing in front of Katie and snarling at my ex.

"What are you doing here? Get out!" I shouted.

Lightning flickered across the sky and thunder cracked, loud, nearly overhead. The lights flickered as if to punctuate my demand.

When the lights came back on, my ex held a gun pointed right at my dogs. And, by extension, Katie who stood right behind them.

"Stan! What the hell are you doing!"

"Call off your damn mutts or I'm going to do what I should have done years ago." His eyes were wild, but his hand was steady.

I hadn't even known he knew how to shoot a gun.

"Creek, Shiner, get back here."

Before I could retrieve my dogs, my ex's gaze hardened.

I ran forward to throw myself between him and the dogs. The world slowed around me as I saw his finger tighten.

"No!"

Thunder cracked, the lights flickered again, and the clatter of hooves on wooden floors filled the resulting silence. The lights came back on. Stan squeezed the trigger.

The resulting bang was muffled as a herd of ghostly reindeer plowed into my ex and trampled him to the ground.

The two paranormal investigators pointed, mouths dropping open, and I tackled my dogs to the ground.

They yelped, but more in surprise as I hit them than in pain. Where had the bullet gone?

We sprawled and I twisted, but Katie was still standing, eyes wide, hands clutching her chest as if surprised she were still alive. She'd had a direct view down the muzzle of that gun, too. I scrambled to my knees and reassured myself that the dogs were fine.

Grandmother appeared in front of me and pointed up. I looked and saw a ladder in the hallway going up to the ceiling.

"What the hell?" *The attic!*

My ex was shouting now, and I knew we only had moments before he got himself under control again. I scrambled to my feet, grabbed Katie's arm and ran for the stairs.

"Come now!"

The dogs were already ahead of me by the time the words left my mouth. I thought they might have been following the teen, who they'd taken quite a liking to.

I did have a moment to see that my ex was wiping ectoplasm from his face, and I hoped it hardened before he got it off. Asshole.

"Hide the gun," I hissed as I ran, hoping they'd take care of it if they hadn't already.

Creek was trying to make it up the ladder when I dragged Katie up the stairs.

"They can see us," she protested. "They'll know where we're at."

HIDDEN!

The words splashed across the nearest wall, dripping blood and Katie slapped her hands over her mouth, stifling a shriek.

"Thanks, Butcher. They've got us hidden for now. Hurry."

In a desperate feat of strength, I grabbed Creek around the chest and hauled him up the ladder and tossed him into the attic I'd never explored. Nothing up there could be worse than my ex.

Risking splinters, I slid back down and grabbed Shiner before hauling him up. Neither dog resisted, though it had to be uncomfortable for them. They knew things were bad and they simply let me drag them up and plop them in the dark.

As soon as Katie was up the ladder behind me, it shot up into the air as if on its own and the trap door shut.

"Holy fuck," Katie breathed out. "It really is haunted."

"Yeah, appreciate it if you didn't tell anyone, thanks," I muttered, trying to see, but the attic was dark.

Until another bolt of lightning flashed, revealing an attic window. I rushed over, wondering if we could get out that way. A quick look let me know that while I might be able to, I doubted Katie could and the dogs wouldn't make it. I might be able to strap one of them to my back, but that still left Katie with the other. Not to mention the downspouts and lattice were old and probably not that sturdy.

The ghosts had hidden us, but how long would it take Stan and his cronies to find us anyway?

I pulled out my phone, but there was no reception. I killed the sound just in case and turned airplane mode on and off to see if I could get it to connect. Katie did the same. Nothing.

"Did they block it?" she whispered.

"Or the storm took the tower out," I replied as quietly. "We should move." I pointed to the far end of the attic near the other window. This would put other parts of the house between us and my ex and his gun. The wood wouldn't stop a bullet but maybe we could get out of the line of fire.

The dogs, now covered in dust, spiderwebs, and suspiciously glowing goo, scrambled the way I pointed.

A greenish light hunkered down by the window.

"Petey?" I whispered as I got closer.

A stack of ancient, yellowed papers lifted then fluttered to the ground.

"They have names?" Katie hissed.

"Of course. Petey was a teen. He's the poltergeist. The dogs really like him."

I heard a grown man scream downstairs. It wasn't my ex, so likely one of the other men.

Words splashed across the attic wall, illuminated by Petey's faint glow.

THE TWINS LIKED THE MOVIE

I snickered despite the situation. "I showed them *The Shining* the other day."

Katie mumbled something incomprehensible under her breath. "Great, so introduce me to your other friends later. What do we do now?"

I winced as something crashed below. "Wait for the cops to show up, I guess. The security system will have triggered. I think."

Katie shook her head. "They'll be a while. Everyone's out on a water rescue."

"How do you know?"

Katie winked. "Small town."

"Uh huh."

"For real, Debbie saw the boats head out, and Rachael over at the hair salon told her it was a bad one. The salon has a scanner."

222

The idea of the hair salon having a police scanner was both ridiculous and completely reasonable at the same time.

"Right. We need a plan." I again glanced at the window and bit my lip.

With one last crack of thunder the skies let loose killing any idea of escape. I'd freeze in this weather before I could get to help, and the storm was bad enough I might just get lost trying to get to town.

No, we were going to have to save ourselves. I just wasn't sure how.

Chapter 31

Bloody Mary

Sensing a disturbance in the house, I surfaced from the depths of my mirror, pushing off sadness and despair to peer out into the living world. My mirror lived in the teen's room. It was a mess, showing his agitation.

I floated in the mirror for a while, imagining how I would move through the room, picking up the pieces of his life and putting it back to rights, if I were his mother. If I had lived long enough to become one. The fantasy sustained me for a bit, before another surge of disruption in the house caught my attention.

Quickly, I jumped to the entryway mirror. Here I stared, trying to make sense of what I saw. Sound traveled strangely into the mirrors, and I couldn't completely make out what was being said, but what I could see was chilling enough. I pressed my hands against the cold glass, one of the only sensations I could still feel, and watched, horrified. Three men had come in and threatened Violet's friend and her magnificent dogs. Sometimes they would press their noses to the glass, and I could pretend I was petting them for a time.

I pushed away from the outside world, swirling in agitation, helpless, unable to do anything. The temptation to sink back into the depths of the mirror was strong, but I couldn't abandon my new friends. Even if all I could do was watch. That was more than anyone had done for me, back when I walked amongst the living.

The glass was cold against my hands, but I saw Violet, the dogs, and her friend racing away from the men. Ectoplasm covered one, and the other two were staring out the door. I sensed the strange looking deer the butcher had found for the dogs and pieced together what had happened.

My friends weren't out of danger yet, but they had a reprieve.

I jumped up to the mirror in the attic. Dust and webs covered the glass. I could see enough. My friends hid as far away as they could. Now they were trapped and it looked like their communication devices—their phones, I reminded myself of the correct term—weren't working by the looks Violet and her friend gave them.

There had to be something I could do. I swirled again, jumping from mirror to mirror, trying to find a solution.

The men had gotten themselves back on their feet. They looked to be arguing while one of them searched the floor for something.

I put on my fiercest expression and plastered myself in the mirror, hoping to scare them off. I screamed, though they couldn't hear me, reaching as if to take their souls. If only I could.

One of the men saw me, pointed, yelped in fear and made as if to run. The one crawling on the ground, looking for something, shouted at the man then threw a candlestick at my mirror. I ducked back as it shattered, sinking to the depths.

Nothing… Nothing I could do. They needed help, but the others were tethered to the house.

I was tethered to the house.

No one could leave.

But I had to. I could leave. I might never return. The energy it would require… The courage.

I hadn't been brave enough to leave before and it had gotten me here. If I wasn't brave enough now… Violet might join me in the mirrors, and I didn't wish that for her. The thought of Violet never being able to pet her fluffy dogs again drove me to the depths of the mirror web in the house. I flitted around it until I found the one strand I'd never been brave enough to follow. The thin one that was merely a wisp. The one that would shatter if I went down it.

The one that led out.

There were other mirrors I could jump into in this area, but who would know to help?

The man.

Violet's man.

The dogs' man.

The man who had seen me and knew I lived at Hill House.

Ian. I had to find Ian.

I prayed to God, hoping HE hadn't abandoned me completely. I prayed that Ian would understand. I prayed I had the strength to do this thing for Violet. I hadn't been able to save myself, but maybe I could help save her.

I *had* to find Ian.

Chapter 32

Ian

Once I'd gotten over my fear of storms, they'd come to be my favorite weather. Especially since I lived at the lighthouse. Curling up with a warm cup of cocoa, a blanket, sometimes a fire, and a good book had become one of my favorite rituals. Until I'd spent a storm with Violet and her dogs, and now they just weren't the same. My lighthouse cottage was empty without the three of them, and the fierce storm lacked some of its allure.

I'd turned the lights down, though I hadn't lit a fire, and I stood by one of the windows and watched lightning flash across the sky. I had a cup of hot chocolate, but it had gone cold while I stared and brooded.

There had to be something I could do to help Violet. I also very much wanted to win her back, and I suspected my poor handling of our friendship didn't have as much to do with her pushing me away as I'd originally thought. Debbie had called me and filled me in on some of what she knew about the current situation. I needed to convince her that she didn't have to push us away to keep us safe. I also didn't want to be overbearing.

"Ugh!" I took a sip of my cold hot chocolate and wrinkled my nose before stomping over to the sink and setting the cup down. I might reheat it. I might not.

Then I wandered through the house. My once cozy sanctuary away from the rest of the world felt empty. I enjoyed solitude or I wouldn't have rented the cottage at the base of the lighthouse. The lighthouse keeper was an older man I waved at daily, but didn't otherwise interact with much.

He had a small house close to here and didn't need the cottage which is how I'd been able to rent it. He just stayed in the lighthouse itself when the storms were raging, so he could care for it.

I almost went and knocked on the door that connected the lighthouse to the cottage to see if Burt was busy. Instead, I stormed around the house again. This was ridiculous. I needed to go talk to Violet. Even if she still said no, I wanted to apologize again and see if we could figure something out. I hadn't even kissed her, but I couldn't imagine my life without her. Or her ridiculous dogs.

The height of the storm was over the top of me right now and the flashes of lightning were so constant I didn't need lights to safely navigate my house. Resolved to talk to Violet tomorrow, I headed to my bedroom. Maybe I could read a little before bed.

When I went into my bedroom, the hairs on the back of my neck and my arms stood up as if I were about to be hit by lightning. I looked wildly around, wondering if the house was about to take a direct hit. Something caught my eye, triggering an icy tingle of fear down my spine, but I wasn't sure what.

I turned slowly and yelped, jumping backward. A woman floated in my old mirror, hair floating around her skeletal face. Her sunken eyes were sad, and her boney hands reached to the mirror glass from the other side.

"M-M-Mary?" I stammered.

The apparition nodded.

I shuddered, took a deep breath, and then made myself step forward to the mirror. I touched the glass, and she pushed her fingers against mine from the other side of the mirror.

"Is something wrong?"

She stared at me for a moment, head tilted, before she slowly nodded.

"With Violet?"

Her nod got more urgent.

"Is she in danger?"

Mary swirled back from me, spinning in agitation.

"Okay, okay. Let me call the cops, then I'll go over, okay?"

She settled, nodding.

"Mary, thank you." I touched the glass again, then ran back to my kitchen where my phone was on the counter.

Cell reception was out, which wasn't completely surprising. These storms sometimes took out the tower.

I picked up the landline and dialed 911.

"What is the address of your emergency?"

I recognized the dispatcher's voice. "Leeann! Something's wrong at Hill House. Can you get someone out there?"

"Ian, that you?"

"Yes."

"It'll be a little while. Everyone was out on a bad water rescue. They were able to put in, but the storm pushed them down to Fryville. Deputy Maxwell and Ranger Milton are on their way back up, but with the storm everything is taking a while."

"Get them on their way, please."

"Do you know what is going on?"

"Something with her ex." That was the only thing I could think of that would have made Mary find her way to me.

"All right. Be careful, Ian. Don't do anything dumb."

"Promise, Leeann." I hung up and struggled into my rain gear. This drive was going to be bad enough without getting soaked in the process of getting to my car. It was parked in a sheltered spot, but that didn't mean a whole lot in this type of weather.

"I'm leaving, Mary! Make yourself at home!" I had no idea if the ghost could hear me from the other room, but I wanted to make her feel welcome. As ready as I could be, I charged out into the storm, slammed the door shut behind me, and raced for my car.

Even with the rain gear, I was wet before I got into my car. Thankful for the all-wheel drive, I set the wipers to max and sped out of there as fast as I could.

With the rain and the urgency I felt, the trip to Violet's took an eternity. When I got close, even though it made it nearly impossible to see, I killed the headlights and was glad that the storm would cover up the sound of my vehicle. The gate was wide open, and a strange vehicle was parked close to her van. The rain obscured most of the details, but I could make out the shapes. Staying near the fence line and hoping I wouldn't hit anything with my car, I drove around to the back side of the mansion, threw open my door, got a face full of rain and managed to slam it behind me before the car could get soaked too badly. Me, on the other hand, well, I was dry in patches.

I ran to the house and hunkered down on the side near a small utility shed that was built into the side of the house. I wondered if Violet even knew it was here. Needing to get out of the rain for a minute so I could think, and stop flinching every time the lightning cracked, I jerked open the door and let myself inside.

The lightning gave me enough illumination to see it was a standard tool shed with its share of horror-movie implements.

"Okay, what now?" I stood there dripping and stared around me. At my cottage it had seemed simple, call the cops, go help Violet until they showed up. But I didn't know what the situation was, and I was sure Violet's ex was dangerous. Not that I wouldn't put myself in harm's way to save her, but I didn't want to needlessly get hurt.

One of the implements shifted.

"Who's there?" I felt like a psychic in a show asking if someone's grandmother was with them, or late husband or something, but the ghosts were real and I hoped one of them would find me.

Lightning lit up the shed long enough for me to read bloody words on the back of the door.

BUTCHER AND PETEY

"Oh, good. Okay, so what do we need to do? The cops are coming but they'll be a little bit."

DISTRACT THE BAD MEN

"Okay."

PROTECT VIOLET AND DOGS AND FRIEND

I wondered who the friend was, but it wasn't time to ask.

"Yeah. Petey you can move things, right?"

Some chains rattled in reply.

"Can you like, wear the chains and that tarp and fly around like a, well, like a ghost?"

The tarp rustled then settled into a ghost-like form. I had no idea if Petey was under the tarp or just controlling it, but it was convincing.

I grabbed the chains and settled them around the ghost's neck.

"That okay?"

It rose off the ground and the chains rattled.

"Great. What else?" I cast about and found some jars of nails and screws, and I saw a couple of tin buckets. I dumped the nails and screws into the buckets, mentally

233

apologizing to the neat soul who had sorted them for disrupting their system.

Then I threw a tarp over me, found a mouse eaten hole in a reasonable spot so I could see, grabbed the buckets, and went back into the storm, Petey's ghost following behind.

We could run through the house and hopefully distract the men long enough to keep them from looking for Violet.

It was a terrible plan, but if nothing else, I could hit them with a bucket. That was a better plan. Let them get close enough to disable. Maybe Petey could do something with the chains and the other tarp.

I'd noticed a side door that Violet never used and hoped it wasn't locked, or that my key would work in the door. I'd lost the gate key, but I hadn't lost the house key she'd given me.

Hands shaking, I fished out my keys and, after a quick glance through the window to see that the hallway was empty, I fit the key I thought was hers into the lock. It didn't work, so I tried the next one.

Lightning cracked overhead and the resulting thunder was almost palpable. My hands were slick with rain, and I jumped, dropping my keys.

"Damn it."

They floated up into my view and I snatched them. "Thanks, Petey." Now they were sticky with ectoplasm too, but that was the least of my worries.

I finally found the actual correct key and got the door unlocked. I waited until another crack of thunder and pushed it open. The squeal of unused, rusty hinges made me wince, but I was sure the thunder covered any sound I made.

Then, thinking I really hadn't ever wanted to be an actor, I did my best impression of a ghost as Petey and I clattered down the hallway.

One of the doors opened and a pressure shoved against me. I let whoever it was push me inside, just as the thunder of human feet reached my ears. I ducked down behind the door, which I belatedly reached up and twisted the lock on.

Petey zoomed on down the hallway, getting shouts from the men.

My door unlocked on its own, and I took that as an invitation to leave the room. I ran out, rattling my buckets, and diving into another room.

Boot steps pounded after me and this time I stood next to the door. One of the investigators ran in and I slammed a bucket full of nuts and bolts into the back of his head.

He staggered and went to his knees. Before I could hit him again, a broom rose from the ground and wacked him across the back of the head, dropping the guy like a sack of potatoes.

For a moment a woman in old style housekeeper's garb appeared over him. I held up my hand and she went in for the high five…. Sliming me in the process.

I shook off my hand and laughed. "Can you watch him?"

She nodded, then ectoplasm dripped down, pinning the guy to the floor. It probably wouldn't keep him for good, but it would slow him down, and with any luck he'd be out for a while.

I ran out into the hallway with my remaining bucket to see the other paranormal investigator struggling with the tarp and chains. I held up my bucket and Petey snatched it out of my hand. The bucket raced through the air, hovered over the struggling man, then dropped on the top of his head, sending the man off to lala land as he crumpled to the floor.

"You're not a ghost," someone I hadn't seen hissed, and grabbed me around the throat.

I let my legs collapse, taking him and me to the ground. Until I saw the flash of a gun barrel through the hole in my tarp, I still had the upper hand, but I couldn't do much against a gun. Especially since I was still under a tarp.

He yanked the tarp off me, and we both got to our feet, him holding the gun steadily pointed at my face, and me with my hands out to the side.

The storm was starting to lose some of its strength, moving further inland, and the flashes of lightning were less, but the lights flickered back on, and the man's expression turned gleeful.

"Oh, good, the boyfriend. If you're lucky, you'll live through the night."

The expression on his face didn't give me much confidence.

I saw Petey lift something behind Violet's ex. I didn't even know his name. She always just referred to him as the ex. I shook my head, and the object lowered.

"Violet!" the ex shouted. "Get your worthless ass out here, now! Or your boyfriend will join your dogs in the afterlife."

White hot rage rolled through me. If he'd hurt those magnificent creatures, well, I had friends with boats who wouldn't ask questions, and my fantasy would become a reality.

I saw something red splash on the wall near the basement.

DOGS ARE FINE

That let me take a few breaths and think again. How Butcher had known I was losing my cool, I wasn't sure, but I was glad to know that the ex was lying about the dogs. Though, maybe he didn't think he was?

Moments later, Violet came down the stairs, her hands out to the side to show they were empty.

"Get over here, bitch."

My vision went white again. I managed to calm myself once more. I could handle myself in a fight from growing up on the fishing boats, but the ex was too quick with the gun, and it was aimed at Violet before I could jump him from behind.

She obediently went over to him.

"Okay, now you're going to take me to that treasure, and we all walk away from this."

Violet and the ex couldn't see it, but I saw something splash up on the wall in blood.

BASEMENT

I glanced and the door that we couldn't unlock was now standing open.

"Violet, it's not worth it. Just show him the basement."

She glanced at me, eyes wide and I gestured before her ex could glance at me. Her eyes widened further as she saw the open door.

"Yeah, it's in the basement," she said, voice trembling.

It was the hardest thing I'd ever done, to let her go down there alone, with that creep pointing a gun at her back.

I might not have managed it, if one of the ghosts hadn't glued my boots to the floor with ectoplasm. The time it took me to get out of them was enough for the basement door to slam shut behind the two. I just had to hope the ghosts knew what they were doing, and that whatever lurked in the basement wasn't worse than her ex with a gun.

Or maybe I did hope it was worse. A lot worse… as long as it didn't hurt Violet.

Chapter 33

Violet

The basement.

I didn't even hesitate.

I'd rather deal with whatever was down here than my ex with a gun on one of his power trips. It was likely my best chance of survival, and I'd have to thank whatever creature called my basement its home somehow, if I survived this.

Cold tendrils curled around my ankles, sent spiky pricks of pain up my calves and dug into my thighs and hips. But the tendrils didn't impede my motion, so I accepted the pain and moved down a few steps into the dark.

"Where's the light, bitch?"

Even his insults were unoriginal.

Before I could answer, a light snapped on. A bare bulb sent a sulfur glow throughout the surprisingly clean space. No cobwebs, no dust, no droppings, just rows of empty shelving where food or other things could have been stored, bare brick walls, and a concrete floor with a few cracks running through it. The furnace was in the corner, and I'd wondered if I was ever going to be able to get to it or not, along with a water heater and a few other things. There was another room around the corner, but I couldn't see into it from where I was at.

The shadows were thick, but nothing hid in their depths that I could see.

239

"Where is it?"

"The other room." I pointed.

He shoved me in that direction. The whatever-it-was now wrapped around me up to my midsection kept me on my feet and I relaxed. Whatever was down here was on my side. It might not like me, and it was hurting me a little, but it liked my ex less and I suspected it would hurt him a lot more.

As we walked, tendrils of what looked like black frost spread across the freakishly clean floor and walls, slithering and swirling, spreading frost patterns everywhere, then retreating again. I wasn't even sure my ex noticed them.

I didn't even try to talk to him, just trusted the basement dweller.

We turned the corner into the other room and the lights blanked out. The creature grabbed me and shoved me down just as a loud bang deafened me. I saw the muzzle flash, but it was as if I looked through thick colored, leaded glass. The light flicked back on, and my ex looked around, confused.

"I'm going to kill you for that, bitch."

He didn't even seem to notice the smear on his polo. I couldn't tell from behind the protection of the creature, but it looked like he'd gotten hit from the ricochet, though I doubted it was serious. Probably just brushed along his ribs.

I crouched in the corner behind whatever barrier protected me and watched as he swung the gun this way and that, looking for me. Finally, his gaze settled on something in the corner.

The first thing that caught my attention was the remains. There was literally a skeleton in my basement.

I shuddered.

My ex rushed over and shoved the skeleton away, revealing a chest of an old style I'd only ever seen in movies or in museums. Wooden, iron bound, certainly looked like it could have treasure in it.

He opened the lid and stared, before turning around and shouting.

"Where is it!"

He seemed to be looking right at me, but he clearly didn't see me. Instead, his eyes widened and his gun came up, pointing at the door.

Shadows writhed as if alive, the light overhead flickering a few times before catching steadily again and casting that sick sulfur glow as tendrils of black frost reached for my ex.

He backed up, away from the door. Some movement drew my attention, and I turned back toward the skeleton. A wall of black undulated toward my ex. White spots that seemed to blink in and out of existence like dead fisheyes all focused on his back.

I whimpered and shut my eyes, curling up into a ball and wrapping my arms around my knees.

"Where is it!"

Behind you a sickly voice hissed.

The smell of brine rose on the air.

I heard my ex's feet shuffle, then a sharp inhale before he let out a soft moan of fear. The astringent scent of urine joined the brine scent, and the gun barked four more times in rapid succession before it clicked empty.

The sound was muffled, protecting my hearing, and though I heard the ping of the bullets, nothing touched me.

I sank deeply into myself and rocked back and forth, hoping never to see what could only be described as the ghost of a sea monster ever again.

***

241

"Violet!" Warm hands grasped me and pulled me into an embrace.

I surfaced from wherever I'd gone to hide and threw myself into Ian's arms as soon as I recognized it was him that was shaking me.

"Are you okay?"

Nodding, I looked around. My ex was still standing there, eyes blank, mouth open, a bit of drool on his lips.

Deputy Maxwell and Ranger Milton were trying to get his attention, but he didn't respond. Finally, they pulled his arms behind him, cuffed him, and forcibly marched him out of the basement.

The room was empty now. No skeleton, no chest, no monster, no lines of black frost anywhere. Deputy Brody was looking around, but not as if he were inspecting the place out of curiosity, no, he was collecting evidence and taking pictures.

"The paramedics are on the way. Let's get you out of here."

I cast one last look around before letting Ian help me to my feet. He was wet and we were both shivering, but I didn't move away from the comfort he offered.

Half of his face was splattered with what I recognized as drying ectoplasm, as was one of his hands and his forearm. I didn't care that he was getting it all over me.

When we got into the larger room in the basement, I stopped for a minute and looked around.

"Thank you," I said.

A faint scent of brine rose then settled.

Ian shifted uncomfortably. He'd noticed, too.

Getting back up the stairs took more energy than I had left to spare, but I managed with Ian's help. By the time I was in the living room, paramedics rushed inside. One of them came over to me and Ian with warm blankets while the others tended to the unconscious paranormal investigator who appeared to be glued to my floor.

"There's another one in the back room," Ian said.

"What is this stuff?" One of the paramedics tugged on the guy's arm, trying to free it from the ground.

"Salt water will get it off," Deputy Maxwell said, coming back inside.

That started a whole different conversation that, fortunately, I didn't have to be part of.

A bark from the attic reminded me I still had to get my dogs back down, along with Katie.

Fortunately, Deputy Maxwell and Ian felt better than I did, and they helped my dogs and Katie back down to the main level.

"Oh no," I said with a desperate laugh. The dogs were coated in slime and dirt and cobwebs. They looked brown instead of black and white.

"It'll clean," Ian assured me.

I didn't have time to get too worried about it because Creek and Shiner mobbed me, then sat on me and refused to move, even for the paramedics. They finally checked my vitals around the dogs.

The cell phones were working again, and someone called Charlotte. She sat in over speaker while Deputy Maxwell asked all the questions he could think of, while carefully avoiding the topic of ghosts though he clearly knew what had happened. At least enough, anyway. At some point maybe I'd have to ask him if his house was haunted, too.

Everything seemed to take hours, but finally it was just me, Katie, Ian, the dogs, and the ghosts.

"Fuck." I finally said, not sure what else to say in this situation.

"Fuck is right, kid," Katie said. "What a mess."

"Uh, the housekeeper will help clean it up."

"I can't believe how clean that basement is," Ian blurted out, then blushed, as if embarrassed.

"Yeah, it's really weird. But, if that's the way the basement dweller likes it, well, then it can have whatever it wants. Well. Within reason." I shuddered.

"What was it?"

"I don't want to talk about it, Ian."

"Fair. If you change your mind—"

I shuddered again. "You don't want to know."

He squeezed my hand and let it drop.

"Ian, how did you know to come, and to get help?"

"Mary jumped into one of my mirrors."

"Damn it, Ian. You knew the ghosts were real and you didn't tell us?" Katie swore at him.

Ian looked abashed. "It wasn't my place to tell."

"Ian, you staying here with Violet tonight? Or are we taking her someplace?"

"I can stay here. My ex is behind bars. I'm safe now."

Katie looked around the house, a doubtful expression on her face.

"Even the creature in the basement protected me," I said. "I'll be fine. Ian, you don't have to stay."

"If you want me to leave, I will. Otherwise, I'd rather stay with you, Violet."

Creek got off my lap and plopped down on Ian's, settling the matter.

"Besides, you'll need some help getting these two clean." He rubbed Creek's ears.

I took a breath. *Accept the help, Violet.*

"Okay, thank you, Ian. Katie, you can take the van, if you want."

"Why don't you take my car," Ian said. "It's around back. You're more used to that style of vehicle and some of the roads will be slick from the storm. You can come get me later, or Violet can give me a ride if she's willing."

244

I nodded.

"Okay. Do you want any help before I go?"

"No, get home to Debbie. I'm sure she's worried. Ian and I can handle this." I finally dislodged Shiner and got to my feet. Ian did the same with Creek and took my hand in his while we walked Katie to the back door, which was closer to the car.

Ian patted his pants and cursed. "Keys."

Before we could start looking, his set of keys floated into view.

"Thanks, Petey." Ian took the floating keys and handed them to a pale Katie.

"You all have fun," she said and hurried out into the cool, now calm, evening.

"Think she'll be okay?"

"Yeah. I don't even think she'd be leaving if she didn't want to give us some time alone."

I turned to look at him. "Ian, I'm sorry. I just didn't want you to get hurt."

"It's okay. We have a lot to talk about, but nothing has happened that we can't work through."

He brought his free hand up and brushed some dirt off my cheek, then laughed. "I just made it worse."

"Oh well. Good thing I have a lot of salt."

He laughed, then leaned forward. "Can I kiss you?"

At that moment, I wanted nothing more than to melt into his arms. And why not?

"Yes, Ian. Please do."

He pressed his lips to mine, and it was the softest, most fiercely protective kiss I'd ever received.

I melted into his embrace and parted my lips, deepening our kiss into something soul feeding, letting him feel all my pent-up passion and even love that I'd never really been able to share before.

245

Broken pieces inside of me slipped back into place and started to heal when I was able to show that emotion and feel him respond just as fiercely.

Was there a long road ahead? Yes. Could I finally move on from my past? I thought so. And I had no doubt that Ian wanted to walk that road with me.

Chapter 34

The Twins

"**R**ing around the rosie, pocket full of posey…" We giggled as we sang and danced around in a circle. "We knock the bad men, and they all fall down."

We both collapsed to the ground while Grandmother watched with approval.

"We sure did, little ones. Now, just because that was fun, doesn't mean we can go around knocking other people down."

"We know, Grandmother! Just the bad men!"

We got up and danced around again, entranced with our new song.

"Ring around the rosie…"

Chapter 35

Violet

The last couple of weeks had been some of the best in my life. Ian and I worked a few lingering things out and spent all our spare time together. And the Halloween event I'd planned was going fantastically.

Ian had, yet again, stolen Creek for the costume contest. This time we had a non-partial judge, so I'd entered Shiner.

Ian and Creek were currently running around in the stage area, Creek chasing him with a wooden stick in his mouth—supposed to be a stake but not sharpened. And he wore a collar that mimicked a priest's collar. Ian was dressed up as a vampire.

"You'll never *get me*," Ian said, stressing the last two words so Creek would keep chasing him around while the audience lost it, laughing.

Finally, Ian slowed and whispered "up" so Creek jumped on his back and Ian fell to the ground for a dramatic death scene.

"I didn't realize it was a play, too," I said with a laugh when Ian came back over to me.

He gave me a quick kiss on the cheek. "Last minute decision. Glad you're teaching me his commands."

Creek had the biggest grin on his face as he dropped the wooden stick at Ian's feet. I pet my goofy dog and then looked down at Shiner.

"That act is going to be hard to beat, buddy." Ian's willingness and even eagerness to learn how to do things with my dogs was filling my heart with much needed joy.

He wagged his plumed tail which he held curled over his back.

"I don't know, Violet. You went all out on this one." Ian gestured at Shiner.

My very green-colored dog.

It was a temporary dye, and dog friendly, but because Shiner was mostly white with only a few black patches, I'd dyed him green and drawn lines all over his fluff. Then I'd given him a collar with studs out either side and he was wearing a black thing I could only call a hat perched between his ears to mimic the flat top and hair of Frankenstein's monster. I wore a Bride of Frankenstein wig, a black dress, and had white makeup all over my face with lines drawn on it.

Shiner wagged his tail again, then when it was time to go on stage, he strutted his stuff as if he were at a show. No way did he want to lose to his brother. I wouldn't tell him if he did, but because Ian had done an act, I cued Shiner into a heel then worked him through a really quick dancing routine that we often used for warmup before freestyle competitions.

He kept his eyes focused on me while we danced together, him crossing his legs when I did, then doing some spins around me. The weave through my legs was harder because I was wearing a dress, but we sorted it out.

The crowd lost their minds when I had him put his paws on my back and we waltzed out of the stage area.

"Okay, you totally win," Ian said with a laugh when I returned to his side.

"Oh, I don't know. I think the girl with the dog dressed like a unicorn has a good shot." She did, too. "I was thinking, maybe you could spend the night, tonight?" I asked before I could chicken out. I'd been wanting to ask him for a while, but I kept losing my nerve. This time I just blurted it out. He'd stayed for a few nights after my ex had attacked me, but that had been in another room. He knew that wasn't what I meant now.

"Yeah, I'd like that." Ian hugged me to his side and held me there.

I appreciated that he didn't make a big deal of my request, though by the way he was digging his fingers into my arm, he was absolutely into the idea.

Now that I'd asked, anticipation and nervousness had me feeling like I'd just drank an entire pot of coffee all at once.

Ian leaned over and kissed my cheek. "You okay?"

"Yeah."

"Someone excited?" he murmured so that no one else could hear.

If I hadn't been wearing thick makeup, I probably would have been very obviously beet red to anyone looking.

"Yeah, maybe just a little," I finally replied instead of squirming away as my first impulse wanted me to do. I was working very hard on not shying away from things like affection and my feelings. It was tough though.

"Good." He kissed me again, then gently shoved me up to the stage area. "You won," he said when I gave him a confused look.

"Oh! Come on, Shiner." He trotted happily next to me. The girl who'd done the unicorn costume got second and Ian tied for third with a kid who had dressed his dog up like a lighthouse.

The prizes were baskets with various things from the local businesses, similar to last time.

"All right, last round of giveaways, and then you can go home and get ready for trick or treating!" Debbie called out.

I went over to the table I'd put up for the dogs.

"I have an idea about the house, too," Ian said quietly.

"Oh?"

"Yeah, later. Just wanted to let you know I was thinking about it."

"Thanks, Ian."

Katie came over then. "Why don't you two get out of here?"

"Are you sure you don't want me to help clean up?" I protested while Ian, seizing the opportunity, tugged on my arm.

"Nope, go, have fun." She waved us away with a wink.

I let Ian pull me away and once we'd loaded the dogs and gotten into the van, for which I had to take my wig off because it was otherwise tall enough that it annoyed me when it brushed the top of the driver's area, Ian told me his plan.

"Obviously we have to talk to the ghosts, but what if we turn it into a haunted house? This time of year, we'd get a ton of business, and the rest of the time we could cater to the investigators. It probably wouldn't pay all the bills, but I bet you'd make enough to pay for the heat and electricity through the winter. Isn't that your biggest worry?"

"Yeah, that's certainly part of it." I frowned. "I don't know, Ian. That's a lot of strange people wandering through my house."

"Yeah, I get it, and if you don't like the idea, that's totally fine. But I think it would work."

"Well, let's run it by them. If nothing else, they can decide. And they do have to haunt. I'm sure chasing me around every day does get boring."

"Speaking of ghosts, has Mary ever shown back up?"

"No, Ian. No one has seen her. Maybe we should detour past your house and see if we can find her there? She shouldn't miss Halloween."

"As interested as I am in getting you back to your house." Ian mock-leered at me. "Let's go see if she's still in my antique mirror."

"I hope she's okay." I took the turn toward Ian's cottage. "No one has seen her for a couple of weeks, and I am worried."

Ian gripped my arm for a moment. "I'm sure she's okay."

The trip out to the lighthouse went quickly. We let the dogs out and they beat us to the door, tails wagging. They loved coming over here. It didn't hurt that Ian always had a special treat for them.

I unlocked the door. The dogs, seeming to know what we were up to, ran straight for Ian's bedroom. I followed with a brief thought that we could just stay here, instead, but I sort of wanted to spend Halloween with the ghosts, too.

"Mary?" Ian called when we got into his room.

Nothing, but I remembered the summoning from my childhood. "What if we actually have to call her?"

"Oh! Right." He dimmed the lights and we both went to the mirror, and each put a hand on the glass. "Ready?" Ian glanced at me.

"Yes."

"Bloody Mary, Bloody Mary, Bloody Mary," we called together.

For a moment nothing happened, then both Creek and Shiner put their noses on the glass, too. The dark mirror turned cloudy, and slowly our terrifying Mary rose from the depths. She touched the glass where the dogs were pressing their noses against it and made motions as if she were caressing them.

"Mary! You're okay!" I pressed my forehead against the glass, and after a moment she matched the movement. "Thank you so much for helping save me. If Ian hadn't shown up when he did, well, I don't know where we'd be. He distracted them long enough for the cops to show up. You saved us."

I'd never seen Mary smile before, but, moving slowly as if she wasn't quite sure she remembered how, her gaunt features turned from sorrow to joy, and her lips turned up into a grotesque smile.

"Mary, can you leave the mirror?" I kept my hand pressed against the glass.

She studied me for a moment as if trying to figure out what I'd said before she slowly shook her head. Her hair floated around her as if she were underwater.

"If we take this mirror back to my house, will you be able to rejoin the ghosts?"

She nodded again.

"Okay, well, let's do it then," Ian said, studying the vanity.

Before we could start to dismantle it and remove the mirror, a shaft of bright light beamed down from the ceiling directly onto the mirror. We all jumped back, shocked.

Where the light touched Mary, her skin filled out and her features shifted to that of a beautiful young woman. Her hand, still in shadow, was skeletal, but when she brought it to her face to touch her skin, it also shifted to a normal hand.

She looked into the light, then between Ian and me, then back to the light.

"I think you should go, Mary," I whispered. "Take your rest."

Mary glanced at her hands again, then back to the light.

"You are so brave," Ian said. "You saved Violet, Katie, Creek, and Shiner. If you want to rest, you should."

She took a deep breath, chest and shoulders rising and falling, before she beamed at us.

Mary stepped from the mirror, not hesitating until she stood in the shaft of light between Ian and me.

Then she kneeled. Shiner and Creek came right up to her and her lips parted in delight as she pet the dogs for the first time. Both leaned in for solid scratches. We gave her all the time she wanted but finally, she straightened, the dogs stepped back and she turned to Ian.

He held out his hand and after a moment, she put her hand in his. He raised it to his lips and after a look for permission, kissed the back as if he were in an old-fashioned movie.

Mary's smile was luminous.

When she turned to me, I wrapped her in a hug.

"I hope you don't ever feel the need to return, Mary, but know you're always welcome under my roof and in my mirrors."

Her entire being went radiant and she pressed her lips to my cheek before turning and walking into the light.

Creek and Shiner lifted their noses to the sky and howled.

We stood there for a while as the afterimage of the woman going to her final rest faded from our eyes and the sound of their howls faded from our ears.

Ian took me in his arms, and I brushed a few tears from my cheeks.

"We'll have to tell the others."

"Yeah." He held me tightly for a few minutes and then we quietly left his cottage and headed back to my place.

It was getting late by the time I turned onto the drive to Hill House. We wouldn't have trick-or-treaters out here, so I wasn't worried about getting home on time, but maybe next year? Maybe if the ghosts liked Ian's idea, we could have a Halloween party out here? I felt bad charging for a party, but maybe it could be donation based. Potluck, bring candy to share, stay for the haunting, donate a few bucks? It wasn't a terrible idea. Especially with the reputation this place had.

"I'm so damn proud of her!" Ian blurted out.

"Mary?"

"Yeah! She did it. She crossed over."

I grinned at Ian through a fresh set of tears. "Yeah, I am too."

Ian jumped out when I stopped by the gate. His key, now secured with a ring instead of a string of leather, was already in his hand. We might not have to lock the gate as strictly as we used to. I still wasn't comfortable leaving it open. It turned out that Jason had seen Ian's key when he'd barged into my house and stolen it. That's how my ex had gotten in.

Ian grabbed the mail out of the mailbox and shut the gate behind me.

"Hey, you've got a letter from that kennel club you're a part of. Is that good?" He climbed back in, and I drove the short distance to the house.

"I do?" I wasn't expecting anything.

"Yeah." He showed me the envelope, but I didn't take it from him. We still had a few things to do, like unload the gift baskets we'd won. We'd also picked up some treats for us earlier in the day. We'd planned on hanging out this evening even before I'd asked him to stay.

We got the dogs out, grabbed the things we'd gotten from the store, and headed inside.

"Hey, everyone, I have an announcement!" I said it loud enough to make it clear I was talking to the ghosts. When the air chilled even more than it already was—I couldn't turn the furnace on. I'd tried—and a few pillows shifted on the couch, I continued.

"Mary crossed over. We were going to bring the mirror over here from Ian's house, and instead she was able to step out of the mirror and walk into the light. She even got to pet the dogs first."

There was a general lightening of the atmosphere, and everyone manifested, even the teen who almost never did. The housekeeper clapped her hands together. Grandmother pressed her hands together in a prayer pose and bowed her head. The butcher did a ghostly happy dance, and Petey actually smiled. The twins hooked their arms together and spun themselves around in a circle.

"Also, Ian's spending the night. No peeking!"

There was a general wave of mirth and agreement.

"And we'll have haunting hour soon. If you all have any requests, let me know?"

LOOKING FORWARD TO IT

Butcher splashed the bloody words onto the wall then Housekeeper cleaned them off.

Ian and I went into the kitchen, and he started putting things away while I stared at the letter from the kennel club. What could it possibly be?

"Ian, have I ever told you that you are the most useful man I've ever met?"

"How so?"

"You can do things. Like, with your hands."

"I intend to show you what other things I can do with my hands, too."

I gasped. "That's not what I meant."

257

"You don't want me to do things with my hands? What about my lips?"

That got me to laugh. "That's not what I meant, either. I just meant, like handy things. Putting stuff away, cleaning, fixing things."

He'd fixed up a lot of things around the house in the last couple of weeks.

"You're welcome. I need to look at that furnace, too. Think it'll let me go downstairs?"

"You'll have to ask." I shivered. To distract myself from the thought, I opened the letter.

"What is it?" Ian asked while I read.

"Oh! It's my official acceptance to the invitational show in the spring." At first excitement filled me. I'd been waiting for this for a long time. We'd qualified and I'd be able to actually go because my ex wasn't around to tell me no. Then reality sank in. There was no way I'd be able to afford it this time around. Maybe next year. Except there were no shows nearby, so I wouldn't qualify next year, either. I sighed.

"Great, when are we going?" He clapped his hands together.

I laughed sadly. "It's in the spring, and there's no way I can afford to go. The hotels alone would cost several months of pay. It's okay though. I'm just proud that we made it this far." I put the letter on the table and set about getting part of our meal ready. I hadn't eaten in a bit.

"Silly, let me do that. Unless you want to wear streaky white makeup. It is theme appropriate." Ian gestured toward my face.

"Oh, uh, right. Thanks." Heart feeling incredibly full, even with the disappointment of not being able to make the invitational, I headed toward the bathroom to cleanup while my amazing Ian made up our dinner for us.

Chapter 36

Ian

"**O**kay, it's getting very cold and one thing I don't do is chop wood. So… let me see if I can talk the basement dweller into letting me down to check the furnace. The pilot light is probably out. Wouldn't hurt to check the filters, either, but it's so dang clean down there, that they might be okay. Depends on how old they are." I was a lot more afraid of going down there now than I had been before, but we had to get the furnace going.

"Be careful, Ian."

"I'm going to ask. Besides, we can't get down there before it lets us, anyway, right?"

"Yeah." Violet crossed her arms over her chest and hunched her shoulders.

Taking a deep breath, I knocked three times on the door. "Hey, I know you don't want anyone in your space, but I was hoping I could come down and check the furnace. It's getting very cold, and we need to heat the house."

We waited for a while, and I tried to remain patient while I let the creature think. Not once did I think this was ridiculous. In fact, asking permission was probably vitally important to my continued well-being, if the condition Violet's ex was in was any indication. He had clearly checked out of reality and had no intention of returning any time soon.

After a tense eternity, the lock clicked, and the door silently opened.

"Thank you." Not feeling nearly as confident as I probably sounded, I put my foot onto the first step. "Uh, may I have some light, or would you rather I find a flashlight?"

Another small eternity passed, and then the bulbs flicked on in the stairwell and in the main room of the basement where the furnace was. It was still as clean as the last time I'd been down here, though no scent of brine colored the air.

Saying a small prayer to whoever was listening, I went down into the depths of Violet's basement.

It was one thing fearing basements because they were creepy. It was entirely another knowing there really was a monster in the basement.

Still, we had to have heat.

Nothing happened to me as I made my way down the old wooden steps. The door at the top stayed open, and the light stayed steadily on.

Focusing completely on the furnace and not looking around, I crossed the open expanse of the floor.

"You're a fantastic house cleaner, by the way. I'm impressed. Also, I wanted to thank you again for helping save Violet."

The faintest hint of brine scented the air, before it went back to general musty basement smell.

I reached the furnace and spent some time inspecting it. It was clean, as I'd anticipated, and I was right, the pilot was out. The gas had been turned off.

After quickly reviewing all the instructions, I got the pilot going and manually flipped on the furnace. It hummed along as if it were brand new. That was a relief, at least.

"Okay, I think the thermostat should control it for now. Um. Is there anything we can do for you?"

NO

The words scrolled across the furnace in black frost lines.

I clamped my lips shut on the whimper that threatened to escape.

The words vanished, and I nodded sharply, turned, and hurried back to the steps. "I'll just be going then. Happy Halloween."

THE BARRIER IS THIN

The words scrolled across the brick wall in front of me.

"Yep!" I squeaked, hoping that was basement monster speak for "Happy Halloween." I definitely ran up the stairs.

The door closed silently behind me and the lock clicked shut.

"Ohmygod," I gasped.

Violet pulled me into a hug. "That was amazing. Did you really wish the basement dweller Happy Halloween?"

"Yep. It replied, 'the barrier is thin.'"

"Oh, shit, it talked to you?"

"Wrote on the walls. Anyway, let's just hope it maintains the furnace for us, and we can leave it alone. I appreciate everything it's done, it's welcome to the basement, and I'm happy to leave it in peace."

"Same." Violet shuddered in my arms. "Thanks for doing that."

"Of course. The house should warm up soon. Let's get this party really started. Wine?"

"I'll go get it." Violet headed for the kitchen.

"Okay, ghosts, who wants to do a dance party for haunting hour?"

"A dance party?" Violet laughed when she came back with the wine and meat and cheese platter we'd put together.

"Yeah! They chase us around all the time. I thought we could do something different."

Grandmother manifested then and curtsied before holding out her hand.

"See?" I grinned at Violet before taking the old woman's hand and spinning her around.

"Well, we'll need music. Give me a moment."

Before Violet could do anything, an old-fashioned record player floated down from upstairs and an old rock ballad started up, likely from Petey's collection, though I supposed the old woman could have liked rock and roll.

She silently laughed when I spun her around.

Dancing with a ghost wasn't too difficult, and they were more substantial than normal because of the day I guessed.

Violet danced with Butcher, then Petey, and I danced with the housekeeper. The twins hooked their arms together and spun and skipped around in circles.

After we'd made the rounds with the ghosts, Violet and I joined hands. She looked at me, biting her bottom lip.

"Ian. Thank you. This is amazing."

"Violet, I love you, your dogs, your ghosts, and your house. You're amazing."

Her eyes widened and she sucked her lip in between her teeth.

"Also, you don't have to feel the same way about me. I just want you to know how I feel. Take your time."

"I… I do love you, Ian. I've just not been able to say those words without ridicule for so many years it's hard."

My heart broke for her, again, and I kissed her forehead.

"It's okay, Violet. You can pick other words, or just keep letting me come over and dance with your ghosts."

Her expression lightened. "Thank you."

I pulled her into my arms and danced her around to the music. The ghosts paired off and joined us as we waltzed around the furniture. Both dogs had some chews and lay on their beds concentrating on the treats.

The lights flickered, though the music kept playing. Black frosty tendrils twined up through the floorboards.

Violet sucked in her breath before holding out her hand. One tendril wrapped around her wrist. It spun both of us around as I still had a hold of her. After one spin, the tendril vanished, and the lights glowed steadily again.

Eyes wide again, Violet looked at me.

I fought through my fear and smiled.

"Basement dweller wanted a dance too." Then I kissed her forehead.

The other ghosts had all paused, as well, and slowly they resumed their dance as I held Violet close and swayed to the current song.

She melted in my arms, and I couldn't wait to have her melting in other ways, too.

Dakota Brown

Chapter 37

Violet

The evening had been perfect, and while I was anxious for the rest, I was also really nervous. I'd never been with anyone but my ex, and that hadn't been a great experience. Thanks to the toys I'd been gifted, I had some higher expectations, but I still wasn't completely sure what to expect.

I shifted in his arms where we cuddled on the couch while Petey played ball with the dogs. Ian tightened his grip, seeming content to wait until I was ready. I appreciated that, but I wasn't truly sure I'd ever be ready.

Finally, Grandmother manifested in front of us and pointed toward the bedroom, before putting her hands on her hips, though she was grinning.

"I think we have orders," Ian whispered with a laugh.

"I think you're right." Silently I thanked her, or I might never have gotten off the couch, despite how much I wanted this. I unfolded myself from Ian's embrace and tugged on his hand. He followed, pulling me into his arms again once we were in the bedroom and kissed my neck.

"If you just want to cuddle, I'll hold you all night if you want. We don't have to do anything you're not ready for."

I turned in his arms so I could look at him. He was serious.

"I…" I'd never really had a choice before.

265

"If that's all you're ever ready for, that's fine with me, Violet. Take your time."

"Okay." I took a breath, partially in anticipation, partially to ground myself. "Kiss me. We'll see how far I get."

Ian did just that, leaning over and pressing his lips to mine. I let myself feel how he held me, how he supported me, and how different he was from anything I'd ever known. His lips were gentle, questing, responding to my motions as if I were leading the action.

I parted my lips, asking for more and Ian gave me exactly what I wanted, deepening the kiss, pressing with his tongue and kissing me as if he were trying to heal my soul with his love. Maybe he was.

Hesitantly, I ran my hands over his back. He had surprisingly firm muscles for a weatherman, and I knew that came from his childhood on a fishing boat with his family. He tightened his grip, pulling me more firmly against him. I responded by digging my fingers into his ass.

He murmured happily in response.

When I tugged on his shirt, he shifted back and let me unbutton it. He had a happy grin on his face when I pushed the shirt off his shoulders. He had a bit of soft chest hair that I ran my hands over.

"So, put on flannel and crawl into bed?" He ran his hands through my hair.

I'd forgotten how much I liked having my hair played with, and the feeling made me melt a little. I shut my eyes, and went still, enjoying the tingles of sensation at the roots of my hair as Ian caught on and continued to thread his fingers through my hair. It had gotten longer since I'd moved out here. I hadn't had time to cut it, but also, I'd chosen to let it grow, too. Short and stylish was what I'd been expected to do, but now, I could wear it however I wanted.

"You have such talented hands," I said, then felt dumb. I shouldn't say things, they always came out dumb.

"Thank you," Ian replied. "I appreciate that."

It wasn't dumb?

He traced his fingers through my hair, then ran them lightly down my neck.

"Let's skip the flannel," I said.

"But the flannel has pumpkins on it. It's Halloween flannel."

I snapped open my eyes. "When did we get Halloween flannel?"

"I might have gone shopping." Ian ducked his head, embarrassed. "We and the dogs have matching flannel PJs. Well, the dogs have sort of cape like things because I didn't think they'd appreciate the full outfit with all the fur they have. And, well, I'm going to make breakfast, and we're going to wear Halloween flannel. Um, if you want too, that is."

I just stared at him for a few moments before I giggled. "I very much want to wear matching flannel PJs for breakfast. But, like, maybe we can skip it tonight?"

"Oh, okay. Yeah, I'm good with that." He made an exaggerated sigh of relief. "Breakfast fantasy saved."

I laughed harder. "You really got the dogs matching outfits?"

"Yep."

I shook my head. "That's amazing. You're amazing. Thank you."

"What would you prefer to sleep in?"

"Ummm, I'm thinking we can skip the sleep for now, too. Bare skin would be fantastic." Also something I'd never done with my ex. He'd always expected me to leave my nightgown on and just taken what he wanted. I pushed away the memories. Tonight was about new memories, and Ian. And apparently matching flannel PJs.

"I haven't had a lot of partners. Really only two, but, they both taught me a lot. Also, I did get tested after my last partner and I am clean."

It took me a minute to figure out what Ian meant. "Oh. Right. Uh. I'm so bad at this. I hadn't even thought about any of that."

"No, you're not." He caught my hand in his and brought it to his lips.

"I did get tested. Fortunately, I'm also clean. But I'm not on birth control. I'll, uh, get that taken care of as soon as I can."

"I came prepared." Ian blushed a little. "But, also, I'm still totally fine if you want to wait."

"You did?" That blew my mind even more. My ex would have never.

"Of course."

"Okay, yeah, I think we're fine with condoms this time. I'll get on birth control, and we can see how we feel after that."

"That's totally fine. Whatever you're comfortable with. Forgive me if I'm being an ass, but I'm guessing you don't have a lot of ideas about what you like and don't like?"

It was my turn to blush. "Yeah, not a lot, but, uh, I was given some toys when I first moved in and so, I, well, used them, and… Yeah."

Ian's expression brightened. "Oh, good. We can even use some of them if you want."

I felt my eyes widen. "Really?"

"Oh, sure. Toys are great."

"I. Well. Uh. They're in the nightstand drawer."

"Good place for them." Ian grinned. "Any time you want to stop what we're doing for whatever reason, just say so. Okay?"

"Yeah."

"I'm serious, Violet. I want you to know that we have to discover what we like together and if you don't like it, I don't want to keep doing it."

I took a breath. "Okay, yes. I promise I'll say something."

"Good. Okay. Give me a second." Ian went and retrieved his overnight bag. He first held up matching his and hers flannel pajamas with pumpkins on them as promised, then showed me the dogs' costumes that matched.

"How?"

"The internet. You can find anything on the internet. Though, I admit, this one was a little bit of a stretch."

After he showed off our morning outfits, he pulled out a handful of condoms. "They're new, I just didn't bring the entire box. So they should be in good shape."

"Thank you, Ian. This really means a lot to me."

"Me too, Violet."

Ian came up to me and wrapped me in a tight hug.

I leaned my cheek against his chest and sighed happily. Then, stepping back, I tugged off the t-shirt I'd changed into earlier and reached for the closure on my bra.

"Can I?" Ian waited until I nodded before he reached around and unhooked my bra.

I let it slide off my arms and lay on the floor with my and Ian's shirts.

"Okay?" he said, reaching for me.

"Yes, please, touch me."

He did. Running strong hands over my bare skin, exploring, caressing, cupping my breasts. The feel of his hands on my body sent tingles of warmth shooting through

269

me, out to my fingertips and down to the tips of my toes and then traveling back to settle into my core.

"Okay if I lift you onto the bed?"

"Yeah."

Ian grabbed my hips, and, in a quick display of his understated strength, he had me up on the edge of my thick mattress.

Then he leaned in and kissed the curve of my shoulder where it met my neck and then trailed down until he was pressing soft kisses against my breast.

"Is this okay?"

"Yes."

"Are you enjoying it?" Ian looked up for a moment.

"Oh, yes, it feels wonderful." I thought for a moment, then realized I wasn't giving him any feedback. "How should I tell you if I'm enjoying something?"

"Well, you can outright tell me, or make encouraging noises, or both. We can figure out what you're comfortable with as we go."

"Okay. I'll try."

Ian studied me for a moment before shaking his head. "If the basement monster hadn't already handled him, I'd be talking to some friends with boats about turning your ex into lobster food."

Surprised at Ian's bloodthirsty statement, I hesitated for a moment before nodding. "I'd be helping." I shied away from the memory of him shooting at my dogs before I could get there to shield them. The reindeer had saved them, I was sure. I was going to have to process that memory somehow, but right now I shoved it firmly away.

Ian went back to his exploration, and I experimented with making sounds and actually telling him when he hit a good spot. It took some concentration, but before too long he'd managed to get me close to incoherent anyway and I just dug my fingers into his shoulders and moaned or gasped encouragement.

Ian slid his hand over the button on my pants. "Okay?"

"Yeah, please," I managed to get out.

I helped him get me out of my pants and then he moved me further up on the bed, climbing on himself and kneeling between my legs. I tried not to be embarrassed about being completely naked, but I was, a little.

"You're lovely," he said after he let his gaze roam my bare skin, hunger in his eyes.

I didn't reply, just arched up my stomach when he returned to his exploration of my skin with his lips. I was surprised when he went lower, but he didn't object that I'd let my hair grow from when I'd kept it waxed, and his enthusiasm as his lips met my lower ones distracted me from other thoughts.

"Oh, that's good," I gasped out as his lips found my clit and he sucked.

A now familiar pressure was building inside of me. I wouldn't have known what it was if I hadn't had those toys to play with, and I was grateful, and excited that I was getting this far with Ian. I hadn't expected to even get close to having an orgasm unless we used a toy, but between Ian's skillful mouth and hands, and the trust and love he made me feel, I was well on my way.

Ian slid a finger inside me, curling it and hitting an extra sensitive spot inside that just amplified the feeling. I hadn't expected it, but I was wet, and ready, and it just felt natural for him to be inside me.

My actual orgasm surprised me, and I cried out as my body shuddered, electric tingles of pleasure coursing through me.

"Holy shit, Ian," I gasped.

"Good?" he asked, wiping his face off on a shirt and coming to lay next to me.

"Yeah."

"Well, I enjoyed that, a lot. Let's get another." He reached over me and slid my drawer open, coming up with the massager. "Let's play with this. That okay?"

"Oh, yeah, of course. But, uh, what about you?"

"You do understand that you can have all the orgasms you want, but I pretty much only get one or two, right? And I tend to pass out for a while after, so, let's go for a while, and then we'll take a nap." He waved the massager at me.

"That sounds kind of amazing, actually."

Ian's eyes lit up.

Somewhere along the way, he'd learned how to use toys in ways I hadn't even dreamed of, yet. And I was going on several orgasms by the time I tugged at Ian's pants.

"I want you inside me, Ian."

"You're sure?"

"Yeah, completely sure."

He hopped off the bed and shed his pants.

I would have helped but my limbs were practically boneless by now. So I lay there and watched, licking my lips in anticipation. I didn't have a lot to go on, but Ian seemed reasonably well endowed, and I was looking forward to this.

"Like what you see?" He winked.

"I'll like it even more when it's buried inside me," I replied.

"Oh, you're getting the hang of pillow talk already." Ian grabbed a condom after he climbed back up on the bed, sheathed himself and kneeled between my legs again. "Any requests?"

"I want to look at you."

"You want to be on top?"

"Uh, I don't think I can support myself right now. You wrecked me."

He laughed. "Okay." Ian lined himself up with my entrance then met my gaze. "You sure?"

"Very sure. I'm aching to be filled by you, please don't make me beg." I was about to apologize but Ian made a joke before I could.

"Right, save begging for some other time." He lifted my legs and pulled me a little closer, before pressing against my entrance.

I groaned. "Yes."

Fortunately, he didn't make me ask again, just gently slid inside me. I was already wet from everything else, and it didn't take much effort for him to get fully seated inside me.

"That's so good, Ian," I moaned and shifted feeling him inside me and feeling where we were joined, and everywhere our skin touched. I dug my fingers into his ass and encouraged him to move.

"It has been a while. I may not last too long."

"I'm not going to judge, Ian. Trust me."

"I do."

With that, he gave a few experimental thrusts. I cried out, body extremely sensitive. I'd never felt like this before, and I lost myself in the sensation of him moving in and out of me.

"Ian! Just like that!" I shouted when he hit the perfect rhythm. He managed to hold it long enough that I found myself clenching down on him, just on the edge of another orgasm.

"Violet, you feel so good," he breathed out as he moved in and out of me.

"I'm so close."

Ian found my clit with his finger while he managed to keep up a good pace and sent me crashing over the edge one more time. He cried out, following me with his own orgasm. He curled forward, hugging me close and holding me while we both trembled with the aftershocks.

Once we'd come down enough that he could slide out of me, he clung to consciousness long enough to quickly clean up, then passed out next to me, one leg thrown over mine, and an arm over my stomach, holding me close.

I didn't try to hold off sleep, either. Knowing we'd both probably wake up again before long and we could get back to it. And I knew I wanted this man in my life for as long as he'd let me keep him. It wasn't just the best sex I'd ever had, but the way he made me feel—safe and loved— and that he'd embraced my life and shown me his. He made me feel loved for the first time in a very long time.

Chapter 38

Ian

I woke up buried in dogs and curled up with the love of my life. It couldn't get better than that. I wondered if we should get another dog. It would be fun to raise one from a puppy. Maybe Violet could teach me to show it, and we could do those sorts of things together. She already enjoyed my favorite activities, and the dogs could hike with us.

But first, we had to have a ghost meeting. And I needed to make breakfast.

When I stirred, Creek grumbled, and Shiner got up and shoved his nose into my face.

That woke Violet.

I was still holding her, and she startled before she glanced over at me.

"Shiner!"

"Oh, it's fine. I've accepted the dog life." I reached up and ruffled Shiner's ears.

"I don't remember letting them in."

She still sounded worried.

"Grandmother probably did and I'm glad. They're part of your life and I'm sharing it with you. The dogs shouldn't be excluded from things they are used to. If they sleep on the bed, well, it's a good thing you have a large bed."

She laughed uncertainly. "I did get a large one because of them."

"Good planning. So, I was thinking, do you think they'd like a little brother or sister? Because I'd love to have you teach me how to raise a puppy and show one and all that."

She burst into tears.

Guessing her tears had nothing to do with me and everything to do with her ex, I pulled her into my arms and let her cry. She dug her fingers into Creek's thick mane, and Shiner delicately licked her cheek.

She sobbed for a while, and when her tears subsided, I kissed her forehead.

"Sorry." She wiped her face.

"As long as you're not upset at the idea of getting another dog, we're good." I gently teased her.

"No. Not at all. I just... you have no idea how much I had to fight to get my dogs in the first place. I only managed it because they're ultra rare and my ex thought they would be good show pieces. Which, he was right in that regard. They get a lot of attention. And then you just casually mention getting a puppy after getting crushed by dogs for half the night? It's just, a lot. In a good way," she added hastily. "And, like, after last night? That was amazing. And, I guess I just had a lot of emotion."

"Don't apologize for crying, Violet. And if it's ever my fault, well, then I'll be the one apologizing." My heart ached for her. "I'm serious about wanting a dog, though. One like yours. You'll help me find a good breeder and all? It'll be my dog, but, like, you'll have to teach me so much. If that's okay?" Suddenly I wondered if I should be asking that of her. Maybe she didn't want to raise another puppy?

"I love puppies, Ian. I'll absolutely help you find a dog. Maybe after breakfast we can talk about what owning one of these dogs takes. These two make it look easy because they're so well trained, but they are a high energy working dog."

"My other favorite activity is hiking, so I think that's okay."

"Your other favorite?" She twisted so she could prop herself up on her elbow. "What's the first?"

I let my gaze travel what I could see of her bare body. "Last night was my other favorite." Then I winked. "Honestly, just spending time with you is my other favorite right now. But also, weather. Long walks on the beach, and occasionally going out on boats, but I prefer very calm weather."

"Understandable." She sighed. "I feel terrible because I didn't realize you liked hiking so much. I just thought you were indulging me. I've been so wrapped up in my problems..."

"Violet, your problems were trying to murder us. Besides, there will be a time when I get to be wrapped up in mine and then you'll have to deal with moody introverted Ian. It'll be fine. We'll work through it. And yes, I love hiking. This spring I'm going to take you to all my favorite dog friendly places."

"That sounds amazing."

"As much as I'm enjoying being buried in dogs, Shiner just sat on my bladder." I stared at the dog, who had just plopped down on my stomach and was staring at us.

"They probably need to go out." Violet sighed, then shifted out of the bed.

The dogs jumped off the bed, Shiner launching himself off my bladder in the process. I grunted.

"Sorry," Violet apologized.

"For what?"

She opened her mouth to apologize again, then shook her head.

"Oh, hey, pumpkin flannels!" I got out of bed, shivering in the cool air. The heater was working, but Violet didn't have it turned up very high. I supposed with dogs with such thick coats, she'd probably want to keep it down for their comfort. Not to mention the cost of heating this place. She was right, that was a real worry. I quickly put my pajamas on, then dressed the dogs.

Violet came out of the bathroom, and I handed her the flannel nightgown.

"I'm going to have to get some slippers to leave over here." I'd put on socks, but I didn't prefer them if I could avoid it.

"Yeah, I finally got some of my own." She put them on, eyed the dogs with a laugh, then went to let them out. The matching set had actually been a custom order, but I didn't want her to think I'd spent too much money on them, or that I was a giant dork. She'd find that out soon enough if she hadn't already figured it out. It was totally worth it, and I was absolutely getting a picture later. Since her dogs came self-equipped with blankets of fur, I'd had the person just fashion it like a rain jacket style for dogs, with the flannel going over their backs then it fastened with Velcro around their necks and legs. Their tails were free to curl up over their backs, and hopefully it wouldn't be too warm for them to wear at least long enough for pictures after breakfast. Since Shiner was still dyed green, he matched the flannel pretty well. Briefly, I wondered how Shiner felt about the dye job, but I knew Violet wouldn't do anything her dogs didn't like and he seemed perfectly happy.

I made my way to the kitchen and got started on my self-proclaimed famous pumpkin pancakes, threw some bacon in the oven, and started water for tea. Normally I put chocolate chips in the batter, but I guessed the dogs would like the pancakes too, so I left them to put on the side.

I was deep into my cooking groove when Violet came in.

"What can I do?"

"Just make your perfect tea. I always over steep it. Food will be ready in a few minutes. Okay if the dogs have some? It's all dog friendly. I left the chocolate chips for the side."

Violet froze, took a deep breath, and nodded. She turned and I saw her scrub at her face.

"Yeah, they can each have a pancake."

"Great!"

We settled into the routine of feeding the dogs, feeding us, and drinking perfectly steeped tea. I could easily see myself doing this for the rest of my life with Violet and I toyed with the idea.

The letter from the national kennel club caught my eye when she moved it over to a safe counter. I started toying with another idea, too.

"Ian, this is delicious." Violet leaned back in her chair and patted her stomach, a satisfied look on her face that reminded me of last night.

The dogs had scarfed their pancakes up quickly, so I assumed they approved, too.

"Thank you." I grinned at her. "I only make them once a year, otherwise I'd live off them. I'm glad you are enjoying. After we're done, how about we see what the ghosts think of my idea. Unless you don't like it?"

"No, we should ask. It's not a bad idea. If it'll pay enough to cover the heating costs, that will take a huge pressure off me. Katie and Debbie are giving me as many hours as they can, but this is way more house than I thought I was buying. No regrets, but I didn't have 'heat a haunted mansion' in my budget."

I chuckled. "It'll work out, Violet. Okay, why don't you gather the ghosts while I clean up?"

"Oh, let Housekeeper do it. She says it gives her purpose. It was hard to get used to just leaving stuff like this, but they assured me she wants to clean up after us."

"Wow. Thank you," I said, assuming she would hear.

A cool breeze tickled my cheek before dishes rattled on the desk.

"That's our signal to get out. Let's walk the dogs for a few minutes and then we can propose your idea to the house."

***

"So it turns out the ghosts love the idea of hosting a haunted house in the fall. Obviously, we're a little late this year, but we can start working on getting the place fixed up and ready for next year. Also, they're interested in potentially being a tourist attraction, for a fair fee, of course. Violet is right, heating that place this winter will be expensive."

Debbie was staring at me, incredulous. Katie had a smirk on her lips that made me think Debbie hadn't actually believed the place was haunted.

"Hill House is actually haunted? Come on, you're having a go at me." Debbie looked over at Katie who gave her an "I told you so" look.

We'd gotten together at the coffee shop and no one else was around, so I felt okay sharing all this with family. This part of the family, anyway.

"No, it's really haunted."

"We're giving Violet as many hours as we can, but we're still not busy enough to have her on full time or give her more of a raise than we already did," Debbie said.

"Yeah, that's why we're trying to work something else out, too. I don't think she'll let me help. Yet. But assuming we get to that point I'll give up the cottage and help pay the house bills."

That got Debbie and Katie grinning.

"Should we be planning a wedding, then?"

I laughed. "I'd ask her tomorrow, today even. But I don't think she's quite ready for that, yet. One thing at a time. However, I do have a request for the spring. Do either of you know anything about dog shows? Or, like, well, what this really means?"

I'd used my phone to scan the pages the kennel club had sent to Violet and printed them at home.

Both Katie and Debbie read them.

"Oh, I don't know much but I know this is a really big deal. Maybe Betty knows something." Debbie pulled out her phone and touched the screen. After a minute the groomer answered.

"Hello, Debbie. What's up?"

"You got a minute? We have a dog question."

"Oh, yeah, sure. But where's Violet? She knows way more than I do."

"It's a surprise. Just come over if you can." Debbie glanced at me, and I nodded. She'd caught on.

"Yeah, okay, give me just a minute. Business sure has picked up, but I was closing for the day anyway."

"Great, see you in a few minutes."

They hung up and we sat there in anticipatory silence for a while. When Betty finally joined us, Katie had a cup of her favorite coffee ready.

"Okay, so what's up?"

"Well, Violet got this letter yesterday and she's all sad because she can't afford to go. But, I was thinking I could pay for the trip and make it a surprise. But I don't know anything about entries or whatever." I handed over the letter.

Betty's eyes widened. "I had no idea she and her dogs were this good. Look at all the titles those dogs have." She pointed to the letter.

"I have no idea what I'm looking at," I confessed.

"Okay, these are her dogs' registered names and these letters in front of and behind the names are all the competitions they've won titles in. There are a lot. And," she scanned the paper, "They're qualified for quite a few classes. I can help you fill this out, but how much did you want to enter her in."

"Um, everything? Is that reasonable?"

Betty stared at the entry form. "I have no idea."

"Well, let's enter everything and she can decide what she actually competes in." I studied the paper as if I could figure out what it all meant.

"Ian, this will be a several thousand-dollar trip, with hotels and stuff. You know that, right?"

"Betty, I've been saving up for a vacation for a long time and I know this will mean a lot to her. It's fine."

"It's also several months away, what if you two break up?"

I took a breath. "I want to do this for her, even if she breaks up with me. If nothing else, it'll be an investment in her recovery from her ex. I'm planning on asking her to marry me if the next couple of months go okay and she still wants me around."

"You're not going to ask her at the show, are you? Because that's a lot of pressure." Betty frowned.

"Oh, no! I'll ask her before we go. Like, before she even knows she's going. That way if she says no, or that she's not ready or whatever, she won't have to associate the trip with it. And I'll make all the arrangements so that she can go without me, if things between us don't work out. Honestly, though, I think we're going to be just fine."

"You're a sweet boy, Ian." Betty patted my hand.

I wanted to remind her that I was in my thirties, but she'd known me when I was a baby, so I let it go.

"Okay, this is how you fill out this form."

I spent the next few hours arranging a trip that did, in fact, cost a lot of money, but would be more than worth it. I was actually really excited to dive into her world. Sure, I was doing this for her, but I imagined I'd have a lot of fun, too.

Chapter 39

Ian

Spring

Wind drove rain against the house, battering against the shutters on the windows and pounding on the roof. Wind rattled in the chimney, thunder rumbled, and lightning flashed in the sky. It was perfect weather to survey the renovations we'd made over the winter. The last several months spent in close proximity to Violet had been the best in my life. And I figured if we were still speaking to each other after doing home renovations, we could survive anything. The thought made me smile, and I put my hand in my pocket and fingered the small box I'd stashed there.

Between Violet, the ghosts, and I, we'd come up with a series of reasonably affordable renovations to make the house even spookier. We also had our first haunted tour lined up the following weekend. It turned out that the idea was popular, and we'd booked out for a few months already.

We'd also hired a local teen to run the tours and come up with some gift shop trinkets including shirts, some pins, mugs, things like that, many of them featuring the actual ghosts and some had the dogs, too. I'd funded the gift shop since it was my idea. We'd even come up with a solid business plan and the ghosts all had their scripts.

We hadn't told the teen we'd hired that the place was actually haunted. Hopefully, she wouldn't quit after the first tour.

Violet stood next to me and the ghosts swirled around us as we surveyed the living room.

"It looks amazing," she said.

The lights flickered after an extremely close lightning strike.

"Especially with the storm." I laughed. "I never thought I'd renovate a house to look creepier, but this came out perfect." We'd done our best to make it look like a lived-in mansion, but we'd also taken a long look at a lot of horror movies and shows to give us inspiration and I thought it had turned out spectacularly.

The sitting room, originally the dogs' room, was the final destination where the tourist shop was. We'd put up a door to the hallway that led to the back part of the house. It kept tourists out of the bedroom, the new dog room which turned out to have been the twins' room, and we'd taken the last room in the back hallway and set up a private living room area just for us, so we could have private space. The rest of the house, with the permission and help of the ghosts, we'd set up for the tour. Though we had moved Mary's mirror out of the teen's bedroom and into our own. That felt a little too personal to share with the world, though we had developed a display, of sorts, toward women in white ghosts and mirror dwellers. We'd also put up other things for people to read about other different types of ghosts. I thought they'd love it.

We'd made sure our basement monster was kept informed, but that it understood it was in no way obligated to participate. Though we had requested that if it chose to, to not destroy people's minds. It hadn't replied, but the other ghosts had said they were sure it understood and agreed.

The lightning knocked out the power completely, which happened now and again.

I tugged on Violet's arm, and she and the dogs followed me over to the light from the fireplace.

A few visible orbs bobbed around us, and I guessed everyone was present. It took a lot of energy for the ghosts to fully manifest so most of the time they just used glowing orbs to let us know when they were around if they weren't otherwise interacting.

"Violet, I have a question for you before we start our afternoon training with the dogs." The show was in a few weeks, and I'd made sure we rarely missed a chance to practice, even though she had no idea we were going.

"Yes, Ian?" She turned to face me, and I took her hand in mine.

"These last few months have been the most amazing in my life. I think you are amazing, Shiner and Creek are amazing, the house and our ghost friends are amazing, and I want to spend the rest of my life with you and all of this at my side. So, I'm going to ask you to marry me, but before I do, I want you to know that if you're not ready, tell me and I'll wait until you are. If you decide you never want to officially get married and just remain as we are, that's a hundred percent okay with me. And if home renovations have destroyed me in your mind and you're just too polite to tell me to leave, well, that's okay too." I grinned at her when she laughed.

I pulled the ring box out of my pocket and kneeled, opening it and holding it up. Before I could say anything, Creek booped the box then sat, expecting a treat. Shiner sat and put his paw on my arm.

Violet looked horrified. I just burst out laughing.

"I mean, we've been working really hard on their tricks. I'm just sorry I don't have any treats to reward them. I'm a failed dog dad."

She laughed, relaxing. She'd gotten used to my acceptance and even enjoyment of her dogs' antics, but sometimes she still got worried.

"Good boys," I said, lowering the ring long enough to give them both pets. "Okay, you two lie down."

They both did as I asked, tails curled over their backs and wagging.

"Okay, Violet, will you marry me?" I'd thought of trying to come up with a big old speech, but in the end, I just wanted to make sure she knew I was okay with no, then ask her the question.

"Ian, you're the most amazing man I've ever met. You love me, my dogs, and you've made my life better than I could possibly imagine. Yes, I'd be honored to marry you."

Hands shaking, I pulled the ring out of the box and slid it onto her finger. I hadn't been sure she'd say yes, after all. Not with everything she'd gone through with her ex. Relief flooded through me.

I got to my feet, and she folded herself into my arms, pressing her lips to mine.

The ghosts chose that time to manifest, clapping their silent hands. Something crashed upstairs, which I took to be Petey's version of congratulations, and the twins skipped a little dance.

Before I could tell her about the trip I had planned, Shiner and Creek bolted upright and turned toward the basement.

The lights flickered back on, and the basement door stood wide open.

Violet and I stared at each other wide-eyed, before glancing at Grandmother and the other ghosts.

They all stared at the door, too.

The light in the stairwell flicked on.

"Um, I take it that's an invitation?" I tightened my grip on Violet.

She took a deep breath and nodded, stepping away and leading me to the stairwell.

"Stay," she said to the dogs, and then we both went down.

"Oh my," Violet gasped as we went into a transformed room. It appeared to be a smuggler's stash, with some ancient style weapons, a broken apart sailing ship somehow crammed into the basement, old fishing nets, and crab cages and things like that. The human skeleton was a nice touch, and I had no doubt it was real. Or had been at one point.

"This is amazing," I said.

The shadows wavered, and Violet stepped into my arms again, shaking.

No writing appeared this time, but in the middle of the scene a tarnished silver platter with barnacles on it sat on a box. On that platter were two rings, a man's and a woman's.

"Is this for us?" Violet finally breathed.

A line of black frost circled the rings then vanished.

We went forward together and picked up the rings. They were crusted by dirt but the details I could make out were remarkable. Fine engraving on what was probably gold for the man's ring, and some sort of gem set into the band. The woman's ring had quite a few more gems, though I wasn't sure what kind, and matching engraving as near as I could tell.

"We're honored," I said. "Is it okay if we take them to a jeweler to get cleaned?"

The circle of black frost grew around the platter again, but more slowly.

"I sense hesitation. How about we take them to get cleaned, but don't leave the rings with the jeweler, we stay until its done."

This time the circle appeared almost instantly.

"We're honored," Violet repeated my earlier statement. "Thank you." She gestured toward the display. "If you decide to participate in the haunted tour, just open the door. We'll need the stairway light for safety, but that will probably be enough with all of this. Maybe some strategically placed flickering fake candles. I'll put them by the door and if you want them, you can take them, okay?"

The black frost lines grew from the floor and twined about both of our legs, before vanishing.

Though I'm sure we were both thinking that the entire thing was creepy, as well as touching, neither of us said it as we left the basement. I had no desire to insult the basement monster.

"We'll have to do a display on smuggling and sea monsters," I said when we got back to the main level.

"Good idea." Violet's voice sounded a little too steady and I guessed she was as shaken as I was.

We put the rings on the counter. Both dogs put their front paws up and sniffed at the rings. Neither had ever done anything like that before, not even for their favorite treats, so Violet didn't scold them, just let them sniff.

Finally, they both wagged their tails and trotted off as if everything was fine. The ghost orbs swirled around too, before Grandmother manifested with a smile on her face and a nod.

"These are incredible," I said after everyone voiced their approval.

"Yeah. That was really touching of our basement friend. You, uh, didn't have any like specific idea on rings, did you?" Violet twisted her hands together for a moment.

I gestured to the counter. "I do now."

She smiled. "Great. Okay, so when?"

"Halloween, if you don't mind a somewhat long engagement." I'd already thought pretty hard on that.

"Halloween is perfect. We can have a Halloween party as the reception. Everyone can come in costumes. It'll be great."

"I also have a celebration trip planned. Now, before you say anything, I had this trip planned so that if you didn't want me to come along, you could still go. You deserve a vacation, and it's all paid for. But I'm hoping you're okay if I join you."

"Ian, you didn't have to do anything like that."

"No, but I wanted to. I'm excited about it, too."

"Okay, I accept."

She was getting so much better at accepting gestures of affection and of offering them, too.

"Where is the trip?"

"It's a surprise, but here are the dates." I pointed at the wall calendar. "And I already set it up with Debbie and Katie."

"You just thought of everything, didn't you?" She glanced at the dogs. "Okay, um, we'll have to find dog sitters."

"No!"

She raised her eyebrows.

"Sorry, no. It's a family vacation. Dogs included. In fact, you know that breeder we were talking to? I might have, uh, committed..." I held up my phone and showed her the little boy puppy we had both really been wanting.

"I thought she wanted a show home?"

"Why do you think we've been doing all this practice?" I grinned at her shocked look. "I know we don't live close to stuff, but we'll be able to travel, and I can work from anywhere, so while you'll have to take time off, hopefully between my work and the business, we'll be able to afford to show enough not to make the breeder regret giving us a show quality dog."

She wiped at her eyes. "We're picking the puppy up on the vacation?"

"Yeah, that's part of it. I have other plans, too." I waggled my eyebrows to make her think I meant sex, which certainly wouldn't break my heart.

Violet laughed. "Okay. Do you have a name picked out?"

"Ace sound okay?"

"Sure, but, like, his official show name."

"Oh! No, not yet, but you can help me with that."

"I think I need to tear your clothes off now." She gave me a hopeful look.

"I'd like that very much."

The storm, still raging outside, took our power out again. Violet glanced around, pulled the thick blanket off the back of the couch and threw it on the ground in front of the fire.

Before I could ask her what she was doing, she dragged me over, pulled the t-shirt out of my pants and was tugging it over my head.

Oh, she'd been literal when she meant tear my clothes off.

Glad that she was finally comfortable enough to do things like that, I helped her undress me then I did the same for her. We'd been together enough by this point that we didn't need to ask what the other wanted, and the dogs knew to leave us alone. This was the first time we'd had sex in front of the fire, though.

I pulled Violet against me. The heat from the flames warmed my bare skin in the places that weren't warmed by the heat from her body. Our lips met and we explored each other's mouths before she went to her knees in front of me.

Groaning as she took my length into her mouth, I buried my fingers in her hair though I did nothing to take control of her head. She'd been practicing and I enjoyed every minute of it.

Legs shaking as she hummed softly while she sucked on my length, I did my best to keep my feet and not come in her mouth. When I'd reached the point where I was either going all the way or needing her to back off, I tapped her on the shoulder and Violet released me.

"That was really good," I said.

She smiled up at me.

I sank to my knees and lowered my lips to her shoulder, kissing gently and easing her back onto the soft blanket.

She made soft, encouraging noises as I worked my way down her body, stopping to spend some time with her breasts, before kissing my way down her stomach and ending when I could get my lips on her clit. I slid a finger into her and curled it, finding her G-spot. She bucked underneath me as I found my mark. She cried out, enjoying being able to make noise and express her pleasure. Her urgency increased as she thrust back against my hand, and I grabbed her hip to help keep her steady as I worked her into her orgasm.

Violet cried out, soaking my hand as she came.

I leaned back and studied her as she lay sprawled in the firelight.

"You're beautiful," I said reverently.

She flicked her eyes open and smiled sleepily. "And you're talented."

"Ready for more?"

"I want to be on top, today."

"My favorite position." And it was. I couldn't wait to watch her ride me as the firelight flickered across her bare skin.

We traded positions and she took me in her hand and guided my shaft into her. Watching her eyes flutter shut as the firelight played sinuous shadows across her skin, and feeling her warmth cage me inside her, nearly undid me before I was ready. I got a handle on myself, just watching as she straddled my hips and gave a few experimental rocks.

When Violet opened her eyes, I took hold of her hips and between the two of us we set a rhythm that soon had us both crying out as we shattered one after the other.

We collapsed together and lay in the radiant warmth from the fire.

Until the dogs started barking.

"Shit, aren't Debbie and Katie supposed to be over soon to see the renovations?" Violet bolted upright.

"Yeah, and Cynthia, so she can practice the tour. Crap!" Embarrassed that I'd forgotten, but not at all regretting the fun we'd just had, I scrambled to my feet, helped Violet up, and, grabbing the blanket from the ground, we sprinted for the bedroom, just as someone knocked on the door.

Giggling, Violet darted back and grabbed our clothing, and our phones, then we shut the hallway door behind us.

"I'll text them and tell them we'll just be a minute," she said as she headed for the bathroom.

"I'm sure they won't mind waiting a minute," I replied as I hit the shower for the fastest rinse off ever. "Take your time. I'll handle them."

She gave me a grateful look as I dressed and headed back out to give my family the good news.

Chapter 40

Violet

"**W**hen do I get to find out where we're going?"

"In a while." Ian gave me this pleased grin, and I wanted to shake him. I trusted him, so I wasn't worried about our destination, but I wanted to know where we were going. Especially since he'd taken off with Shiner and Creek while I was at work and returned with professionally groomed dogs. Even more surprising was that the dogs hadn't been trimmed. Normally groomers couldn't help themselves but trim feet and all, but the dogs were natural, just clean and very fluffy. Shiner was as white as I'd seen him during our show days and Creek's black shone. He'd even insisted that we not get them dirty because he wanted to enjoy how clean they were for a little while. I understood that, but it was so weird. Maybe he wanted to impress the breeder we were getting Ace from?

We'd been driving for hours, and I'd expected that a dog friendly vacation would take us someplace in the country, or in general toward the breeder we were meeting up with sometime soon. He'd been a little cagy about that detail too, other than showing me the registration papers that already had our names on it.

I reminded myself that I trusted him, but we were getting deeper into the city and when we took the exit to Queens, I got really confused.

"Ian?"

"Just… let me have my surprise. We're almost there."

I took a breath. "Okay." I watched the surroundings for a while. I'd never been out this way before. When I'd traveled to Maine, I'd taken the northern route across New York.

When Ian pulled up in front of a fancy hotel a while later, I frowned. "This is dog friendly?"

Ian glanced at me and raised an eyebrow. "You still haven't figured it out?"

"Figured what out?"

Just then I saw a woman walk past on the sidewalk with a poodle in full show coat. I stared, then something clicked.

"Wait."

Ian grinned.

"But…"

He shrugged. "It's important and I'm excited to be here, too."

"But… only entered dogs can stay at the hotel."

Ian leaned over and fished some papers out of the glovebox before handing them to me.

I glanced over them, jaw dropping. "Ian!"

"You were qualified. You deserved to go."

"But!" I didn't even know what to say. Then I looked closer at the entry confirmations he showed me. "Oh my god, Ian, this is… this is everything! You entered every single class we're qualified in!"

"Well, Betty and I had no idea what we should actually enter you in, so we figured you could pick and choose."

"That's…. not quite how this show works." My head was swimming at the logistics of managing all of this. "Well, okay, yeah, we can certainly pull from some things, but you lose the entry fee."

"Oh, I figured. No big deal."

"Ian!"

"Do you want to do something else?"

"No!" I got a hold of myself. "But, I don't have show clothes." Then I stared at the conformation entries. Both dogs were entered. "Ian, you're going to have to show Creek."

"What?" He blurted out.

"I can't show both dogs in conformation at the same time. They'll both be in the ring. You're going to have to do it if we can't find someone else, but, like, I'm not sure we'll find someone else with no notice."

"Um, okay. Hell, he knows what to do. We'll be fine. We've been practicing." He nodded and pulled the van forward to the unloading spot as soon as it cleared.

"We have to find you a blue suit."

"Blue?"

"To show up properly. Uh, the dogs, for the dogs to show up properly. Blue is what you want to wear to showcase a black and white dog. Like, royal blue."

"Okay. So hopefully we can rent something. Let's get checked in and we can go over logistics."

I took another deep breath and shook my head. "I hope you're prepared for a wild ride." I knew the dogs would handle it, but we were all going to be exhausted by the end of this. Still, I couldn't believe he'd gone to all this effort to bring me to this show. I'd always dreamed of being here, and while I did not feel ready at all, that wasn't really the point. We weren't big name handlers and dogs, we were just "good enough." And we'd have fun, and that was that.

On top of that, I refused to let myself feel guilt. Was this extravagant on Ian's part? Yes. But he'd done it a hundred percent on his own and I just needed to enjoy being here.

With that mindset, I allowed myself to gawk at the fancy hotel, the other dogs parading around, and the people.

Creek and Shiner saw the other dogs and immediately went on display. They knew we were here to show off, and these dogs loved showing off more than just about anything else, except possibly being criminals.

Ian handed the dogs over and got our bags out of the van. "We leave the show stuff, right?"

"Yeah. We'll need to take that over to the show site, shit, tonight. In a few hours."

"I cut it a little tight, didn't I?"

"You didn't know, Ian. And this is all amazing. We can make all this work, just enjoy the ride and know it's going to be chaotic."

"Yes, ma'am."

Getting checked in and taking a few minutes to decompress from driving in our fancy hotel room was nice. I eyed the bed, but we did not have time for naps, or anything else.

Ian arched an eyebrow when he saw me looking. I laughed. "If you're hoping for lots of sex in the extra comfortable bed, you're probably going to wish you'd planned a different vacation."

"Violet, we're here for the dogs and the show. Anything else is extra. We get to have lots of sex at home." He winked.

"Okay, great. So. Uh, you didn't happen to grab my bag of show clothes, did you?"

"I think so. Hanger bag? It's in the van."

"Oh, good. That will save some trouble. We need to get you taken care of. I bet the people at the front desk can help."

I took charge and dragged Ian from the room and into the show week whirlwind.

We found a bright blue suit. Ian bought it, saying if he were going to be showing dogs again in the future, he'd need it. The shopkeepers were so delighted with Shiner and Creek that they gave each matching blue bowties and I promised they'd wear them when they could this weekend. It was show week, and a lot of shops normally closed to dogs were allowing the show dogs inside, and the suit place was no exception.

The next day Ian was the perfect show partner. He followed my instructions exactly, knew just enough to be helpful, and was pretty good at staying out of my way. Not once did he get upset when I was short, or in a hurry, just helped me change clothes, or carry ribbons, or hold dogs. He even got very good very fast at keeping track of arm band numbers.

I didn't actually need him to go into the ring until later that day for our first round of the conformation competition and by the time we got there, Ian had a chance to watch a few of the other rounds and he had an idea of what to do.

I could tell he was uncomfortable in the bright blue suit, but he didn't say a word as I handed him Creek's show leash. He did relax after he saw some of the outlandish colors some of the professional handlers were wearing, men and women.

There were a few other Yakutian Laikas here, and I recognized several of the handlers, but I wasn't sure if I should say hi or not.

As soon as they saw me, they came over, however.

"Violet! You made it!" That was Melissa Harrington.

"I did. Everyone, this is Ian. My fiancé."

"Fiancé? You finally get rid of that awful husband of yours?" She grinned and slapped Ian on the arm.

I glanced at the ground for a moment before looking up. "Yeah. He's behind bars."

"About damn time." She proceeded to introduce me to a few people I didn't know.

Then it was ring time.

"Remember, Ian, have fun."

He laughed. "Don't get mad if I mess this up."

"Ian, just don't get excused and we'll be fine."

"Wait, that can happen?" His expression turned panicked, and then they called his number, and he turned his attention to Creek and went in.

In the end, only one dog can win the class, and Shiner got first. Ian and Creek took third. There were enough dogs in the class, that he was ecstatic with third place. The female dog beat us when we went in the ring with the top female, but I was still thrilled, especially after more than a year out of the show ring. And we still had plenty of showing left to do.

When we stumbled back to the hotel room that night, all exhausted, Ian still had a grin on his face.

"Creek and I won a ribbon," he kept saying.

I laughed. "I think you might be hooked."

"Maybe," Ian admitted.

"The ribbons aren't always this pretty, just so you know."

"Oh, that's okay. I've seen your collection."

I laughed. "Did you dig through the totes? Because that's where all the plainer ribbons are."

"You have more?" The awe in his voice was entertaining.

"Yes, Ian. We have a lot more. There are a lot of shows where I used to live."

"Okay, great, well, we will just have to travel."

I shook my head.

The next few days were the same. A whirlwind that Ian seemed to enjoy far more than I would have expected. By the final day, we'd amassed quite a showing and Creek and Ian had even beaten us in the ring once, which I suspected I would hear about for a while. We'd set aside Ian's ribbons, and he kept looking at them with a grin on his face.

On the last day, I was downing an unadvisable amount of pain killers when I remembered the puppy.

"Hey, when are we getting Ace?"

"Tomorrow. I thought with the show and all we'd have plenty to keep us occupied today and I wanted to make sure we could focus on the little guy."

"Perfect. Is the breeder meeting us here?"

Ian nodded.

"Great. It'll be nice to have a day to relax before we head home."

Ian laughed. "Yes, it will."

"Are you two ready to show one more day?" I looked at the dogs.

They both perked up when I grabbed their leashes.

"I'm amazed they're not exhausted," Ian said.

"They probably are, but they love showing off. They'll be glad for a few days off, though."

"What do you think, Creek, can we win one more ribbon?" Ian pet the dog, who wagged his tail in reply.

I kissed Shiner on the top of the muzzle, and we headed for the show.

***

"That was amazing, Violet."

Ian and I lay in the very comfortable hotel bed after the last day of showing. He was the proud bearer of another couple of very big rosettes and I knew he was well and truly hooked. Which was good, because we were picking up his future show dog tomorrow.

"What do we have to do to come back next year?"

301

"Uh, well, we have to get to enough shows and do well enough to qualify. You can start showing Creek in some of the other events so you can hopefully qualify in those, too. Then it'll be a little easier for me only showing one dog. Ace probably won't be ready for the big time, but the year after you could show your very own dog."

"If I wasn't completely exhausted and already falling asleep while we talked, I'd say I wasn't going to sleep tonight from excitement."

I laughed. "I'm pretty excited, too, Ian."

"Do you think the dogs will like their brother?"

"Oh, probably eventually. It'll take a little time."

"Should I be worried?" Ian rolled over to look at me.

Creek grumbled at the end of the bed at being disturbed.

"No. It'll just take a little time. I'm sure everything will go smoothly. It took a couple of months before Creek and Shiner were best friends."

"Oh, okay."

"Relax. They're overall a very social breed. It won't take long before the three of them are committing all sorts of crime together."

He laughed. "I love you, Violet."

"I love you, too. Ian. Now get some rest."

***

Ian was up early the next day, bouncing around the hotel room like a kid at Christmas. I was really glad he was excited for his new puppy. I just hoped he knew what he was getting into. I'd tried to explain what it had been like with Creek and Shiner as puppies, but then Ian had pointed out that much of my stress had been related to the ex and that he wasn't worried about cleaning up messes and he understood that he needed to be attentive to prevent them,

302

and if things got chewed, things got chewed, and that he'd do everything in his power to keep the little guy safe.

We were going to have a harder time with training classes and stuff, but we'd found a place an hour away and Ian said he didn't mind the drive. So, we were getting a Yakut puppy. And I was nearly as excited as Ian was. I thought my only real reservation was that he wouldn't like an untrained dog, but he was right, most of that came from my experiences with my ex.

When I finally climbed out of bed, Ian glanced at his watch for the millionth time in the last few minutes.

"Why didn't we say ten? Why did we say noon? These are going to be the longest hours of my life," he whined dramatically.

I laughed. "Well, since you just got done with a week at a dog show, I guess that's a good sign of how you felt about the show."

"The show was fantastic. I can't wait for the next one. And I'm really excited you were able to reconnect with a few of your friends."

That had been an unexpected benefit. And, not surprisingly, they'd universally hated my ex and loved Ian. I hadn't really had real friends before, and maybe I'd be able to develop those casual friendships into something stronger, even though we lived in different parts of the country. Katie and Debbie had also become close friends, and I was slowly making more around town.

"You have no idea how glad I am to hear that, Ian. Let's get breakfast and then we can wait impatiently for it to be noon." I laughed.

The couple of hours passed more quickly than I think Ian thought they would. I managed to get him involved in a game of cards and when she called Ian's phone to let him know they were here, he almost looked surprised.

"Okay, I'll stay with the dogs, you go bring them up," he said.

"You don't want to be the first to meet your puppy?"

"I'm so nervous I'll do something dumb." He sank down onto the floor as if he were going to wait there for me to put the puppy in his lap.

"Okay, Ian. I'll be back in a minute. Now, remember, the puppy might be uncertain at first. It'll take a few days for Ace to settle in."

"I know." He took a deep breath and clenched his fists.

I couldn't laugh. His feelings were valid, and I had felt that way when I'd met Creek and Shiner as puppies too. I'd especially been worried that the breeder would change her mind once she met my ex, but somehow, he'd managed to not scare her off and I had my two furry best friends.

The elevator ride down went quickly, and I scanned the lobby until I saw the woman with a dog carrier next to her and a Yakutian Laika puppy in her arms.

"Hi! Kimberly? I'm Violet."

"Oh, hello there. Where's Ian?"

"Hiding in the room, terrified he'll make a fool of himself. Hi, little Ace," I said when the puppy noticed me.

He squirmed and Kimberly handed him over. "You carry this little monster; I'll carry his stuff."

I laughed as Ace tested to see if my finger were a chew toy or not, but he settled into my arms and sniffed my face. Unable to resist, I kissed his nose, and he wagged his tail and licked me back.

"Okay, he's not shy."

"No, ma'am, not a shy bone in this dog's body."

He wasn't fazed by the elevator and when I knocked on the door, it took a moment for Ian to answer. I was willing to bet he hadn't moved from the spot on the floor until I made him get up.

He zeroed in on Ace and his gaze was glued to the little guy.

"He's perfect!" Ian held out his hands and when I handed Ace over, he snuggled him close. Which Ace was totally fine with. Though he did nibble on Ian's nose right away.

"Already starting the crime, I see," Ian said with a laugh. "Oh, uh, hi, I'm Ian."

Kimberly laughed.

"Okay, come in, and you can meet Shiner and Creek while Ian and Ace get to know each other." I grinned at Kimberly.

Ian sat down on the floor and Ace attacked his shoelace.

"He's such a beautiful gray color," I said. "The pictures don't do him justice."

"He's got big shoes to fill I see."

We'd left all the ribbons on the table, and Kimberly was studying them.

"Creek and I even won one of our classes," Ian exclaimed. "We beat Violet and Shiner. This is my first show."

She laughed. "How'd you end up getting into a show this big as your first?"

It was my turn to laugh. "I wasn't going to come. Long story, I didn't think I could make it. Ian had other ideas, but he entered both dogs in everything. I actually had to pull a few entries because there was just no way."

Ian shrugged. "I didn't know what I was doing, I just wanted her to be here."

"That was very sweet of you," Kimberly said.

"So he entered Creek and Shiner in confo, and, well, I can't show two dogs at once, so Ian had to do it. He did a great job."

Ian beamed.

An impatient woof reminded me to go get the dogs.

I brought them both out on leashes. They both said polite hellos to Kimberly, then Shiner caught sight of Ace.

He perked his ears, curled his tail and stared.

Creek noticed Ace in his person's arms and grumbled.

"Creek," I said sharply.

He looked at me indignantly but settled.

Ace saw the other two dogs and toddled over. Shiner rolled over and invited Ace into his space. Creek huffed, but didn't object.

"Well, that's good enough," Kimberly said. "Good first impressions all around. They'll get along great in a few days."

"Thank you so much for meeting us up here," Ian said. "Let me get the rest of your money for the transport."

"You're welcome, Ian. Violet, it was wonderful to meet both of you. I'm excited to see what you accomplish with him. Don't hesitate to reach out if you need anything. And remember, if anything happens, I will always take him back."

"Oh, he's not going anywhere," Ian assured her.

"I have no doubt," Kimberly assured him. "But if something happens to you, he will have a place to land. Okay?"

"Thanks, Kimberly. We really appreciate it."

She stayed for a little while longer, said goodbye to Ace, who was already cuddled up with Shiner, and then left.

Ian glanced at me with a raised eyebrow.

"That's normal, Ian. If you get a dog from a proper breeder, they'll always take the dog back if something happens."

"Oh! Okay. It looks like at least two of them are happy," he said looking at the dogs.

"Go pet Creek. He'll be fine as soon as he realizes you haven't abandoned him."

"Creek, buddy, I'd never abandon you." Ian sat down next to Creek and soon had him rolled over for belly rubs.

"See, he'll be okay. Now, let's see if we can get everyone in for a selfie."

I swore Ian had tears in his eyes when we managed to arrange everyone for a picture.

"I can't wait to get him home so he can meet everyone." Ian held the sleeping puppy a few hours later.

"Me either." I was gathering up our things so we could leave promptly in the morning. The vacation had been nice, but I was excited to get back home. Once I had everything packed, I climbed onto the bed with Ian and Ace and got the other two to join us.

"It's like we're one big happy family," Ian said with a grin.

"I couldn't be happier. Thank you so much."

"Violet, I love you, so much. I'm so glad you and your dogs came into my life."

"I love you too. You're the best thing that ever happened to me."

"Me and the dogs, right?" He winked.

I laughed. "You, the dogs, and a haunted house."

Chapter 41

Grandmother

The three dogs charged around the house like kids on a sugar high. It didn't help that Petey and the twins were playing chase with them. The guests were all dressed in Halloween costumes and punch, candy, cake, and other more savory foods covered the surfaces. Butcher wandered about with Housekeeper, overseeing the food and making sure things stayed in order as much as a pair of ghosts trying to remain at least partially hidden could.

Ian and Violet had told us that we could reveal ourselves if we wanted, but we liked keeping some of the mystery to the place and most people were convinced that the haunted house was an elaborate hoax. Even a lot of the investigators that came weren't convinced, though we did put on a good show, if I did say so myself.

At first, I'd been concerned about a Halloween themed wedding, but after months of planning, I could tell that Violet was thrilled with the idea. And I supposed she'd already had a traditional wedding.

Ian had dressed up as a vampire. Violet had been running around in her Bride of Frankenstein costume, but Debbie and Katie had claimed her to get her changed into her wedding dress. It was still themed, just a little more elaborate.

When Ian saw her vanish, he also ducked into the back room to clean up a little. They'd agreed to ditch the costume makeup, but he was keeping the vampire tux.

Us ghosts had all agreed that Violet coming to us was the best thing that could have happened to our house. Our lives were fuller than they ever had been in life, except possibly mine, and even Petey—forever a teen—was a lot less sullen these days. Even the monster in the basement was a little less terrifying to deal with on the rare occasion we had to interact. Though, in its case, I thought that might be because it wasn't starving as it had a real gift for terrifying the tourists and it fed off fear.

Well, it wouldn't be getting any fear today. Today was about joy.

"Okay, everyone, let's gather!" Debbie came out from the upstairs room they'd designated as the changing room for Violet and clapped her hands together.

The dogs stopped charging around like chaos monsters, though Ace, still clumsy on occasion, plowed into Ian's legs and almost took them both down.

The local preacher, Charlie—I'd known his father and his grandfather in life—had agreed to perform the unorthodox ceremony. He was a good kid.

He and Ian gathered at the bottom of the stairs and the dogs, all three wearing bowties, stood at Ian's side. The rings, now polished, sat on a tarnished silver tray to the side. The monster hadn't wanted the tray polished for whatever reason.

It was an odd sort, but decent enough once you got beyond all the eyes and the screaming and the frost tentacles. We'd actually gotten along quite well after a rocky start. It currently was arranging our gift to Violet and Ian in their bedroom, where they would find it after the party. The rumors of treasure were overstated, but not untrue. The rings were just part of it, but if they sold the artifacts, as we intended for them to do, they'd never have to worry about heating Hill House again.

"Oh, hush, it's starting!" someone in the crowd exclaimed.

They keyed the music. A haunting rendition of the traditional song. Violet appeared at the top of the stairs with a little ghostly help with the theatrics. The crowd gasped, and I saw her grin at the reaction.

Ian's gaze was glued to his bride as she came down the stairs. Her gown was beautiful, orange and black, and covered with lacy cobwebs, pumpkins, and bats. Elegant but very Halloween. The train draped behind her on the stairs. It was just absolutely lovely.

I wiped ectoplasm from my eyes.

Housekeeper sobbed on Butcher's shoulder.

The twins and Petey stood silently by as Ian and Violet exchanged vows, and when they slipped their rings on each other's fingers and kissed, a bright light flared and for a moment our very own Mary stepped through the veil to witness the end of the ceremony.

She was only there for a moment, but I'd be sure to let the happy couple know she'd made it.

Violet tossed a bouquet of black roses and then the party resumed with Ian and Violet's first dance.

Ace took an opportunity for crime and pounced on Violet's train, stopping the dance. Laughing, Ian scooped up the miscreant and ended the dance with Violet and the young dog in his arms. For the next dance, both Ian and Violet performed with Shiner and Creek, though Ace tried to help and tangled them a few times, but the couple was going for fun, not perfection, and in that they succeeded happily.

The evening passed too quickly, and once the last guest had filtered out, Violet held up her phone.

"Selfie time! Get in here, everyone. I want some ghost orbs in this picture. We're a big happy family now."

We were happy to oblige, and all gathered around while she snapped the picture.

"And now, it's time for the groom to carry the bride to bed!" Ian declared, scooping her up in his arms. The dogs followed, Ace getting dragged by the train he had his teeth latched into. The rest of us swirled around to enjoy the remaining hours of a holiday dedicated to ghosts while Ian and Violet celebrated their official union.

I was so happy for the radiant couple. Their joy lit up the house, and their love filled all the once empty spaces in all our hearts and, like they'd healed each other, they healed our hurts, too.

When we heard their door open, we all paused and listened, delighted by the twin exclamations of shock when they found our wedding gift to them.

And then we swirled back into our own Halloween dance, excited for what the future would hold for all of us.

The End

Welcome Home, Ace♡

Winners!

We said "I do!"

Author's Note

Thank you so much for reading my reverse harem tale! More is coming soon! Reviews are so very important and are greatly appreciated! Even a line or two will do!

About the Author

Dakota has two passions in life: writing and cinnamon tea. Tea so strong she ought to be able to see her future when she drinks it, and the writing? Well, she hopes it makes you see stars when you read it. She creates reverse harem romance novels filled with things that go bump in the night. That handsome werewolf walking down the street? The suave vampire you're just dying to get a taste of? You'll find them enraptured by charming, smart ladies ready to make those bad boys work for their affection. When not writing, Dakota can be found on the back of a horse out on the trail or tending the animals on her farm.

Other Works

Mountain Magic Trilogy (complete)

Becoming
Demon's Touch
Reckoning

Pizza Shop Exorcist (complete)

The Price of Possession
The Price of Exorcism
The Price of Magic
The Price of Souls
The Price of Rebellion
Demons Don't Do Christmas
Monster's Price

Horsemen Against the Apocalypse Duet

Seeking War
Apocalypse Interrupted (forthcoming)

Dreambound Trilogy (Complete)

Nightmare's Dance
Nightmare's Fall
Nightmare's Flight

Companions of the Convergence
Only Human in Strangeville (stands alone)